# GUARDIANS OF THE DRUMS

## A KEALOHA ISLAND THRILLER (BOOK 4)

## BY

# CHUCK MORGAN

Printed in the United States of America

First printing 2025

ISBN 978-1-968179-47-2 (Paperback)

LIBRARY OF CONGRESS CONTROL NUMBER

2025922727

# Chapter One

## A Stolen Legacy

The call came at 4:13 a.m., breaking through the pitch dark with a low-level vibration and the blue-white pulse of Leilani's phone. Honolulu's city lights had been blotted out by a lingering night rain, and Detective Leilani Kealoha stood in a puddle in the Bishop Museum parking lot, waiting for the world to come into focus. She fished a protein bar from her jacket, tore off the wrapper, and chewed as she surveyed the museum's eastern wing. The building's broad concrete steps looked slick, and the Koa wood doors reflected the glow of police floodlights. Three patrol cruisers idled in the loading zone, blue and white lights painting the columns in an uneasy rhythm.

By the time she finished her breakfast, the campus security team had gathered in a shivering knot under the overhang, trading cigarettes and nervous glances. Leilani swept her jacket aside, revealing her gold shield, nodded at the officers, and flashed the tired, professional smile she reserved for long nights and senseless crimes. She stepped inside.

The entryway was bathed in shadow, and she moved towards a uniformed officer. Every light in the building was on. Officer Jimmy Pahoa, a seasoned veteran with over a decade in patrol, met her in the lobby.

"This way, Detective," he said, waving his hand towards an open set of doors.

Leilani followed him through the first gallery, past the watchful stare of hand-carved tikis and the silent shimmer of shell necklaces. Somewhere above, a leaky A/C unit pinged onto marble tile.

At the far end of the room stood Director Akamu, small and formal in his khaki suit, pacing back and forth in front of an exhibit titled **The Living Royalty of Hawai'i**. He looked like he hadn't slept in a week. When he spotted Leilani, he stopped pacing, smoothed his tie, and gestured her over. There was a display case at his side, or more accurately, what was left of one. The glass had been neatly punched through at its top corner, leaving a neat arch the size of a basketball, as if a pro had scored a perfect three-pointer with a rock. Fragments of safety glass littered the mat beneath.

"Detective," Akamu started, his voice raw from worry. "This is catastrophic. We just finished renovating this gallery for the royal collection."

Leilani bent to inspect the hole, careful not to let her hair fall in her face. "I understand this held King Kamehameha 1's cape?" she asked.

"Yes," the director said. "Eighteenth century. Hundreds of thousands of 'i'iwi feathers, all hand-sewn." His hands hovered over the edges of the display, trembling. "It's priceless. There is nothing else like it in the world."

She circled the case, shining her light along the perimeter. She counted five pieces of glass on the mat, none larger than her palm. On the far edge, near the brushed steel frame, was a greasy smudge. She kneeled and pressed a clear acetate sleeve over it and bagged the evidence. She wondered how many cops had touched it already. Probably all of them.

"You have cameras?" she asked.

Akamu nodded. "Of course. But our night security saw nothing. Not until the alarms triggered at 2:42 a.m. That's when the guards called me, and I called the police."

Leilani grunted. "Nobody saw or heard a thing for the previous half hour?"

"Nothing," he said, almost pleading. "I have no idea how they got past the sensors."

She turned to one of the blue-uniformed forensics techs, who was crouched at the threshold, adjusting the f-stop on a battered Nikon. "You got prints?" Leilani asked.

The tech looked up, thick glasses magnifying her eyes. "There's a smudge on the metal. A partial thumbprint, clean." She paused. "Also, there's this." She held up a small plastic bag containing a fiber, not a feather, but a tiny red thread. "From the border of the glass."

Leilani took it and held it in the flashlight beam. It glimmered with a finish she'd seen before. "Koa wood varnish?" she asked.

The tech shrugged. "I'll confirm with the lab, but you've got the eye, Detective."

She grinned. "Let me see the pedestal."

The museum director led her around the crime scene tape to the raised platform. She crouched, mindful of the damp carpet, and traced a gloved finger over the pedestal. Under the forensic light, a thin splay of droplets glowed faint blue—likely sweat, or the tail end of a cleaning solution. Someone had wiped this down recently. But they'd missed a corner: a print, perfectly outlined, where a left hand had steadied itself. She flagged it for the forensics team.

"Who cleaned in here last night?" she asked Akamu.

He took out his phone and tapped rapidly. "We use a contracted service—Big Wave Janitorial. But they're on a set schedule, always done by 11:30."

"Check the roster, please," Leilani said.

She heard voices echoing from down the hall— another officer, and a man in a navy blazer with the rumpled look of overnight work. The night guard. Leilani took a last look at the scene, then headed over.

The guard's name tag said "Lito." He looked more bewildered than guilty, but years on the force had taught Leilani that the guilty rarely looked like anything at all.

"Lito, right?" she asked.

He nodded, hands in his pockets, rocking on his heels. "Yes, ma'am."

"You walked this floor last night?" Leilani pressed.

"Two times," he said. "First pass at midnight, everything was tight. Second pass, around two. No problems. After that, I was up in Admin on a bathroom break. Came back down around two-twenty-five, that's when I saw the case alarm on my panel."

She narrowed her eyes. "Did you see anyone lingering in the halls? Any maintenance or cleaners?"

He shook his head. "No, ma'am. The place was a ghost town."

The silence stretched. "Nothing unusual, huh? No doors ajar, nothing out of place?"

Lito looked at his shoes. "I heard something in the archives, but I figured it was the A/C again. It clanks sometimes." He glanced at her. "That's it, Detective."

Leilani nodded, pocketed her notepad. "You smoke, Lito?"

He looked startled and shook his head. "Trying to quit."

She looked back at the cluster of security guards, then at the forensics techs. "Keep working the print, and I want a full log of every badge scan since midnight," she called over.

Akamu returned, face red, holding up a phone. "Janitorial finished at 11:12 p.m. I checked with their manager."

Leilani's mind wandered through the gaps— whoever took the cape knew the schedules, knew the cameras, and left what they wanted her to find. She sighed and walked to the admin office, tracing the likely escape route.

In the lobby, another officer handed her a tablet loaded with security footage. "You're gonna want to see the timestamp between 2:15 and 2:40," he said.

She clicked through to the time frame. The gallery

was empty, and in night mode, the case glowed white and ghostly. At 2:17, a faint flicker in the lower left of the frame. Static, or a shadow. She advanced by frame. The image dissolved, pixelated, and cut to black for three full minutes. When the video came back, the display case was broken and empty. The feed cut to Lito's sprint down the hall.

Leilani grunted. "Nice trick," she muttered.

Akamu hovered behind her. "We had our system upgraded last year. This shouldn't be possible. And yet."

She set the tablet on the nearest desk. "Can I get a map of the galleries? I'd like to see all exits and entry points." She pinched the bridge of her nose and felt the pressure headache start its morning shift.

"Yes, of course." Akamu darted away. He returned a moment later with a glossy tri-fold floor plan. She spread it on the desk and traced a route from the Royalty Gallery to the staff corridors, and to the rear service exit. The lock on that door had a keypad; she checked the maintenance logs—the last code change had been six weeks prior. Too long.

"Director, who had access to the security codes?"

He hesitated. "Myself, my deputy, and the night manager. That's it. The janitors don't have the code—they have to sign in at the main entrance."

Leilani wrote the three names in her notebook, double-checking the spelling. "Okay. Has anyone from your staff gone on sudden leave, acted strangely lately?"

He shook his head. "We're a small team, Detective. Everyone knows everyone."

She doubted that but let it go. "I'll need personnel files for all overnight staff for the last week. Can you please have your cultural preservation specialist meet me here?"

Akamu hurried off to make the call.

She let herself breathe for the first time since arriving, blinking up at the vaulted ceiling and the phosphorescent blue of the emergency lights. The place seemed haunted by more than a missing cape.

The forensics tech returned, waving an evidence bag. "You were right about the varnish, Detective. Koa resin, fresh application on a red cloth."

Leilani arched an eyebrow. "Means our thief's a craftsman. Probably spent the last day or two prepping tools and rehearsing on a mock-up." She looked at her watch, realized she'd been on her feet nearly an hour, and wandered toward the break room, hoping for coffee.

The small kitchen smelled of burned beans and cleaning chemicals. She poured herself a cup and leaned against the counter, scrolling through the preliminary reports on her phone.

A soft voice startled her. "Detective Kealoha?"

Leilani turned. The museum's cultural preservation specialist stood at the threshold: a slight woman in her fifties with salt-and-pepper hair pulled back in a braid, arms crossed over a flowery blouse. She introduced herself as Dr. Mahina.

Leilani offered her the chair. "You know what was taken," she said.

Dr. Mahina nodded, eyes downcast. "I helped restore it. Twice. It's not only an artifact—it's a story, a part of the monarchy. The feathers were gathered over generations." She hesitated. "If someone wanted to sell it, they'd have to destroy it. That's the only way it would move on the black market."

Leilani sensed a chill. "So, they'd strip it for feathers, or chop it up?"

The curator looked sick. "They'd cut it, rework the fabric, and sell the feathers to collectors. The rest would go in the trash." She drew a shaky breath. "It's not about money, Detective. Someone took this because they wanted to erase what it means."

Leilani thanked her and promised to keep her updated. She jotted a final note in her book: *this wasn't some spur-of-the-moment job. The thief knew exactly what to take and why.*

She found Director Akamu by the front entrance, talking in urgent tones to a man in a faded Hawaiian shirt—probably the janitorial manager. Akamu waved her over, handed her a folder of badge logs and code access printouts. "This is everything from the past month," he said.

"Thank you," Leilani said, slipping the files under her arm. She nodded at the officers, and they parted, letting her out into the damp predawn. She stood on the steps, breathing in the salt-tinged air. The city stretched awake beneath the pink clouds.

She flipped open her notebook and ran through the details. Prints, fiber, varnish. A perfect three-minute blackout and a thief who worked with surgical precision.

Leilani exhaled. The city never lacked ambition, and this crime was bigger than any single artifact. She took out her phone and dialed her sergeant, Tano Pualani.

"Hey, Tano, it's Leilani," she said. "This was no amateur job. Call in anyone who hasn't shown up yet. We've got work to do. Forensics should be in shortly; they're wrapping up here. Get the conference room set up for the morning briefing, and we'll add this in."

"You got it, ma'am," said the sergeant.

Leilani laughed. "Tano, what did we talk about? Call me Leilani, or Lei or Lani. My mother is Ma'am.

Tano laughed. "Sorry, Ma'am. Oops, sorry, boss."

"Boss will do for now, but don't get used to it," she chuckled.

She hung up and let the adrenaline drain away.

Somewhere in the coming dawn, the city buzzed with the prospect of a new day, oblivious to the gaping hole in its history. Leilani ran a hand through her long, damp hair and glanced back at the museum.

It looked smaller now, older, and in need of protection. She took a deep breath, turned, and walked into the museum.

Leilani found the administrative offices blessedly empty. The rest of the city's bureaucracy never started before seven, and most museum staff wouldn't be in until after sunrise. The reception area, all gray walls and battered cane chairs, was lined with glass trophy cases, each housing a decade's worth of dusty community awards—best educational program, best visitor experience, a framed commendation from a senator. A faint whiff of mothballs drifted out from under the records room door.

She carried the folder of badge logs and code access reports to the staff lounge, dumped her damp jacket over a chair, and spread the paperwork across the table. Somewhere overhead, the ancient HVAC thrummed and cycled. It was the office ambiance that made every whisper of movement seem illicit.

Leilani dug in. The badge log printed out on crisp white paper. The columns of names and times lined up with mathematical precision. Her eyes flicked from name to name on the handwritten sign-in sheet the museum kept as a backup. In the first week of the month, every badge scan matched an entry on the log—except, curiously, for two entries last night. There was a swipe by Heidi N., the janitorial crew supervisor, at 11:15 p.m., but her name was missing from the sign-in. She flagged it with a pink sticky note.

Next, she opened the access code change report. The gallery security keypad had been updated five times in the last year; each update logged by Director Akamu, Deputy Director Samuels, and, recently, night manager Hiro. All changes, including last night's, trailed a digital signature and timestamp.

A tickle of intuition: she cross-referenced the badge log with the keypad report. At 2:14 a.m., less than thirty minutes before the alarm triggered, someone had entered the gallery using a code updated by Hiro.

She circled the timestamp, fished her phone from her pocket, and dialed the number Akamu had listed for his night manager. It rang six times before an answering machine picked up. "This is Hiro. I'm probably on the museum floor. Leave a message and I'll call back."

Leilani hung up. She would circle back to that.

A vibration from her phone: a text from the forensics lab. The fingerprint lifted from the metal case was already being processed, but no hits in the immediate police database. The technician had, however, confirmed fresh, high-end Koa varnish on the print and on the trim of the case. She made a mental note to request a list of woodworking shops and furniture refurbishers in the area.

She started with the inventory records. The museum's collections database was a digital relic, one of those outdated systems where each exhibit change required a slow, manual update. Leilani paged through entries on her laptop, moving from the Royalty Gallery to Polynesian Artifacts to 19th Century Curiosities. Her suspicion grew with each scan.

A folder titled **Incident Reports–Private** revealed more. Three weeks ago, a set of rare fishhooks—hand-carved and ancient—had vanished from a display in the Polynesian wing. The theft wasn't publicized, and the only sign that anything had gone missing was a single incident report marked as a minor inventory discrepancy. Two weeks ago, an 1830s ivory lei was found missing from a locked cabinet, the security alert dismissed as a sensor malfunction. Each case involved objects with deep cultural significance, but relatively little market value compared to European fine art or precious gems.

A pattern. She could sense it coalescing behind her eyes.

Leilani sat back, pressed her palms to her temples, and forced herself to slow down. She paged through the log again, making sure she didn't miss any smaller incidents. There were other, unconnected losses—an office laptop, a batch of supplies—but nothing with the same flair or focus as these artifact thefts.

She glanced at the clock on the wall—5:53 a.m. The city would stir soon. She rose, stretched, and walked along the corridor to the museum's small research library, where Dr. Mahina was setting up for her day.

The preservationist was pulling folders from the rolling cart, lining them up in neat rows on the worktable. She looked up as Leilani entered, and the detective noticed the burden of her own rumpled T-shirt and low ponytail compared to the doctor's crisp, pressed linen.

"What can I do for you, Detective?" Dr. Mahina said, not unkindly.

Leilani smiled. "I need to ask about the cape. What makes it so important—and who might want it, aside from the entire auction circuit?"

Dr. Mahina gestured to a chair. She pulled a heavy manila envelope from the bottom of the cart and slid it across. "I made copies of my research notes," she said. "This cape, as you probably know, was started by Kamehameha himself. It took over a million feathers and at least three generations of artisans to complete. But there's something else. Legend says it's more than a symbol of kingship. It's a ward, a spiritual shield, woven with the old kapu—strict, sacred law."

Leilani whistled low. "That's what can drive people to extremes."

Dr. Mahina nodded. "On the surface, it's a beautiful artifact. But for some, it's an obsession. Every few years, we get a call from someone claiming to have found a lost royal cape in their attic. But nobody has ever gotten this close. Whoever took it knew exactly what they were after."

She paused, lowering her voice. "And Detective…if they did it for money, they'd have to sell it to a collector. But no legitimate collector would ever buy this piece. Its loss would be public knowledge within hours."

"Which means," Leilani said, "they either took it for themselves, or they're planning something else."

The doctor's face paled. "You think it's a ransom?"

"I think it's a message," Leilani said. "There've been other thefts, right? Little things from the Polynesian wing. Fishhooks and an ivory lei. Things missing from other museums?"

Dr. Mahina blinked. "I hadn't heard."

Leilani explained what she'd pieced together, pushing over the incident reports. "The pattern says it's not random. Someone's building a set—or a shrine—or they're pulling a con nobody's figured out yet."

The doctor looked unsettled, as if she'd never considered the gallery might be anything but a haven for old treasures. She rubbed her forearm, silent.

"I need you to make a list of everyone with access to this room," Leilani said. "Staff, docents, and the contractors who renovated the display."

Dr. Mahina nodded, already jotting notes. "I'll have it by midday."

A call buzzed through Leilani's phone. She answered. "Detective, this is Mele. We found something weird with the footprint impressions. Can you meet me in the Royal Gallery?"

Leilani excused herself and walked to the gallery where the forensic team had set up a small lab. She found Mele hunched over a portable workbench, surrounded by black powder, gels, and a high-res scanner.

"We got three good shoe prints from the platform," Mele said. "Two are consistent with Lito, the security guard. The third's interesting."

She swiveled the screen to show a digital outline. "This is a Nike Free Run 5.0, women's, size 8. We've done some checking and haven't found anyone on the museum's staff who wears this."

Leilani blinked. "See if it matches the janitorial supervisor from the badge log—Heidi N."

Mele nodded. "According to the employee roster, she's been on maternity leave for the past month."

"Who swiped her badge last night?"

"That's the thing," Mele said. "We pulled the CCTV from the employee entrance. At 11:15 p.m., someone in a hooded sweatshirt used the badge but kept their head down. Could be anyone."

Leilani ran a hand over her mouth. "So, it's a clone, or a borrowed badge."

Mele grinned. "I'm betting on borrowed. It beeped through the system on the first try, so they had the PIN as well."

Leilani took the scan, then called up the photo of the partial fingerprint. "Is there any chance we can tie this to anyone in the system?"

Mele looked up. "No hits yet, but we'll keep at it."

Back in the admin wing, Leilani gathered her findings, compiling a list: the badge entry, the shoe print, the security code change, the timing of the theft. Each clue narrowed the focus. She walked to the director's office, found Akamu in a freshly pressed shirt, and presented her findings.

"I think someone used inside information to get in and out without leaving a trace," she told him. "They timed the security blackout, wore gloves, and knew which artifacts to target. If I had to guess, they scoped the place weeks in advance."

Akamu slumped into his chair, rubbing his temples. "We try to run a tight ship here, Detective. But if someone wanted to exploit a weakness, I guess they'd find it."

Leilani looked at the office walls, at the framed

diplomas and awards. "When's the last time you changed all the codes, not only the gallery keypad?"

He hesitated. "Never. We do it for the main doors, but the internal systems, not so much. People come and go—it's hard to keep up."

She nodded, scribbling in her notebook. "I need you to put together a list of everyone with access to administrative passwords. IT, security, and consultants."

Akamu nodded. "I'll have my assistant get on it."

"Good," Leilani said, "and please email me copies of all personnel files for last night's staff."

She scanned her phone, reading over the last message from Mele: **We're working on the fiber. Will let you know if we get DNA.**

Leilani stood at the window, watching dawn turn the rain-soaked streets gold. She felt the tension, the sense of something poised at the threshold between ordinary and catastrophic.

She flipped open her notebook one more time, jotting two names: *Hiro* and *Heidi N.* Next to them, she wrote, *access, motive, opportunity*. She underlined the words three times.

This was not a single act of theft. It was a campaign, and the next move could come at any time. She took a last look at the case file, buttoned her jacket and stepped towards the exit, ready to bring the pieces together before anyone else could take from her city what little remained of its past.

The windows of Leilani's Explorer were steamed

on the inside from the morning's rain, and she wiped them clear with the sleeve of her denim jacket. She slumped behind the wheel, the folder of badge logs and security codes heavy on her lap, and the museum's stone facade looming in the rearview like the ghost of a crime she'd failed to prevent.

She flipped open her department-issued tablet and logged into the digital evidence vault. The interface was clunky, but she'd grown used to its stubborn logic. First, the photos: close-ups of the broken glass, the feather-flecked mat, the clean crescent where a gloved hand had cleared the surface. Next, the thumbprint, a shimmering whorl left on the brushed steel of the display case. She zoomed in, cross-referencing with the morning's email from forensics—no hits on AFIS, but a "high probability" of a match once they combed through state employment databases.

She toggled to the security camera stills, advancing frame by frame through the empty gallery, the flicker, the three minutes of darkness, and the sudden absence of the cape. The theft seems personal. Not rage, not vandalism—precision, patience, and a sense of purpose.

She set the tablet on the dash and dialed the number for Special Investigations. The line picked up on the second ring, a voice answering, "Espinoza, SIU."

"Tommy, it's Leilani," she said, pinching her nose. "Got a live one. Bishop Museum, 2:40 a.m., Kamehameha I's feather cape is missing. Forensics found a partial thumbprint and a high-end Koa varnish. It could be that our thief works with high-end wood. The perp used a cloned or stolen badge and seems to have had inside knowledge of code updates. I'm sending you employee information. I need full backgrounds and social media on every staffer with overnight access, especially the janitorial supervisors and night managers."

Espinoza grunted, typing as he spoke. "Is that the same cape from the cover of National Geographic?"

Leilani smiled, despite herself. "That's the one. Print off a picture of the cape and take it down to the patrol captain. See if he can have his folks check pawnshops and antique brokers for anything that matches the 'i'iwi or mamo feather profile. If we're lucky, our thief is stupid enough to try fencing it locally."

Espinoza said, "Copy that. I'll push it to the top. You want BOLOs on the staff?"

"Start with badge access for the last month. Expand the search if you see overlap with other artifact thefts. This isn't an isolated job. The pattern says there could be a ring working the museum circuit, or someone's building a private collection."

She could hear the hum of the open-plan office on the other end, the rattle of keyboards, the distant wheeze of the ancient HVAC. Espinoza said, "Are you still up for the 10 a.m. debrief?"

"Wouldn't miss it," Leilani said. She hung up and glanced at her laptop, now containing half-complete notes and grainy screenshots.

A wave of fatigue washed over her, sudden and complete, as if her bones had finally caught up to her spirit. She let herself close her eyes for thirty seconds, long enough to picture the feather cape on its stand—impossibly fragile, but more enduring than any badge or bronze.

Her phone vibrated again, a familiar number flashing on the screen. She hesitated and thumbed accept.

"Detective Kealoha?" The voice was precise and clipped.

"Yes?"

"This is Ms. Cabral, vice principal at Kahala Elementary. I'm calling about your son, Kai."

Leilani's heart skipped, then it fell into the nervous rhythm it saved for emergency calls. "Is he alright?"

"He's not hurt," the voice assured her. "But there's been an incident in his social studies class. Kai corrected his teacher's lesson about the monarchy, and when asked to apologize, he refused. He's currently in my office, and we'd appreciate if you could come by for a meeting as soon as possible."

Leilani tried to find her footing. "He's ten, Ms. Cabral. Sometimes he… gets stubborn about details. Especially about Hawaiian history."

A faint sigh over the line. "We're very proud of his curiosity, Detective. But it's a question of respect for the classroom."

"Of course. I'll be there in twenty minutes." After finishing the call, she struck the wheel, stuck in the quicksand between responsibility and affection. She rolled down the window and breathed in the city: wet asphalt, hibiscus, and a faint undercurrent of ferment from the storm drains. The parking lot was empty but for the forensic van, a few staff cars, and the gardener unloading sacks of mulch from the bed of a faded Tacoma. She waved, rolled up the window, and started the engine. She put the Explorer in gear and pulled out of the museum parking lot.

The drive across town was muscle memory. She let her mind wander through the case, repeating the list of clues: the badge, the shoe print, the print on the display, the timing of the code change. In the pause between red lights, she imagined Kai in the vice principal's office, arms folded, eyes defiant. She could see herself in the line of his jaw, in the way he refused to yield when dead wrong.

She wanted to be annoyed, to lecture him about time and place, but all she felt was a rush of pride, and a fear she was passing down her own worst habits.

At the last stoplight before the school, her phone buzzed again. It was a text from the forensics tech: **DNA pulled from fiber. Sending to the FBI lab for processing. Will update**.

She typed a quick reply—**Thanks, keep me posted**—and set the phone in the cup holder.

Kai was waiting outside the admin office when she arrived, sitting on a bench with his knees pulled up to his chest, hair damp from sweat and morning humidity. He spotted her and immediately looked away, feigning deep interest in his Velcro sneakers.

She walked up, set her palm gently on his head, and ruffled his hair.

"You in trouble?" she asked.

He shrugged. "They said I was rude. But the book was wrong."

She sat next to him, letting the silence build up before she answered. "Sometimes it's not enough to be right, Kai. Sometimes you have to let other people get there at their own speed."

He made a face, the universal sign for that's dumb, but he didn't argue.

"Come on," she said, standing and offering her hand. "Let's go apologize, and we'll get pancakes. Deal?"

He thought about it, then took her hand. "Deal. But afterwards, can I help you with the case? I want to see the feather cape."

She smiled, full and unguarded. "If you promise to behave."

He made a show of crossing his heart. "Promise."

They walked inside, mother and son, the morning air still fresh with rain. Leilani forgot about the fingerprints, the code changes, the disappearing artifacts, and the responsibility of a city's history riding on her every decision. She still had a job to do, but right now, Kai was her entire universe. She squeezed his hand, took a deep breath, and followed him inside.

# Chapter Two

## Echoes of the Past

The glass-walled conference room perched above downtown was frigid and fluorescent, a world away from the humid streets and open-air markets below. Detective Leilani Kealoha claimed the head of the long, battered table, already loaded with folders, half-drunk coffee, and a department-issue box of powdered malasadas. She cradled a black coffee in one hand and a battered tablet in the other; the stylus pinched like a dart between her fingers.

The evidence board dominated the wall behind her. High-resolution photos of the feather cape, a grid of museum floor plans, the thumbprint overlays, and a badge-log spreadsheet blown up to impossible scale. The scene was less cops and robbers and more PhD dissertation. Every detail was parsed and pored over, every artifact presented with the solemnity of a sacrament. On the left side of the board were eleven pictures. There were five judges, four high-ranking police officers, and two city councilmen. Five of the pictures had red Xs drawn on them. Those were the ones the Special Investigations Unit had put in prison so far. The rest were under investigation and destined to follow their friends.

Detective Isaac Torres, formerly with the FBI and now the lead detective in Leilani's Special Investigations Unit, occupied the far end of the table, his suit so sharply pressed it looked like body armor. He exuded an easy, unhurried confidence—the kind that said, "I already know what you're going to ask, and I have three answers ready." His dark hair was cut regulation short, his jaw clean-shaven, and his eyes flickered with interest as he scrolled through the case files.

Detective Sergeant Tano Pualani walked in and placed his coffee cup at one of the side seats. Tano had been a detective for fifteen years. He was thin and sinewy from years as a competitive surfer. He had dark hair and dark eyes.

Next to arrive was Detective Tommy Espinoza. Tommy had been promoted from patrol, and Leilani looked forward to seeing what he offered. A patrol officer for four years, he was short and athletic with short hair and a small mustache.

Forensic tech Mele Tatana swept into the room in her white coat, jeans, and a T-shirt for a band no one had heard of. She was overweight but still moved with grace, her long black hair tied in two braids.

Rick Caufield was Leilani's liaison from the DA's office. He wore a three-piece suit, and his blond hair was combed back, exposing a high forehead. He wore wire-rimmed glasses and looked more like a college professor than a lawyer.

The last to arrive was their computer tech, Akira. Her dark hair, short and scalped up one side, had streaks of electric purple, and her ears glistened with a constellation of steel. She wore the universal costume of the tech tribe, a threadbare tank top, cargo shorts, and bare feet. She arrived with her usual flair, set down her energy drink and looked at the board.

"This is different," she said. "Have we given up on chasing corruption?"

"No," said Leilani. "This crime has significant cultural implications, and the chief wants us to handle it. Our other cases are still active."

"So," Isaac said, lacing his fingers together. "This is the whole show, huh?"

Leilani kept her eyes on the tablet, but one eyebrow arched in reply. "If you're looking for a PowerPoint, you're out of luck. We do things old-school here."

"I see that," Isaac said, taking in the paper detritus, the handwritten notes taped to the whiteboard. "But you're not old-school, Detective. You're what—thirty-seven?"

"Thirty-five," she corrected. "Flattery will get you nowhere."

Isaac flashed a grin. "It wasn't flattery, but observation." He leaned back in his chair. "So. Walk us through it."

Leilani uncapped her stylus and tapped it on the screen. "At 2:20 a.m. last night, someone with expert-level knowledge of security protocol bypassed the Bishop Museum's motion sensors and broke into a locked display. They targeted a single item, Kamehameha's feather cloak—and left everything else untouched. The job took less than three minutes, start to finish."

"Impressive," Isaac said, his tone genuinely admiring. "No alarms until after the fact?"

"They triggered a silent alarm, but it was too late.

The guard was on a bathroom break when the cameras glitched. When footage resumed, the display was empty, and the case was open like a clamshell." She tapped a grainy freeze-frame from the security footage, and the case was dark and empty. "Our perp knew the exact blind spot and how to exploit it."

Tommy nodded, his eyes flicked to the forensics photos. "That's the partial print?"

"On the brushed steel. Unmatched in our system, but the lab's running it against the employment databases." She zoomed in. "They also left behind a red fiber, likely from a work shirt or rag. But the real tell was the varnish on the display—fresh Koa. Most likely transferred off a shirt."

Isaac glanced at the next board, which listed every Koa wood shop and restoration expert on Oahu. "Nice work."

Akira shrugged. "It's easy. On an island, every craftsman knows every other. It's a small pond, even for sharks."

Isaac grinned. "But this one doesn't smell local, does it?"

Leilani looked at him. "What makes you say that?"

"Too clean," Isaac said. "Every Honolulu job I've ever read up on had at least one idiot with a cousin in the alarm company, or a girlfriend with a big mouth. This seems rehearsed. Either a professional thief or someone who's pulled off similar scores before."

Leilani slid the manila folders toward him. "That's where you come in, I guess. The FBI is supposed to be tracking a ring that's been lifting artifacts from museums and private collections."

Isaac nodded, flipping through the files. "They've had three incidents in the last year—Chicago, New York, Paris. All Polynesian and Micronesian artifacts and always a single, high-value item. Never resold locally. The FBI's working theory is that they're headed for a private collector with specific tastes."

"Is there a name attached to that theory?" Leilani asked.

Isaac shook his head. "No, but my source said they traced two shipments through Manila and Singapore. Both vanished after landing in Southeast Asia. No records, no chatter, vanished."

Leilani's pen clicked against the tabletop once, twice, staccato. "That's a lot of work for a collector's trophy."

"Not merely a trophy," Isaac countered. "Some of these pieces have real cultural weight. Rumor has it, certain buyers want them for leverage—legal, financial, or political. Sometimes, they're offered to the country of origin for a ransom."

Leilani looked unimpressed. "We've got enough crooks at home without importing new ones."

A silence stretched between them. Isaac broke it. "You don't trust the FBI."

It wasn't a question.

Leilani's jaw flexed. "I don't trust outside help that treats this city like a puzzle instead of a home."

Isaac met her gaze. "That's fair. But sometimes an outsider sees patterns we can't from inside the frame."

She let herself smile. "It's like surfing. You can't read the break from the shore. You have to be in it."

He lifted his coffee in mock salute. "Noted."

They reviewed the evidence point by point. Leilani ticked off every badge scan from the night of the theft, cross-referenced with the staff schedule, and circled the anomaly—an access code entered by a night manager supposedly off shift. Isaac flagged a similar tactic in a museum hit in Santa Barbara, where the thief used a borrowed security badge and cloned a staff phone.

"It could be part of a pattern," he said, drawing lines between the incidents.

"It still seems personal. The choice of the target and the way they left everything else behind," said Leilani.

Isaac nodded. "Let's assume it is personal. Who hates the museum enough to spend a couple of weeks prepping a job like this?"

Leilani considered. "Everyone who thinks they could do better. Curators passed over for promotion. Collectors cut off by the museum board. Activists who think the museum exploits the past. Or," she allowed. "Someone who wants to make a statement."

Isaac leaned in, his voice slow and precise. "You ever think it's not about the artifact, but the story behind it? The symbolism?"

Leilani stiffened. "The cape's a sacred thing. It's more than fabric. Taking it is like stealing the island's heartbeat.”

“Our thief is a fanatic or a true believer,” Isaac said. “Those are the hardest to catch.”

Leilani opened her mouth to reply, but her phone vibrated hard enough to skitter across the table. The caller ID flashed: Mom. She pushed the red button and put her phone down on the table. She had opened her mouth when the phone rang again. She silenced the ringer.

“Okay,” she said. “Akira, pull up everything you can find on similar crimes and run a search on social media for anyone taking responsibility. Tano, follow up with patrol and see if their officers have had any luck with pawnshops, and check with robbery and see if they have any gangs working museums. Tommy, grab someone from patrol and visit the wood restoration shops. See what shakes out.”

Everyone stood and left the conference room. Isaac stepped over to Leilani, who was picking up her phone and dialing.

“What’s up?” he asked.

She raised her finger and spoke. “Aloha, Mom. You okay?”

Isaac caught the change in her. He stood silently.

On the other end, her mother’s voice was calm but undercut with a tension Leilani hadn’t heard in years. “Lani, I need to tell you something. There was a break-in at the halau last night. Some damage, but they took the pahu.”

Leilani gripped the end of the table. “When?”

"Right after midnight. I found the door open when I arrived to teach a class. I've already talked to the police, but they said you'd want to know."

Leilani closed her eyes, breathed once. "Are you okay, Mom?"

"We're fine," Naalei said. "But that drum has been with our family for generations. If someone took it for what it means…"

Leilani nodded, though her mother couldn't see it. "I'll be there in twenty. Don't touch anything."

She hung up and stood, already half out the door before Isaac could speak. He caught up with her.

"What happened?"

"My mom's halau," Leilani said. "Somebody stole the family pahu—the sacred drum." Her hand trembled as she jammed the phone into her pocket.

Isaac whistled. "You think it's related?"

"They didn't touch anything else," she said, grabbing her jacket. "Only the drum. Like at the museum."

Isaac stood, pocketed his own phone, and followed. "Let's go," he said. "I'll drive."

She laughed. "Not going to happen."

They left the conference room and locked the door after them. There were still a bunch of officers who didn't appreciate the job her unit was doing, and she didn't want any roving eyes on their evidence.

Down the corridor, the sun was burning through the

city's overcast shell, turning the wet windows gold. Leilani felt the old cocktail of adrenaline and dread, but there was something new—an anger that coiled up from her chest and sharpened her focus.

As she and Isaac hit the street, she almost wanted to be back in that freezing, lifeless conference room. It was safer to talk about feathers and wood than to think of her mother, proud and unshakable, standing beside an empty display that once held the family drum. She shook it off, got in the car, and let the city close in around her.

Senior detective Carl Tanaka watched from his cubicle until he was certain everyone had left the SIU conference room. He stood, stretched and checked the bullpen. Most of the desks were empty. He moved towards the restrooms then veered off at the last minute.

The conference room door was locked, but he reached into his pocket and pulled out a master key he had picked up a long time ago. He was grateful that the police department hadn't changed the locks in the building in years. He slipped into the conference room, closed the door and left the lights off. He walked to the whiteboard and scanned the documents. It looked like Kealoha and her crew had some insight into the island-wide theft of artifacts.

He pulled out his phone, turned off the flash, and took pictures of the whiteboard. He slipped out of the room, closed the door, and walked to his cubicle. He held up his phone, pulled up a phone number from his contact list, and attached the photos. He hit send and waited. The response arrived two minutes later.

**Good. Keep eyes open and send more when available.**

He put the phone away and smiled, knowing he was that much closer to paying off his son's debts.

***

The hula halau was perched on the windward side of town and was painted a washed-out green that faded perfectly into the palms. The parking lot was a patchwork of tire grooves and sand, and a single yellow strand of police tape snapped in the salt breeze. When Leilani and Isaac pulled up, two patrol officers stood by the door, bored and blinking into the morning sun.

They ducked under the tape, nodded to the officers, and slipped inside. The halau's main room was a box of honeyed light and dark shadows, its wooden floor polished from decades of bare feet. The familiar scent—plumeria, sweat, and varnish—hit her in the chest, and she forgot she was there as a detective, not a daughter.

The floor was a battlefield of implements: ʻuliʻuli gourds spilled their red and yellow feathers, pūʻili rattles lay snapped in half, and a trio of ipu rolled in lazy arcs near the back wall. The mirrors along the north side had been left untouched, but every shelf and cubby had been ransacked. On the far side, beneath a high window, a single stand stood bare—the place of honor for the pahu, her family's ancient drum.

Naalei Kealoha stood beside it, her hands folded and hair pulled back in a severe bun. Even in crisis, she wore her teaching clothes—black slacks, a yellow tunic, and a green lei strung fresh that morning. Her expression was unreadable, but the muscle in her jaw worked with every breath. Leilani crossed the room, careful to step around the scattered artifacts.

"Mom," she whispered.

Naalei nodded once, as if accepting a gift she didn't want. "Lani. Thank you for coming."

Isaac took in the room silently as he surveyed the mess. He stopped by the window, squinting at the twisted lock and the clean break in the frame.

Leilani scanned for evidence, every sense hyper-tuned. The drum's absence was like missing a limb—the void still vibrating with memory. She faced her mother. "Was anyone here last night?"

"Auntie Kalea," Naalei replied, her voice steady. "She left at ten, locked up behind her. When I came this morning, the back door was open. Nothing was taken from the office. Only the pahu." Her hands hovered over the empty stand, fingers trembling despite her composure. "It's been in the family for at least a hundred years."

Leilani crouched low, inspecting the perimeter of the stand. On the floor below, a glimmer of red drew her eye. She pulled a pair of nitrile gloves out of her pocket. She plucked it up—varnish, still tacky, smeared along a sliver of wood.

She glanced at Isaac, who kneeled by the door, examining the pried lock with a jeweler's loupe. "Tool marks are clean," he called over. "Straight blade, probably a lock shim. No damage to the glass."

Leilani held up the wood flake. "You see this? Koa, fresh coat. Same as the museum display."

Isaac straightened, his lips pursed. "You thinking what I'm thinking?"

"Same perp," she said. "Or at least, the same tools. Means they hit the museum, then came here."

Isaac pointed at the jumbled floor. "Only one thing was taken, yet here, the perp damaged other artifacts. What else might they have been looking for."

Naalei smiled a sad smile. "Most of these items are reproductions. Other than the drum, there was nothing of value."

Leilani turned to Naalei. "Was there any word? Anyone asking about the drum, trying to see it?"

"No one unusual. Only students, their parents, and other kumu."

"You sure?" Isaac pressed, his tone gentle. "No odd phone calls, strangers hanging around after class?"

Naalei smiled, with an icy edge to it. "I've been teaching for thirty years, Isaac. I know every scam that walks through these doors. This was no amateur."

Leilani experienced a surge of pride at her mother's iron. She pulled a zip bag from her pocket, carefully sealed the wood fragment, and labeled it in block letters.

Isaac moved through the room with a predator's patience, taking mental snapshots. "No prints," he said, gesturing to the doorframe. "You can see where they wiped it down."

Leilani nodded. "Whoever did this was careful. They didn't want souvenirs, didn't want to be seen. Only the pahu. The damaged items bother me."

A knock sounded at the front door. One of the patrol officers poked his head in. "Detective? Got a neighbor who says they saw a car idling down the block. White panel van, no markings."

"Get a canvass going and pull any outdoor cameras within two blocks."

The officer nodded and ducked out.

Naalei remained by the empty stand, her composure now beginning to crack. "I want you to find it, Lani," she said, her voice low. "Not for us. For the halau. For the island."

Leilani moved closer, placed a steady hand on her mother's arm. "We will," she promised. "I swear it."

Naalei drew in a breath and let it out slowly, the tension rolling off her like a surf at dusk. "Thank you, daughter."

The three of them stood there in the circle of sunlight and loss until Isaac gently cleared his throat. "If the thief is targeting cultural items, they may try again. Are there any other pieces that would matter as much?"

Naalei considered. "The kapa. Or the lei niho palaoa in the Bishop's archives. But nothing like the drum."

Isaac turned to Leilani. "We should notify the museums. Have them double up on security."

"I'll call it in," she said.

They walked Naalei out, past the debris of practice and memory, into the clear air. The officers lingered nearby, taking orders from a patrol sergeant.

When her mother was gone, Leilani turned to Isaac. "You think it's the same buyer as the feather cloak?"

He nodded. "If not the buyer, then someone working the same list."

She stared back at the halau, at the shattered quiet inside. "I thought this city was finished taking from us," she said.

Isaac's eyes softened, but he kept his distance. "We'll get it back."

The sun had climbed over the mountain by the time they walked back to her Explorer. The day seemed impossibly bright, the case suddenly a living thing with its own momentum. As they got in, Leilani set her jaw and made a silent promise to herself, her mother, and to every artifact that had survived the city's endless appetite for forgetting.

Nobody was taking anything else. Not on her watch.

She fired up the engine, Isaac at her side, and aimed the explorer towards downtown.

The hunt was on.

# Chapter Three

## A New Player Emerges

The Honolulu Museum of Art looked like it belonged in another city—Boston, or San Francisco—if it weren't for the wall of humidity and the perfume of plumeria drifting in through the open doors. Leilani stood tall in the glamorous marble lobby of the Honolulu Museum of Art, her black clutch tightly clenched in one hand. Her minidress, a jewel-toned confection, accentuated her curves and showed her firm thighs as she fidgeted with the strap. The rich blue color stood out against the white marble floor. The silk tight against her skin. Her long black hair was pulled up from her neck in a beautiful bun; the gold and jeweled butterfly hairpin sparkled in the lights. Her six-inch stiletto heels accented her sculpted, tanned legs. She was stunning, and Isaac couldn't help but notice, as did several other men and women when they walked in.

Isaac Torres, standing beside her, wore his suit as if it were an extension of his own body. The lines were perfect, the tie a subtle blue. He looked the way the museum looked: like he'd been born into this world, and he scanned the crowd with an ease that made her want to elbow him in the ribs. Instead, she whispered, "See anything suspicious yet?"

He smiled without turning his head. "Other than your shoes?"

She stifled a laugh. "Funny. Bet you didn't have to

Google how to tie your tie."

"I did not," he said, nodding at the slow swirl of patrons gathering around the check-in table. "But I had to borrow the shoes. I didn't expect to be working at a party."

A ukulele trio played in the corner, soft and almost lost against the sea of voices. Crystal chandeliers cast halos on the crowd. Waitstaff in white shirts and flower leis circulated with trays of sparkling wine and half-moon slices of fresh mango. The air was equal parts laughter, expensive perfume and the undercurrent of competition—every guest here was auditioning for something.

Leilani accepted a glass and let the bubbles settle before she sipped. She scanned the nametags as people drifted past: gallery owners, media personalities, and at least one state senator. She counted no less than three men with the same lacquered hair and linen suit combo, and two women who might have been in direct competition for "Most Surgical Touch-Ups Per Square Inch of Skin." No one met her gaze for longer than a second, but she clocked each one anyway, matching faces to the files in her head. Honolulu wasn't a big city; the names repeated if you looked hard enough.

"I see two," Isaac murmured, nodding with his chin toward the east gallery entrance. "Blonde woman in the red, and the guy with the thick glasses. He's been to three different tables asking questions. Didn't look at the art once."

"Red is Dolly Burton, a collector," Leilani said. "She's been on the island for about a decade. She got flagged last year for trying to bribe a registrar. Pretty low-level, never charged. And Glasses—" She trailed off, checking her memory. "Docent, I think? He did a lecture series on Polynesian tattooing. Nothing suspicious."

Isaac arched an eyebrow. "You have a weird brain, you know that?"

"I try not to let it show." She scanned for cameras—discreetly embedded in the molding, exactly where they should be. Museum security hovered near the doors, all in matching black suits, the sort that got paid by the hour and wouldn't stop an actual heist if it walked right by.

Through the tall glass doors, the open-air galleries shimmered with reflected moonlight. Leilani could see the silhouettes of guests drifting among the outdoor installations: towering coral sculptures, a line of ironwood benches carved by hand. Somewhere above, on the lanai, a jazz band waited to replace the ukuleles when the night called for more drinking and less decorum.

She and Isaac made their way along the perimeter, staying in the sightlines but never central. She didn't want anyone to remember her unless she wanted to be remembered, which was almost impossible. During a recent investigation, while working as a cocktail server in a casino, the sprinklers were set off during a robbery. Her white shirt became translucent and left nothing to the imagination. Pictures from the SWAT team's body cameras caught every unfortunate minute of her exposure and went viral on both the police department network and on social media. She was still finding the images as screensavers on computers at headquarters.

"I hate these things," she muttered as they passed a wall-sized mural of the Hawaiian royal family. "It's like a debutante ball for adults."

Isaac grinned. "That's the point. Everyone here thinks they're auditioning for the next chapter of Honolulu's power index. They can't help but put on a show."

Leilani eyed him. "You sound like you've been to a lot of these."

"My uncle was in city government on the mainland," he said. "Got dragged to a fundraiser every month. You learn to recognize the species." He let his eyes linger. "But you blend in well. If you smile, they'll assume you're running for office."

She shot him a look. "I don't do smiling."

"That's not true," he said. "You smiled at the last crime scene."

"That was a grimace. Big difference."

Isaac laughed, the sound bright but not loud enough to carry.

They moved through the room in practiced sweeps, taking in every detail. The featured exhibit—Oceania: The Tides of History—occupied the center gallery, its entryway flanked by two massive feather standards called kahili, each topped with a riot of 'i'iwi feathers. It should have looked regal, but to Leilani, it looked like endangered birds had crash-landed in the rotunda.

"Check that out," Isaac said, tilting his glass. "See

the security team?"

"Yeah. Overkill, even for this."

"I counted seven plainclothes and four in-house. And at least two more in the parking structure." He kept his voice level as his eyes tracked the edges of the crowd. "Somebody's expecting trouble."

Leilani experienced a twinge in her chest. She thought of her mother's halau, the gaping hole where the pahu used to sit. "Or they're trying to prevent a problem before it happens. Do you think we'll get through the night without a scene?"

"That depends. If our thief is here, they might want to case the new displays. Or show off."

She scanned the artwork. She recognized several artifacts as part of the museum's permanent collection—war clubs, stone adzes, a quilt of kapa with a note showing it was painstakingly restored by Dr. Mahina's team. But there were also pieces on loan, which meant new targets, new opportunities for someone who'd showed a taste for the irreplaceable.

"I'm betting on show-off," she said. "Whoever took the cape and the pahu wants us to know they're smarter than we are."

Isaac shrugged. "Ego. It's the same with every art thief I've ever chased. The good ones don't want money. They want to be remembered."

Leilani watched a guest in a navy suit glide past the cordon and pause in front of the feather cape display of a lesser chief. He lingered, hands behind his back, head cocked at a precise angle. She made a mental note of his posture, the measured distance he kept from the display. Not reverence—more like appraisal.

She drifted closer, motioning for Isaac to hang back. As she passed the case, she let her eyes linger on the cape. The museum had staged it beautifully: mounted on a headless mannequin, feathers catching the light, every stitch visible in relief. It was almost perfect. Almost. But at a glance, Leilani noticed the tiny imperfection, a patch near the hem, barely off-color, where the original had been repaired after a theft in the '70s. She tucked the detail away.

The man in the navy suit glanced her way, offered a polite smile, then returned his focus to the cape.

Leilani waited until he moved on, and she pivoted back to Isaac. "You see that?"

"I saw you see it," he said. "What are you thinking?"

"He looked at the repair. Not the feathers, not the plaque, not the craftsmanship. The repair." She kept her voice low. "That's not a collector move; that's a craftsman or a forger."

Isaac considered. "Or someone who knows exactly what they're looking at."

They circled the next gallery, where a cluster of older guests whispered in Japanese, their voices soft but urgent. At the far end, two young women with perfect beach hair pretended to take selfies in front of a bronze tiki god. But when Leilani looked closely, the woman's phone camera was aimed at the crowd, not the art.

"Subtle," she muttered.

"What?"

"Fake selfies. Crowd surveillance."

Isaac nodded, lips pursed. "Could be a journalist."

They pressed on, skirting the buffet table, past a group of donors arguing over whether the museum should use native or imported wood in its next restoration. Leilani felt the tension in her shoulders bleed away, replaced by a kind of hunter's focus. She didn't like these events, but she understood them: the rules, the pecking order, and the way the smallest gesture could tip the balance.

She stepped onto the open-air terrace, inhaling the breeze. From here, she could see the city in miniature—lights blooming up the hill, the cathedral spire lit like a match. The hum of conversation drifted out and tangled with the call of geckos in the eaves. She let herself exhale.

Isaac joined her, two drinks in his hands. He handed one to Leilani. "You think the perp is in the crowd?"

"If I had to guess?" She watched a group of men with identical smiles cluster around a woman in a red silk dress. "I'd say yes. And if they're smart, they'll be the last person we'd expect."

"Or the first," Isaac said. "Sometimes the trick is hiding in plain sight."

Leilani sipped her drink and checked her phone for messages. Nothing from the lab yet, nothing from Tommy or Tano. She was on her own tonight.

"Do you ever wish you were on the other side of this?" Isaac asked, eyes on the city. "You know—a person who actually enjoys these parties?"

She smiled, the first real smile of the night. "No. But I do like the view."

He laughed and clinked his glass against hers. "To the view."

They stood together, silent, letting the sounds of the party roll over them. It was almost peaceful. Almost.

A voice—too loud, too practiced—rose above the music.

"Ladies and gentlemen!" The MC, a man in a sharkskin suit, waved his arms like he was flagging in a rescue chopper. "If you'll follow me into the main gallery, we're about to begin the charity auction!"

The crowd surged forward, guests gathering in a tide of eager anticipation. Leilani and Isaac fell in with them, letting themselves be swept into the grand hall.

At the far end, on a raised dais, stood the MC and a handful of museum staff. Behind them, the feather cape of a lesser chief gleamed under a focused beam of light, every eye in the room drawn to it.

Leilani braced herself for the show.

It was time to see who wanted to play their hand.

The main gallery thrummed with anticipation, auction paddles handed out to every registered guest, and with every eye trained on the head table. The museum's director worked the room, shaking hands and nodding graciously to the assembled wealth, but

Leilani only had eyes for the man at his side—a scarecrow figure in an ash-gray suit, his thinness sharpened by the black silk shirt beneath. His face was all bones and angles, a geometric equation made human, and his silver goatee looked like it had been etched with a ruler.

"Sam Worthington?" Isaac murmured, already tracking the man's orbit.

"Has to be," Leilani replied. She watched him greet donors with the offhand ease of a man who knew every power-broker in the room, his handshake more a performance than a greeting. From across the space, she could hear his accent—hard, New England, cut-glass—and the way it made his compliments sound like mild threats. The other guests deferred to him without knowing why.

Worthington's arrival on Oahu had been as dramatic and headline-grabbing as a volcanic eruption. One month, nobody had heard of him; the next, his name was in every society column and business section in the state, always linked to figures with an embarrassing number of zeroes and a backstory that mutated with every telling. Some said he made his fortune in rare earth mining; others claimed it was algorithmic trading; and there were rumors—persistent but never confirmed—about a chain of encrypted data centers in Singapore. What was indisputable was the money: so much of it that the local banking and real estate markets had warped slightly in his orbit, like a black hole bending light.

The official story, the one the PR reps and museum director loved to repeat, was that Worthington had divested his entire tech empire for an "undisclosed sum" rumored to be in the low billions. Afterward, he reinvented himself as the Medici of the Pacific. He bought one of the most ostentatious estates on the North Shore—a sprawl of glass and cedar perched on a bluff with its own beach and three acres of native forest—and put out a press release promising the land would never be carved into parcels, never be paved. He called it a cultural easement. He held summits with local leaders, donated to every rescue shelter and food bank, and announced his intention to make Hawaii the new world capital of art and ethics. The first step, apparently, was to take every available invitation to a gala, fundraiser, or black-tie launch within driving distance of Honolulu.

The locals' reaction was split down the middle: half saw Worthington as a benevolent force, a haole billionaire whose heart might beat to the right rhythm, while the other half waited for the mask to drop, convinced he was one more predator with a more expensive suit. Among the old-money set, Worthington was an oddity—the man who'd drink with the mayor and donate twice as much to the mayor's opponent to keep things interesting. He had no children, no pets, and no visible hobbies beyond collecting Polynesian art and collecting stories about himself.

There was also the matter of his wife. Nobody could remember her name—she was always Mrs. Worthington, rarely seen, but when she was, not without two stemless wine glasses and a stack of thank-you notes to sign. The estate's staff called her the ghost, and the one time Leilani tried to Google her, she hit a firewall so thick it might as well have been classified. Rumors swirled about a daughter back on the mainland, but nobody could ever say it with certainty. What they knew was that Sam Worthington never traveled without an entourage of bodyguards, art curators, and at least one personal chef rumored to have worked for actual royalty.

Since his arrival, Worthington had also begun collecting cultural oddities at a rate that made auction houses salivate and anthropologists nervous. He acquired artifacts through both legal and questionable channels, never hesitating to flex his influence if an item caught his eye. At least twice, Leilani's own department had fielded quiet requests to "assist" when Worthington's agents attempted to repatriate disputed pieces—always through the proper legal channels, of course, but with an undertone that suggested the rules were more like guidelines. To his credit, he made significant donations to restoration programs and museums, and if he won a contested artifact, he would hold a public exhibition. Nine times out of ten, he'd gift it to the people of Hawaii. The running joke among the museum staff was that Sam Worthington bought things for the pleasure of giving them away.

Still, Leilani's instincts prickled. She'd met enough philanthropists to know that nobody spent that much money on the public good without expecting a return, even if it was only the right to throw a bigger party next year. And behind the deference that Worthington commanded, Leilani sensed hesitation. He wasn't a player in the old game; he was the type who wanted to write new rules.

At tonight's event, his presence had already shifted the gravitational field. Curators nervously fussed with their notes, donors checked to see if their families made the seating chart within three tables of his, and the museum director—usually a picture of serene confidence—hovered behind Worthington like a supplicant at court. When Sam Worthington laughed, people turned to see if they were supposed to laugh too. The security detail, burly and bored at the beginning of the night, now gave the impression of anticipating an exam—something Worthington himself could devise, to see if they were focused.

Sam Worthington made his way along the buffet line, taking a single olive off a canape. He used the pause as a pretext to lean into a state legislator's personal space and finish his point. Leilani could see how the man owned every conversation—never waiting for permission, always setting the terms. She half-expected him to pull out a tape measure and start rearranging the art.

Isaac arched an eyebrow. "He's good."

She grinned. "He's terrifying."

They shadowed Worthington as he cut through the crowd, watching him switch modes with every new person he encountered: magnanimous host to one, cool expert to the next, and genial alpha for the money men. If there was a secret code to the room, he'd written it. When the director tried to break away, Worthington reeled him back in with two fingers to the elbow— subtle, proprietary.

Finally, when Worthington's route took him within

range of the feather cape, Leilani signaled to Isaac and they stepped into his path. Worthington stopped, made a micro-adjustment to his posture, and gave them the smile he reserved for potential adversaries. He looked Leilani up and down like a predator looking at its prey. His gaze lingered momentarily on her legs before he looked up and smiled.

"Detectives," he said, his voice not quite quiet enough to be a secret. "I'm flattered. I was told Honolulu's finest would be represented tonight, but I expected brass, not the real brains of the operation."

Isaac shook the man's hand, taking the measure of his grip. "Sam Worthington, I presume. Detective Isaac Torres, and this is Detective Kealoha."

Worthington's grip was dry and fast, as if he couldn't wait to let go and get back to controlling the room. His eyes flicked over Leilani. He had catalogued everything: the dress, the shoes, the unpolished nails, and the tension in her jaw.

"I've heard about you both," Worthington said. "All good, mostly. Is this a social visit, or am I under suspicion for jaywalking on Bishop Street?"

Leilani smiled. "We're here to keep the artifacts safe. But I'd be lying if I said we weren't a little curious about your new project."

Worthington's face lit up, as if he'd been waiting for the pitch. "Ah, the Cultural Center. My pet obsession. It's long overdue—Hawaii's treasures deserve a better home than this repurposed mausoleum. We're raising funds for a world-class center, all local input, no colonial nonsense." He turned the full intensity of his gaze on Leilani, as if she alone could decide the project's fate.

"That's a lofty ambition," she said. "Few outsiders would put their own money on the line for a local cause."

Worthington gave a small, contemptuous snort. "Money is a tool, Detective. Like a microscope or a chisel. I have the means to open doors others don't know exist."

Isaac leaned in, voice dry. "And what is it you're hoping to find behind those doors, Mr. Worthington?"

He looked at Isaac as if he'd asked whether the sky was blue. "Access. Legacy. The chance to be remembered for more than my balance sheet." His smile slipped, but only for an instant. "Isn't that what we're all after?"

Leilani played along. "Some people want to be left alone."

Worthington laughed. "And some people pretend to until you shine a bright enough light on their ambitions."

The MC's voice rolled through the gallery, announcing the start of the auction, but Worthington ignored it. He surveyed the feather cape as if appraising it for shipment.

"Astonishing, isn't it?" he said. "That something so fragile could outlast entire civilizations. The work involved in each feather, each knot—most people observe only the color. But the devil is always in the work."

He pointed, not quite touching the glass. "The restoration on that hem. You notice it?"

Leilani sensed her pulse falter. "Yes."

"Whoever did it was either a genius or an idiot. They matched the technique perfectly, but the dye is off. Too much cochineal. It glows under the wrong light."

Isaac smiled. "You know your stuff."

Worthington regarded him with sudden intensity. "I know more than I'd like. The same could be said for your department, yes? Your special investigations team—what is it you're calling yourselves now? The Shadow Bureau?"

Leilani tensed enough for him to notice.

"I read the papers," Worthington said. "The mainlanders may laugh at your crusade against city corruption, but I find it admirable. You cut right to the bone. That's rare in this town."

He let the compliment dangle, waiting to see who'd grab it.

Leilani chose not to. "We try to do our jobs."

Worthington's eyes crinkled in amusement. "A humble cop. How refreshing."

There was a pause—three, four seconds—where he seemed to weigh something.

"I'll be blunt," he said. "There's a market for these artifacts, Detective. Every major collector in the world has at least one piece acquired by less than legal means. What's new is the level of sophistication. In the last year, the thefts have become art themselves—timing, technique, the vanishing act. I respect that, even as I despise it."

Isaac cut in. "You think it's one crew?"

Worthington shrugged. "Or it's a dozen, all competing. But if I were you, I'd look at the restoration teams. The forgers. They're the only ones with the skill to take a feather cape apart and make it vanish."

Leilani watched him for any tell, but the man was a vault. She tried a feint. "You've never had anything go missing from your own collection?"

Worthington smiled with a touch of venom. "I run my life the way I ran my businesses—risk is calculated, contingencies in place. But the difference between a collector and a thief is always one bad day, isn't it?"

A ripple of laughter erupted from the main stage as the MC finished a joke, but Worthington kept his eyes on her. "I'm happy to show you my holdings, Detective. No secrets, no locked cabinets. If you think I'm involved, come see for yourself."

She weighed the offer, tried to see the trap. But Worthington was already moving, his attention focused on the auction.

"Excuse me," he said, already a half-step away. "Duty calls."

He left them standing there, the afterimage of his smile like a watermark on the conversation.

Isaac exhaled. "That was exhausting."

Leilani grinned. "You get used to it."

They drifted to the back of the gallery, both keeping Worthington in their peripheral vision. The auction rolled on—signed posters, a donated guitar, a morning at the Kahala spa. The crowd applauded politely, then with genuine heat when the MC announced the museum's plans for the new cultural center.

Leilani watched Worthington work the donors, always two steps ahead of the game. He laughed at the right moments, asked questions that sounded polite but cut straight to the core, and never let his own agenda slip for more than a second.

Isaac kept his eyes on the crowd. "What do you think?"

She considered. "He's hiding something. Not the cape, but something."

"You trust him?"

She gazed at Worthington and at the feather cape. "Not at all."

"He seemed interested in you. Couldn't keep his eyes off you," said Isaac.

Leilani laughed. "Yeah, interested like a lion is interested in a lamb." She snickered at the thought that Isaac was a little jealous. So far, their relationship had remained professional because that's how she wanted it, but she knew Isaac was interested in more. She noticed he also had trouble keeping his eyes off her.

The auction ended with a crescendo of applause, the director beaming as he announced a record haul for the museum. Leilani clapped along, but her mind was elsewhere. The entire night had been a dance, every step choreographed. Worthington was the sort of individual who created mazes, subsequently tempting others to become lost inside.

Isaac nudged her. "You want to follow up on his offer?"

Leilani checked her phone—still no messages, which meant the lab hadn't found anything useful. She weighed the risks.

"Let's see what the man's hiding," she said.

As they made their way out, Leilani glanced over her shoulder one last time. Worthington was standing alone in front of the cape, hands behind his back, eyes narrowed in a look that was part admiration, part hunger. She shivered. The city had always belonged to predators, but tonight she knew exactly which one was hunting.

Leilani and Isaac didn't have to wait long. Ten minutes after the auction ended, as guests lingered for photo ops and final flutes of prosecco, Sam Worthington appeared behind them, conjured by the sheer force of his own self-importance. His voice was a saw blade, precise and loud enough for them to hear over the fade-out of jazz.

"Detectives," he called, his eyes flicking from Leilani to Isaac. "You two have the look of people who prefer conversation to cocktails. Indulge me?"

He led them away from the traffic of departing guests, toward a side corridor lined with glass cases. It was quieter here. The only audience was a line of terracotta masks staring from the walls, their features frozen in polite horror.

Worthington didn't waste time. "It's rare," he began, "to meet public servants who care about the artifacts they're protecting. You're not ticking off boxes, are you?"

Leilani matched his tone, easy as you please. "I grew up around these things. My mom teaches hula. Most of our culture is oral, but the physical pieces— they hold the line. They're all that's left after the missionaries and the state park brochures have had their say."

He smiled. It was not a kind smile. "A poet with a badge. There's hope for the system after all."

Isaac interrupted. "We're curious, Mr. Worthington. You seem to know a lot about these recent thefts. More than I'd expect from a collector."

Worthington's eyes glittered. "It's a small world, Detective. I make it my business to know what's being stolen in any city I frequent. The genuine pieces never surface again—unless someone with my kind of money puts up a reward. The thieves are idiots. The buyers, not so much."

"Still," Leilani said, "you know specifics. At my mom's halau, the drum was taken, and it was the only item that had any real value. At the Bishop, it was the cape. You noticed the restoration flaw. None of that's in the paper."

Worthington steepled his fingers, not feigning surprise. "You want to know how I keep up? Simple. I ask. People love to talk if you're willing to listen."

Isaac smiled thinly. "Most don't listen as well as you do."

Worthington shrugged, and in the movement, Leilani caught a faint, oily note—Koa varnish, but sharper, more pungent. It clung to him like a cologne, beneath the real one. He leaned closer to the case, examining the inlaid bowls on display.

"I have a proposal," Worthington said. "If you'll pardon the hubris. I have a private but properly documented collection. Some items are on the edge of legal export. If you're interested in examining them, I'd welcome your expertise."

Leilani tried to read him: the set of the jaw, the hands, the eyes always moving, always gathering. This was not a man who liked to be doubted. But he loved to be challenged.

"I'll take you up on it," she said. "But you have to answer one question straight. Why Hawaiian artifacts? You could fund a dozen galleries of European art. Why this?"

Worthington's smile receded. "The mainland collects its own. No one cares for the islands except the people born here. And frankly, the collectors who do are usually exploiters, not preservationists. I'm hoping to see this city own its past, not watch it leak into the Pacific one piece at a time."

"You sound invested," Isaac said.

Worthington looked at him, then at Leilani. "I am. In every sense of the word."

The man let the silence settle. He fished a card from his breast pocket and handed it to Leilani. She noticed the weight—thick cardstock, embossed, the letters dark and exact.

"You have my number," Worthington said. "Call anytime."

He excused himself with a quick, dismissive nod and strode away, pausing only to bark a command at a passing security guard about better lighting on the next exhibition.

Isaac and Leilani watched him go. They turned to each other.

"Thoughts?" she asked, barely above a whisper.

"He knows way too much," Isaac said. "And he wants us to know it. That's not a collector. That's a player."

She grinned, adrenaline fizzing beneath the skin. "Game on."

They left the side corridor and rejoined the trickle of guests into the humid night. The scent of plumeria clung to their hair. Leilani flicked the card in her fingers, noting the indentation of each letter, the silent challenge implied in the weight.

She slipped the card into her clutch and started the mental list of everything she would need to figure out what Sam Worthington was up to.

It was a short list, but it was growing.

# Chapter Four

## Family Ties

The hula halau was brighter than Leilani remembered. Maybe it was the absence, the vacuum left by the missing pahu, or it could have been the way the sunlight slanted in, turning the polished Koa wood floors to liquid gold. She hovered at the threshold, her eyes adjusting, and inhaled the room's familiar perfume—sweat, coconut oil, and plumeria blossoms crushed between someone's palms. It was still a sanctuary, now stripped of its sacred drum.

Inside, Naalei Kealoha moved with a choreography that defied her age. She stood near the altar wall, her trim figure draped in a blue pareu skirt, silver hair pinned up with a battered, yellow hibiscus. Her hands shaped order out of the morning's chaos—aligning 'uli'uli rattles, straightening stacks of kapa cloth, repositioning an armful of feathered kahili so their colors fanned perfectly. There was more care than usual in the way she handled each object, a deliberate tenderness reserved for the aftermath of violation.

"Mom," Leilani called out, soft enough not to startle. She stepped inside, taking care to sidestep the scuffed groove left on the floor by a toppled ipu heke. The police tape from the break-in was gone but not forgotten.

Naalei turned, her face pre-set for business. She melted into a smile. "Lani, you brought the good coffee, yeah?"

Leilani lifted the cardboard carrier and waggled it. "And malasadas. I stopped at Leonard's."

"Now you're talking my language." The kumu hula shuffled her implements to one side. She headed for the folding table at the back, where they usually hosted post-class potlucks and impromptu gossip summits.

Leilani followed, setting the cups down and tearing open the pink pastry box. She watched her mother's eyes scan the room, cataloging what was out of place and what had survived. There was a new steel combination lock on the door, a chunk of baseboard missing near the rear exit, a pale rectangle on the wall where the pahu's shadow still lingered.

They sat in silence. Outside, the steady drone of weed-whackers, the chitter of mynas. Inside, the two of them and the echo of dancers gone home.

Naalei broke first. "The police called again this morning. Some detectives I didn't know. I told them what I told you—no, I didn't see anyone, yes, I locked up at ten. They wanted to know if we had enemies."

"Everyone has enemies," Leilani said, tearing a malasada in half. She offered the piece, but her mother waved it off, fingers already sticky with powdered sugar. "But I don't think this is vengeance. It's too clean. They wanted one thing, and they got it."

Naalei made a low, considering sound. "What if they come back for the kapa, or the poi pounders? Some of those are a hundred years old."

"No reason to believe they will, since they didn't take them when they took the drum," said Leilani.

"The thief was after one thing. The drum."

Naalei nodded and sipped her coffee. Leilani's words were comforting, but she was still uneasy.

Leilani shrugged, setting her coffee aside. "We're putting a car on the street for the next week. It's probably a onetime hit."

Her mother gave a skeptical squint. "You never say 'probably' when you mean it, Lani. I can still tell."

Leilani smiled despite herself. "You know me too well."

There was a rhythm to their conversation—a give and take, a long silence stretched like taffy until the next beat. Leilani let it spool out before speaking again.

"I had an interesting encounter last night," she said. "At the art museum. The guy running the new Hawaiian Cultural Center—Sam Worthington—he made a point of seeking me out."

Naalei's eyebrows rose. "That man. He came by this morning and left a few minutes before you arrived. Told me he was sad to hear about the break-in."

Leilani's cup halted halfway to her lips. "What did he want?"

"To hire me," her mother said, her voice dry. "Consult on the center's opening. Said I was the only kumu on the island he'd trust to make sure the hula wasn't 'Disney-fied.' His words, not mine." She gave a short, barking laugh, but her eyes flicked away. "He knows how to flatter, that's for sure."

Leilani's jaw tightened. "Did you accept?"

"I told him I'd think about it," Naalei said, looking at her daughter with a little too much challenge. "Lani, this is my world. If they're going to build something, someone has to do it right."

"He's not Hawaiian," Leilani said. "He doesn't know the difference between mana and mayonnaise."

"Oh, he knows plenty," her mother replied, a touch defensive. "He quoted Queen Liliuokalani at me. He brought up my grandmother, the way she started the halau in Waianae. And you should've heard him talk about the museum—the politics, the donors, all the backbiting. It's like he's been here forever."

Leilani remembered the way Worthington had watched her at the gala. The man was a sponge, soaking up everything, then wringing it out in exactly the way you least expected.

"Did he mention the drum?" Leilani asked.

"He did," Naalei said, a shadow passing her face. "Said it was an outrage. He put up a reward—ten thousand dollars, no questions asked, for the safe return of the pahu."

The words hung in the air. Leilani pressed her palm against the paper cup, heat blooming in her fingers. She thought about the case board back at the station, the pattern of artifact thefts, and the way each was surgically chosen. She thought about the cape, the vanished fishhooks, and now her own family's treasure.

"Mom," she said, voice low. "Be careful with this man. He's not what he seems."

Naalei made a skeptical noise, but her hands betrayed her—fussing with the lei hanging over the chair-back. "You always think everyone's a con."

"I'm paid to think that," Leilani replied, but there was no bite in it. "It's not only him. There's a pattern to these thefts. Someone's building a set—maybe for a collector, maybe to repatriate, I don't know. But Worthington's got his fingers in all of it."

"He's not the one who stole the pahu," Naalei said. "Besides the reward, he offered to pay for a replacement if we wanted. Said it would be a donation to the halau. He was very genuine."

Leilani stilled. "And you don't find that suspicious? He was at the gala last night, Mom. Less than eight hours after your drum goes missing, he's here visiting you and offering to replace a priceless artifact. Nobody moves that fast unless they're part of the story."

Naalei bristled, tugging at the hibiscus behind her ear. "What do you want me to do, Lani? Tell him to go away? Refuse to help with the center? You know how many people would kill for this chance?"

Leilani hesitated, searching for the right words. "Please keep your eyes open. If he asks you to do anything weird—anything that seems wrong—I want you to tell me. Promise?"

Her mother's face was a patchwork—part pride, part irritation, part the old, fierce love that survived every argument and disappointment. She picked up the malasada, bit into it, and dusted sugar from her lips.

"I promise," she said, her voice thick with

something Leilani couldn't quite name. "But I also promise not to let anyone make a fool of me. Not even you, daughter."

Leilani smiled as the tension uncoiled enough to breathe.

A shadow moved outside, a flicker of motion across the sidewalk. A patrol car, making its loop. Leilani checked her watch, stood, gathered the coffee cups and dusted off her hands.

"Next week is Kai's birthday," she said. "You're still doing the pa'ina at Kaimana, yeah?"

"Of course," Naalei said. "I ordered the poke already. But you're in charge of the cake."

"Store-bought or homemade?"

"Do you really want to test me on this?" her mother asked, and they both laughed.

Leilani moved to the door. She stared at her mother in the forgiving light—her manner, her bright eyes, the hands still strong enough to guide three generations of dancers through their first 'ami.

"You're the bravest woman I know, Mom," she said, voice almost a whisper.

"And you're the stubbornest child ever born on Oahu," her mother whispered. "You get it from me."

Leilani stepped forward and wrapped her arms around the older woman, snuggling into the solid, unyielding body that had never once let her fall. She let herself sink into the comfort.

"I'll watch Worthington," Leilani said, pulling back

enough to meet her mother's gaze. "No matter how nice he sounds."

Naalei put her hands on Leilani's shoulders and squeezed, hard. "You always do."

They stood like that for a long time, letting the halau fill with the sound of their breathing and the faint music of memory, until the sun dipped lower and the world outside remembered to move again.

***

Home was louder than usual. The first thing Leilani heard as she slipped off her shoes and dropped her backpack was Kai's voice, ricocheting off every surface in the house. The place looked like it had been hit by a crosswind of science fair debris: posterboard on every available flat surface, colored markers uncapped and drying into hard nubs, a scatter of printer paper fanned across the dining table like a magician's trick gone wrong.

She set her keys on the hook, placed her pistol in the lockbox on the kitchen counter and surveyed the chaos. Her son stood in the middle of it all, ten years old and vibrating with the energy of someone three malasadas deep into a sugar binge. His long hair was twisted into a samurai bun, a self-applied tattoo peeking out from under his left ear—a Sharpie gecko, already half-smudged from sweat.

"Mom!" he yelled, but remembered the rule about inside voices and started again, lower. "Mom, you gotta see this!"

She hung her jacket on a chair and made a show of

looking impressed. "Did you start a business while I was out, or is this homework?"

"Project," he said, gesturing her closer with both hands. "It's due next week, but I'm almost done. Wanna see?"

"Hit me," she said, sitting cross-legged on the couch. "Give me the show."

Kai grinned and shuffled through the mess, finally plucking a single sheet from the pile. "Okay, so, we had to pick something about Hawaiian history, right? But no surfing, no tourist stuff. So, I picked—wait for it—How people keep culture alive when everything else changes." He grinned, waiting for her approval.

"That's a heavy topic," Leilani said, proud despite herself.

He shrugged, as if this were no big deal. "I interviewed three kupuna for it—Aunty Keely, Aunty Lena at the hula studio, and the janitor at school. He's not a real kupuna, but he remembers when all the roads were dirt." Kai started laying out the sheets in order, his motions precise for someone who never closed a marker cap in his life. Each page had photos: ancient implements, fishhooks and a side-by-side of two different feather capes.

"I started looking for stories," Kai continued, "because you said before that stories last longer than anything, including rocks. So, I made a timeline, see?" He unrolled a strip of butcher paper that stretched from the coffee table onto the floor. "This is where I got stuck, but it's cool. Look!"

The timeline ran from first contact with Captain Cook to, apparently, that afternoon. Along the line, little illustrations, and magazine clippings: missionaries, plantation workers, a smiling Queen Liliuokalani with a speech bubble that said. "Aloha means more than hello." But what made Leilani lean in was the series of artifact pictures along the bottom—capes, drums, poi pounders—and the way Kai had drawn small, exaggerated X marks over some of them.

"These are the things people tried to take away," Kai explained, proud of the visual. "Like the museum said, sometimes stuff goes missing and they don't get it back for years. Aunty Keely said sometimes the old temple sites got raided, and nobody ever found out where the stuff disappeared to."

Leilani's scalp prickled. "Which temple sites?"

"The one up by the water tanks—remember the hike we did? And the one near Aunty Keely's cousin's house, where the boulders have petroglyphs. She said that when she was little, someone stole a wooden idol, and nobody knows who did it. The papers stopped talking about it."

He made it sound like the punchline to a ghost story, but Leilani sensed her heart kick. "Do you remember what year that was?"

Kai frowned and flipped through his handwritten notes. "Ummm, nineteen-seventy-four? She said it was before her cousin moved to the mainland."

Seventy-four. That was the same year as the feather cape job in the museum's private incident file. She kept her voice level. "And Aunty Lena, what did she say?"

"She said her tutu used to hide stuff in their house—feather things, like hats and leis—because people would buy them to cut up and sell. Or sometimes they'd burn them, so nobody else could have them. Which is nuts, right?"

"Super nuts," Leilani agreed, running a finger along the timeline.

Kai's excitement kept rising. "But here's the best part, Mom. See the red dots?" He pointed to a series of marks that skipped across the paper from left to right. "Those are all the times somebody stole something, and it showed up later somewhere else. Like, in a different museum or a collection on the mainland. It's like a secret path, see?"

She did see. It was a literal red line through a century of thefts. She was about to ask him to slow down when Kai moved into full TED Talk, standing on the coffee table and holding up a pointer he'd fashioned from a broken chopstick.

"Okay," he said. "So, if you connect the dots, it always goes from a small collection to a big collection, and sometimes, to a private person. And every time something gets stolen, there's like a three-year gap where nobody knows what happened to it."

Leilani whistled. "That's brilliant, Kai. You made your own cold case map."

He beamed and slouched into a mock bow. "Thank you. Wait until you see my slides."

She had the impulse to hug him, but she sat a little straighter, her mind racing. The pattern was there, plain as the red ink on Kai's timeline: theft, dormant years, followed by reemergence—always in a richer or more prestigious setting. It was the same MO as the current run on artifacts, but no one in her department had pieced it together with the old stuff. Not even her.

Kai leaped off the table, nearly landing on a packet of goldfish crackers, and looked at her for approval. "Do you think the teacher will like it?"

"She'll freak out," Leilani said. "Lose the part about arson, though. It's a little much for fifth grade."

"Can I keep the story about the guy who stole a shrunken head?"

She considered. "If you promise not to use it for show-and-tell."

He grinned. "Deal."

She took a picture of his timeline with her phone, paying attention to the cluster around 1974. "Do you mind if I show this to someone at work? I think it might help the case."

Kai tried for a nonchalant shrug but failed. "Don't forget to tell Isaac that your son is the next Sherlock Holmes."

Kai had taken a liking to Isaac, especially after he and Leilani showed Isaac how to surf. They had surfed together, two guys, several times, and Leilani had learned to let go a little by not watching them from the sand dunes. She smiled.

"Done," she said. "But you've gotta eat dinner before you become famous. What do you want— ramen or leftovers?"

"Ramen, please. Extra Spam." He dropped the pointer and started gathering up his project, already humming a new tune.

Leilani watched him, her heart thumping with a mix of pride and worry. If Kai could see the pattern, there was no telling who else could. Or who already had.

She ruffled his hair on the way to the kitchen, and he protested but didn't duck.

"Thanks, Mom," he said, halfway lost in his thoughts.

"For what?"

"For always helping me see the story."

She smiled and got out the noodles. In the other room, Kai's project glowed under the lamplight— bright red lines, a century of theft, and the hopeful arc of things coming home. She hoped that this time they'd break the chain.

# Chapter Five

## Threads of Deception

Tommy Espinoza's hands were sweating through the steering wheel as he pulled the Crown Vic into the cracked parking lot of Kaimuki Woodworking. The sun was midday high, and the city was baking under an odd late heat wave. It striped the shopfront's metal roll-up door with hard shadows. Next to him, Officer Winston cracked his neck and squinted at the faded sign.

"Third shop today. Only two more on our list after this one, hopefully the third time's the charm," Winston said. His voice was lazy, but Tommy saw the tension: the way his fingers danced across the grip of his holstered Glock, the way he scanned the storefront with a predator's patience. They had been crisscrossing the island for the past two days, talking to shop owners about the museum theft. It had been a long two days.

"Yeah, if we're lucky, they'll offer us a damn lilikoi pie," Tommy answered, too loudly. He needed the banter, or else he'd start picturing the last place—the cracked paint, the old woman shaking so bad she could barely talk, the way Tommy had wanted to apologize for asking questions.

"Your optimism is blinding," Winston said, opening the door.

They got out almost in unison; the heat slapping them, and the badge lanyard swinging over his untucked shirt. Tommy seemed like an impostor in plain clothes. Working as a detective was still new, and the gun seemed heavier than when he'd carried it as a patrol cop.

Winston turned towards the door. Tommy stepped around the patrol car to join him. He tried to read the shop—big bay window, closed blinds, the cloying reek of fresh sawdust and the sharper bite of glue. No movement. The sign said CLOSED, but the strip-mall dentist next door was still seeing patients.

Tommy was about to ask if they should knock when all hell broke loose.

The glass behind the "OPEN/CLOSED" sign exploded, sending shards cartwheeled past Winston's head. The sound from the rifle—it had to be a rifle, no handgun made a crack like that—hammered Tommy's chest before his brain caught up. Winston jerked back, and for one sick instant Tommy thought the man's face had simply vanished. But it was the force of the shot; the round hit Winston high, right above the vest line, and spun him off his feet, his hat tumbling behind him.

Tommy didn't remember drawing his weapon. It was suddenly there in his hand, arms up and rigid, thumb already popping the safety and finger tight on the trigger. He dropped into a crouch behind the fender and returned fire—three quick pops at the darkness behind the window, because that was where his lizard brain said the shooter was.

"Shit—Winston!" He glanced over the hood. Winston was moving, not dead, dragging himself on his elbows toward the driver's side. The second shot dug a furrow into the asphalt inches from his heel, and he kicked like a swimmer, scrabbling for the tire well.

Tommy ducked and grabbed the back of Winston's collar, yanking him up and over in a clumsy arc behind the car. Winston crashed into the rear quarter panel and curled into a tight ball, cursing wetly.

"You hit?"

Winston's lips peeled off his teeth. "Vest got most, but—son of a bitch—burns like lava."

Another shot shattered the rear glass and sprayed their legs with glittering chips. Tommy swore and tried to think, tried to breathe. He clapped a hand on Winston's shoulder and did a quick body check.

"Stay down," he barked. He pulled his rover radio from his belt and keyed the mic.

"Dispatch, this is SIU 4, officer down! Officer down! Shots fired at Kaimuki Woodworking, Waialae Avenue! I need EMS. I need all units—perimeter up, suspect is still armed—"

He barely got the words out before another round caved in the side mirror and sang a ricochet off the trunk.

Tommy snapped two more shots at the window— one-handed, to keep the bastard's head down. His ears rang with it, and his brain started a quiet, useless countdown: thirty seconds to first patrol, a minute to real backup, three minutes if the guy in there had friends.

"Talk to me, Winston."

Winston was alive. "Oh, fuck," he said. "That fucking hurts."

"Got the breath knocked out," Winston coughed. "Fuck. Could have fractured a couple of ribs. Don't let me pass out, okay?"

"Stay with me, man," Tommy said. He thumbed the slide on his Glock, checked the mag, and tried to slow his breathing.

A movement—shadow on glass, top right. Tommy aimed, focused on the tiny break in the blind. A blurry face followed by another shot punched through the door. This one hit the patrol car's spotlight and sent pieces everywhere.

Tommy fired twice, slower this time, walking the shots up the window frame.

A shape darted left—a second guy? Tommy saw a flash of red cloth. His knees collapsed under him.

"Winston, you see that?"

But Winston had his eyes shut tight.

Tommy moved to the trunk and grabbed the spare magazine. He swapped it in with a click that seemed way too loud. He tasted metal in his mouth and realized he'd bitten his lip. The radio was squawking, dispatch calling for status.

"We're holding the perimeter," he said into the mic. "Suspects are in the building, unknown number, two seen, one rifle at least. Winston is conscious, shot to the vest, non-lethal."

"Hold position, SWAT en route," came the reply.

Tommy rolled his eyes at the hood. "Easy for you to say," he muttered.

The fire stopped. Long enough for Tommy to register the difference between chaos and the potential for real danger.

He risked a look: nothing. No movement, no further shots.

Tommy pressed his hand to Winston's shoulder, noting the twitch of his muscle and the slow, measured breaths. "We're good, Winston. Hold tight, okay?"

"Watch the side door. They always run for the alley," Winston rasped.

Tommy nodded, wiped sweat from his forehead with his sleeve, and shifted his position. The alley. If they made a break for it, they'd have a clear path to the next street over, and into the knot of backyards and open driveways that ran behind Waialae.

He keyed the radio again, voice low and urgent. "Dispatch, watch the rear. Suspects may break for the alley; request units on Hilea and Eighth Avenue."

"Copy, SIU 4."

Tommy steeled himself and set his focus on the front of the shop. His heart jabbed his ribs like a fist.

Seconds stretched into minutes, followed by another. Sirens now, coming from every direction, growing louder.

Tommy heard the crash and flinched. Another window on the front of the building blew out, and a second rifle fired on their position and peppered holes in the arriving patrol cars.

By the time Tommy dropped the mag, reloaded, and stood up for a clean line, the entire area was alive with blue and white lights. Patrol units screeched in, bracketing the alley and fanning out on foot. Bullets punched holes in the arriving patrol cars, and officers darted for cover. The area sounded like a war zone as officers returned fire.

Tommy let his gun hand drop, chest heaving, and slumped down next to Winston, whose eyes were open and wild.

"Back up is here," said Tommy while reloading. They could hear the echo as several shotguns and assault rifles fired on the building, but the firing from inside continued.

Winston sat there, knees up, holding his chest. The stink of gunpowder was thick in the humid air. Sirens howled, and over the wail, Tommy heard Winston laughing, low and disbelieving.

"Next time," Winston wheezed, "we let the lab techs check out the woodworking joints."

Tommy smiled and let it slide into a genuine laugh, shaky and sharp as glass. He returned fire as more officers joined the melee.

***

The sawdust in Kaniela's shop hung so thick, Leilani could taste it when she spoke. Isaac Torres sat beside her at the battered counter, pen poised over his little brown notebook, and together they tried to squeeze a coherent story out of the man's nervous laughter and half-finished sentences.

"Let me get this straight," Isaac said, his accent curling up at the ends. "Someone came in three days ago, asked you to build a replica paddle, paid cash, and vanished?"

Kaniela nodded, stringy hair pulled back into a bun that leaked new wisps with every shake of his head. "Yeah, brah. Told me, 'No names, no address, only a drop at this P.O. box in Pearl City, ya?' It's not the first time, but—"

"But this time, you thought it wasn't for a collector," Leilani prompted. The woodworker shot her a grateful look.

"Right. Usually, it's the mainland guys who want a piece for their man cave. This one? I dunno. This was hinky. Guy kept his sunglasses on inside. And he reeked of varnish, but not mine. High-end stuff."

Leilani nodded, letting the silence invite more. She watched his hands: thick, stained, with the telltale grooves of a man who spent his life pushing wood against power tools. Kaniela's fingers were trembling, even though he was used to holding sharp things.

"Did you get a look at his car?" Isaac asked.

"White van," Kaniela said. "No plates, or they were covered. Thought that was weird, but…" He shrugged, like the weirdness of life didn't need to be explained.

Leilani leaned in, lowering her voice. "If someone came back, would you know it was the same guy?"

"Oh, yeah," Kaniela said, almost eager. "Big guy. Lots of tattoos. I saw a little when he paid me, you know? Spiderweb, here." He tapped his own wrist, right below the cuff of his plaid shirt.

Isaac jotted down the details and closed the notebook with a click. "If you see him again, call my cell. Day or night."

Kaniela nodded, eyes flicking between them.

Leilani was on the verge of thanking him when the world turned chaotic.

A thunder of static burst from her radio. "Dispatch, SIU 4. Officer down! Officer down! Shots fired at Kaimuki Woodworking on Waialae Avenue! Requesting immediate backup. Officer hit. Suspects armed and inside."

Every sound in the room vanished except the radio. Leilani's brain snapped into a single, white-hot thread.

"That's Tommy," she said.

She was on her feet before the second transmission. Isaac was right behind, barely remembering to tip his chair upright as they bolted for the exit. On the run, Leilani keyed her radio:

"Dispatch, this is Detective Kealoha. We're two blocks out from Kaimuki Woodworking, responding."

"Copy, Detective. SWAT is ten minutes out."

Leilani threw herself into the driver's seat and slammed the Explorer into gear. She hit the lights and siren. She took the curb hard and saw Isaac brace against the dash. Two minutes later, they crested the ridge and saw the scene: patrol cars stacked along the sidewalk, officers crouched behind doors, glass everywhere. The sound was deafening.

She parked behind the nearest cruiser and ducked low. From her vantage point, she could see Tommy behind a patrol car. Sitting next to him was a patrol officer with his arms wrapped around his chest. Gunfire spat from inside the wood shop, slapping the cruisers with metallic pings.

Isaac scanned the perimeter, all business. "Front door's a kill zone. Side windows are covered. No line of sight of the alley."

Leilani assessed. The strip-mall had a shared back lot, fenced but open. If the shooters made for the rear, they'd either go over the fence or double back to the street. Leilani moved towards the sergeant two cars up.

"What's the status?!" she yelled over the gunfire.

"SWAT's eight minutes out, ma'am," the sergeant barked, crawling to their position. "They want us to hold."

"We don't have eight minutes," Leilani said. "It sounds like a war zone, and the perps could bolt at any minute."

She glanced at Tommy, who met her eyes, turned, and returned fire as more windows in the patrol car exploded.

"Let's roll the dice," she said, mostly to herself.

Leilani pointed at two patrol officers—one rookie with eyes so wide they looked cartoon, one veteran who moved like a bulldog on four limbs. "You, with me and Torres. Flank the rear. Sergeant, keep their heads down. No heroics."

"Yes, ma'am." He keyed his mic. "All units, friendlies at the back."

Isaac led the way, hugging the low cinderblock wall that ran behind the shops. The four of them moved fast, low, communicating with hand signs—stop, cover, go. When they reached the back lot, Leilani spotted the side door: metal, unpainted, locked but battered. Isaac gave a thumbs-up. She drew her Sig, took a breath and fished the lock pick set from her pocket.

"Three seconds, tops," she muttered, glancing back at the officers.

"Take your time," the rookie whispered, though his voice cracked on the last word.

Leilani popped the lock with a hard twist and braced for the rush of air as the door opened. There was no movement inside—only the sharp, chemical reek of solvent and raw fear.

They moved in single file, Isaac on her left, a veteran cop on her right, and the rookie at the tail.

The wood shop was chaos: benches overturned, saws and planers still humming from an interrupted project. At the far side, a man with a pistol gripped a stool like a riot shield, eyes huge and white against a face smeared with blood. Next to him, a second suspect—tall, sweaty, and wild-eyed—wrestled with a rifle, reloading while the third guy kept firing.

Isaac's voice was ice. "Police! Drop your weapons! Hands high. Now!"

The answer was two wild shots, one splintering a cabinet inches from Leilani's shoulder. She ducked, returned fire—one, two rounds into the plywood rack behind the shooters, sending a shower of splinters into their faces.

The suspects dove. The rookie fired blindly, rounds popping through sheetrock into an office area, while the veteran picked his shots, slow and steady.

Leilani caught movement to her right: a third suspect, small and fast, trying to slip behind a row of file cabinets. She pivoted, squeezed off a single round, and watched the man drop, grabbing his thigh and howling.

The veteran cop barked: "Going left!" and shifted, drawing fire away from the main door. Isaac covered him, advancing three steps and planting a bullet into the rifleman's shoulder. The man spun and collapsed behind the lathe.

The last shooter, now bleeding from a scalp wound and seeing his cover evaporate, raised his pistol and screamed something unintelligible. Leilani advanced, keeping low, and waited for the flicker of motion before she fired. She hit the man in the chest. The gun skidded across the shop floor.

"Suspects down! Suspects down!" she shouted into her rover radio, not sure if her voice would carry over the ringing in her ears.

The silence happened so fast it made Leilani's head spin.

Isaac moved to the shooter Leilani hit in the chest and kicked the weapon away. He checked for a pulse and moved away. The veteran secured the rifleman, hands zip-tied and already swelling. Leilani checked the last suspect, whose leg wound had become a wet, sticky mess.

She exhaled, the pressure of adrenaline burning off.

"Clear," she said, and the word was like a promise.

The rookie nodded, eyes blinking fast. He wiped blood off his cheek and stood straighter.

Outside, the patrol sergeant's voice came over the radio, steady and proud. "Front secure. No movement. Everyone alive?"

"Affirmative," Leilani replied, her own voice shaking with the aftershock. "Three suspects down, building secure. Request EMS to rear."

She stood in the workshop, the sawdust now tinged with the coppery tang of blood and let herself take in the aftermath: the carved paddles on the wall, the chaos of broken furniture, the silent drift of powdered wood in the sunlight.

Isaac checked her and grinned with tooth-baring satisfaction. "Hell of a breach, Lei."

"Team effort," she said, not quite smiling back.

They waited for the next wave: the sirens, the medics, the swirl of investigators and crime scene techs who would measure every bullet, every spray of spatter, every inch of the chaos.

But for now, it was only them, breathing and alive.

Leilani holstered her weapon and felt the full force of the shake in her hands. She watched the rookie collect himself, watched the veteran flex sore fingers, and watched Isaac lean against a bench, chest still heaving, but eyes shining with victory.

She let it sink in. Today, they held the line. Again.

But tomorrow, the game would reset, and the pieces would start moving all over again.

She shrugged. "Let's go see what these guys were so desperate to protect."

He nodded, the tension already falling off his shoulders. "Bet you twenty it's not wood."

"Yeah," she said, already stepping over the bodies, "it never is."

Leilani's teeth pulsed as she swept through the shop. Every surface was dusted with saw debris and the aftermath of violence: bullet holes, splintered wood, the muddy drag of boot prints across a freshly varnished floor.

She was still on edge. As she stepped over the first shooter, hands zip-tied behind his back and already twitching with the telltale signs of withdrawal, she kept her Sig at the ready. Isaac moved in behind her, checking doors with the lazy, predatory gait of a man who'd done this too many times to get spooked by it anymore.

"Clear here," he called, after a quick sweep of the tool room.

Leilani moved toward the back. The office was unlocked. She nudged the door open with her elbow and stared.

There were no desks, but the three long tables inside

were buried—not in bills or order forms, but in clear sandwich bags, all stamped with a blue lotus flower. The contents were a grayish-white powder, compacted and labeled in tidy columns. Next to them on the credenza, two digital scales and a counting machine. On the far wall, six bundles of cash, banded and stacked, sat in a neat row beneath a calendar of Hawaiian surf spots. There were twenty-five banker's boxes on the floor, all filled to the brim with filled bags.

Leilani took a moment to inventory the scene, then reached for her radio.

"Dispatch, Detective Kealoha. Notify Narcotics to respond to our location." She turned to the veteran who stood behind her. "They'll want this one gift-wrapped. We've got product—looks like fentanyl, distribution volume—plus scales, packaging and cash."

A pause followed by Isaac's low whistle from the hallway.

"Check this out, boss," he said. She followed his voice into the shop's rear loading area. Stacked like cordwood on a reclaimed pine table were boxes of fake floor tiles and hollowed-out wood beams. Each was packed with more of the lotus bags, shrink-wrapped and labeled for shipment to every state in the union and several foreign countries.

Isaac pushed around a few bags on another table. "I gotta say, I'm disappointed. I thought it'd be jade carvings or bone hooks. Never suspected they'd be running the oldest hustle in the book."

Leilani flexed her fingers, noticing the ache in her

right hand from the breach. "Maybe the artifact theft was a cover, or we chased the wrong rabbit. Either way, this is the motherlode."

Isaac nodded, his expression cool. "They'll be digging this stuff out of evidence lockers for months."

They made their way outside, where the world had become a circus of uniforms, EMTs and nosy bystanders. In the blur of sirens and flashing lights, Leilani spotted Tommy sitting on the bumper of an ambulance, a silver blanket draped over his shoulders. His eyes tracked every movement, feral and unblinking, but when he saw her, he broke into a crooked grin.

Winston was seated next to him, shirt open and stained, a blue-and-purple bruise ballooning across his chest. A paramedic probed the wound with gentle fingers, checking for rib fractures.

"Hurts like hell," Winston wheezed, "but I've been shot at by ex-girlfriends with worse aim." He nodded to Tommy. "This guy saved my bacon."

Tommy shrugged, embarrassed. "I did what you woulda done, man."

The medic was carefully removing pieces of glass from Tommy's face and arms. Another medic checked a large purple spot on his hip. It probably happened when Tommy slammed into the back of the squad car a little too hard as he dove for cover.

Winston reached out, squeezed Tommy's forearm, and the two shared a wordless, lopsided laugh.

Leilani watched, oddly proud. She remembered her

own first shootout—the shakes that didn't hit until hours later, the way the city's birds sounded too loud for a week after. She saw the tremor in Tommy's hands as he accepted a bottle of water from the medic, and the way he clenched his jaw to hide it.

A shout from the perimeter: "Chief on site!" The crowd parted, and Chief Mori strode in. Gray slacks, white shirt, blue blazer, and a commanding presence cutting through the chaos like a shark's fin.

She took in the scene. The cuffed suspects, the wounded officer, and cops standing proud despite the carnage. She stopped at the ambulance, and her face softened as she regarded Tommy.

"Good work, Detective," Mori said, voice low. "You pulled a man out under fire, held the line, and put three bangers in cuffs. That's a good day by anyone's metric."

Tommy swallowed, eyes bright. "Thank you, ma'am."

Chief Mori clapped his shoulder. "Get checked out and go home. You've earned it."

She pivoted to Leilani and Isaac. "You two—nice hustle with the breach. I heard the whole thing while at a meeting with the mayor. You made the right call."

Leilani inclined her head, but Isaac couldn't resist a grin. "Can't wait to read the next review on our Yelp page."

Mori arched an eyebrow. She moved off, already dialing her phone.

The medical team finished bandaging Winston and

rolled him into the ambulance. Tommy stayed put, watching his partner disappear inside.

Isaac offered Tommy a cigarette, which he waved off. "Gave it up last year," Tommy said, but the longing in his face made them all laugh.

"Come on," Leilani said. "Let's hit the scene one more time and see if our artifact angle wasn't a total bust." She turned to Tommy. "You wait here. Let the EMTs finish checking you out."

Tommy nodded, eyes still wet.

Inside, the wood shop looked different now. Less like a den of violence and more like the set of a dark sitcom: chairs overturned, workbenches pocked with bullet holes, a line of lotus bags gleaming in the evidence bags that Mele Tatana, the forensics tech, was already snapping photos of. She stopped and handed each of them an N95 particle mask.

"Fentanyl, by the pound," Mele said, her gloves dusted with sawdust. "Never seen a setup like this. They must've run everything through the filter in the shop's vac system—explains the chemical stink."

Isaac pointed at the far wall, where a handful of Koa canoes and paddle blades leaned against the cinderblock. "We chase the rabbit," he said. "And ended up in a den of snakes."

Leilani grinned, tired but sharp. "That's how it always goes. One job covers the other until the right people notice the overlap."

Isaac circled the bags of powder. "So, what now?"

"Now," Leilani said, "we hand off to Narcotics, buy

the next round of coffee for the SIU, and pray the paperwork's not as brutal as the breach."

Isaac laughed. "Worth it. Every page."

They stood there, two detectives in a ruined wood shop, as the first wave of news vans pulled up and the sun edged lower in the sky. Sirens faded, but the air still hummed with electricity—like everyone on the block knew that tonight, something had changed.

Leilani stepped outside, walked towards the ambulance, and looked at Tommy, at the pride, the fear and the adrenaline in his eyes. She remembered when that was her, remembered the toll of each case stacking until it made you hard, or it broke you.

She reached out, touched his arm. "Good job, Tommy."

He swallowed, nodded. "Thanks, boss."

Leilani believed that holding the line was enough. That sometimes, when the dust settled, you could win. Even if it meant getting shot at, or buried under paperwork, or holding a partner together with nothing but your own stubborn will.

Tonight, they'd won. Tomorrow, there'd be another breach, another chase, another shop. But for now, Leilani stood in the wreckage and breathed.

Tommy found Leilani and Isaac in the pale wash of the wood shop's side entrance, arms crossed as they watched the narcotics team haul out box after box of contraband. He looked like hell—shirt rumpled, eyes bloodshot, one arm cradled at his side. But his face was set with the stubborn pride of someone who'd survived their own funeral and wanted to brag about it.

"I'll start the paperwork," Tommy said, forcing a smile as he tried not to favor his right side. "And I still have two more woodworking shops to check. With a little luck, one of 'em pans out."

Leilani caught his eye and jerked her chin. "No way, Tommy. You took a gunfight to the face and saved a cop's life. You're done for today. Go get fixed up at the hospital and then go home and get some sleep. Let us handle the rest."

Tommy bristled, ready to protest, but the look in Leilani's eyes made him think better of it. "Yes, boss," he said, softer this time.

Isaac clapped Tommy on the shoulder, careful of the bandages. "Next time, we buy the first round. Get out of here."

Tommy nodded and looked like he might cry. Instead, he squared his shoulders, found a ride from a patrol officer and left the scene.

Leilani waited until he was gone. "He'll remember this forever," she said, not softly enough.

Isaac shrugged, already moving to the next task. "If it were me, I'd want to finish the job too."

She shot him a look but didn't argue. They headed for Leilani's Explorer.

***

The next shop on their list was so close to the freeway on-ramp that the roar of traffic drowned out the chime of the door as they walked in. The space was no bigger than a two-car garage, wedged between a 24-hour convenience store and a laundromat. Inside, the air was thick with the caramel-sweet scent of raw Koa and the sharper undertone of finishing oil.

Behind the counter, a Polynesian man the size of a refrigerator stood hunched over a half-built desk, hands stained black at the cuticles. He didn't look up when Leilani and Isaac entered but kept his focus on the fine brushwork along the drawer face.

Isaac made the opening play. "Excuse me—Mr. Maleko?"

The man grunted and didn't look up. "Yeah."

"Detective Torres, HPD. This is Detective Kealoha. We wanted to ask you a few questions about some work you might have done recently."

The man wiped his hands on a red shop rag—bright, cheap, the kind they sold by the bundle at hardware stores. He set down the brush with a surgeon's care and turned to face them. His face was broad, nose flattened by a hundred scrapes, and his eyes were a deep, liquid black.

"I got a permit for every piece in here," he said. "Don't do custom unless it's by contract. All legitimate."

Leilani smiled, let the silence stretch, and nodded at the half-finished desk. "That's beautiful. Koa's hard to work with, yeah?"

He shrugged, but the pride was there. "Worth the trouble. Every grain tells a story."

Leilani smiled. "My dad loved working with KOA.

For him it was a hobby, but he took great pride in what he built. Working with him growing up was an incredible education."

Isaac circled the desk, running a fingertip along the dovetailed joint. "Do you ever get requests for museum-style displays? Or specialty restoration?"

Maleko snorted. "People come in all the time, asking for a piece that looks authentic. Means they want the old look, but not to pay for the real thing. I say no unless it's a proper commission. Every reproduction I make has a stamp somewhere on it so people know it's not the real deal." He eyed Isaac, then Leilani. "Is that why you're here?"

"Actually, we're following up on a theft. Artifacts—wooden items, feather work. A few pieces are missing from the Bishop, and someone took a drum from my family's halau."

That got Maleko's attention. His hands closed tight on the rag, twisting it unconsciously.

"Nothing stolen here," he said.

Isaac traded a glance with Leilani. "We heard a rumor you'd been hired for some off- the -books work. Koa repair, something that'd need a craftsman's touch?"

Maleko thought hard about his answer. "Last month, I did a patch for a guy from the mainland," he said finally. "He paid cash, wanted it fast, and didn't want any record. Weird, but not illegal."

"Do you remember his name?" Leilani asked, already knowing what he'd say.

Maleko shrugged. "Didn't use one. Gave me a phone number, but it was prepaid. That's all I've got."

Leilani let the silence fill the space, watching the man's breathing. The red rag twisted tighter.

She nodded towards the desk. "Is that for the same client?"

"No," Maleko said, too fast. "Different job. For the new cultural center. Some big shot is paying for a whole set—desks, shelves, art cases. All real Koa, nothing fake."

"Who's the big shot?" Isaac asked, pretending to be casual as he bumped gently into the workbench.

Maleko hesitated. "Worthington. The new haole billionaire everyone's talking about. He's throwing money at every craftsman on the island. Good business, but a little… much."

Leilani's brain lit up. "And he asked for this to be finished by—?"

"Two weeks from now. He needs it for the new cultural center he's building."

Leilani filed it away. "Did Worthington ever ask you to make repairs on any old artifacts? Or mention anything about the Bishop Museum?"

Now Maleko's eyes narrowed. He set the red rag on the bench and wiped his palms slowly down the front of his shirt. "The man treats me well and pays me fairly and on time. Got no beef with him. Now, I've got to get this done before the varnish sets up. You can show yourselves out. If you have more questions, you need to talk to my attorney," he said, his voice flat and rehearsed. "I'm only a craftsman."

Isaac stepped back, putting both hands up in surrender. "We get it, Maleko. Thanks for your time."

As they turned to leave, Leilani glanced back and saw the red rag again—now streaked with a new, oily line of fresh Koa varnish.

She caught Isaac's eye as they hit the sidewalk.

"That's our guy, isn't it?" Isaac said, sotto voce.

"He's not the thief," she replied, "but he's the hands. Someone like Worthington? He hires locals to do the work, keeps his own clean."

Isaac grinned and pulled up the bottom edge of his shirt and looked at the sticky spot and the red fibers.

"Oh, look," he said with a smile. "Looks like I've got something on my shirt."

She nodded. "That, and enough fibers to match against our evidence. Mele's going to love this."

Isaac pulled out a pocketknife, cut a piece of material from the shirt, and placed it in an evidence bag. They crossed the lot to their car, the freeway's noise like a tidal current behind them. Leilani slipped into the driver's seat and grinned. She was thrilled to be back in the hunt.

"So," Isaac said. "What's the next move?"

Leilani checked her notes and started the ignition.

"First, we get the sample to forensics. Once that's done, we pull Maleko's phone records, run them against any incoming calls from Worthington's people.

And we keep eyes on both until something gives."

"Sounds like a plan," Isaac said.

She looked over at him, at the street, and back at the shop window where Maleko stood, arms folded, watching them leave.

"Yeah," Leilani said. "This time, we're not letting the chain break."

She departed, the sky darkening to purple behind the city, and noted the case clicking together, one clean dovetail at a time. This time, they'd catch the thief and bring a piece of the story home.

# Chapter Six

## Auction House Intrigue

The entrance to the Mokulua Auction Gallery looked like the gates of paradise, if paradise were run by an overzealous wedding planner with a gold-leaf fetish. Every square inch sparkled, every edge gleamed. Leilani's stiletto heels clicked on the marble, crisp and merciless, a high-hat riff that made security flinch and heads swivel. Her purple minidress stopped mid-thigh and was tight in all the right places. Her black hair hung loose and was clipped to one side. Isaac glided a half-step behind, his hair tamed, his suit cut lean. Together, they could have been a couple, or two assassins, or two detectives coming down from the last time someone tried to shoot them.

The foyer was a snapshot of Honolulu's ruling class: realtors in hot-blooded silk, white-shoe lawyers scanning the floor for their next mark, and wives lacquered with enough Botox to survive a low-yield nuclear event. Up above, chandeliers the size of rental cars threw rainbows onto the assembled donors. There were only three rules here: smile big, drink light, and never, ever lose a bidding war.

"Overkill," Isaac whispered, nodding at the valet team as they hustled a vintage Mercedes into the cordoned VIP lot.

Leilani scanned the crowd, ignoring the waitstaff who orbited with glasses of Veuve Clicquot and amuse-bouches that looked like jewelry. "Have you ever been inside this place?"

He shook his head. "But I know the security setup. They run old-school—guys in blazers, eyes like security cameras. The back hallway linked to the loading dock with hidden doors on both floors."

She adjusted her clutch—weighted down by her badge, gun and, for once, a lipstick that matched her dress. "All that money," she said, "and none of it buys class."

He snorted. "It rents it by the hour."

They moved past the chattering horde of society-page regulars, letting the line of arriving power-players file in. The big fish tonight was easy to spot: Sam Worthington, alone in the center of the gallery, surveyed the room like it was a chessboard, and he'd memorized every opening. He wore an ash-gray suit, pressed so sharp you could slice fish with the crease. His tie was navy, silk, subtle enough to pass as humility. He let people come to him, shook hands with precision, but retreated behind a smile that showed all the warmth of a safe deposit box.

A bespectacled staffer hit a chime, and the hum of conversation slipped down a notch as the first lot was announced. The floor manager—a young guy with the steely optimism of someone only recently promoted—ushered the VIPs to their reserved seating. Leilani and Isaac slid in near the back, where they could watch both the stage and the crowd.

The MC, a relic in a powder-blue jacket, opened with a florid speech about cultural stewardship and the precious heritage of our archipelago. He was answered by a wave of polite applause as the first item was rolled out: an aliʻi-era war club, wicked as a crocodile's jaw, inlaid with shark teeth and bone.

"The next two hours will be a feeding frenzy," Isaac muttered, unfolding the program and scanning the lot list.

Leilani tracked Worthington's location. He'd taken a seat dead center, arms crossed, a pen balanced between two fingers. Around him, the front row gleamed—oil magnates, retired judges, a sprinkling of imported philanthropists. But Sam was the polestar; everything revolved around him, whether he appeared to notice.

The first few items sold to the expected crowd: a university, a bishop's niece, a CEO in a blue dress with arms like driftwood. Worthington didn't lift his paddle, not once. He watched, he listened, and when the club closed at 95K, fifteen thousand over the estimate, he tapped his pen on his wrist and made a note.

"He's letting them tire themselves out," Leilani whispered.

Isaac smirked. "Then he'll start a real fight."

Lot Four—a feathered kahili standard, bright as a rainbow—came up next. Worthington raised his paddle at the opening bid, not bothering to look up. A woman in a lemon blouse countered. He topped her. She doubled. Worthington escalated in three sharp increments, never flinching, never betraying more than a flick of his jaw.

"Guy's a machine," Isaac said. "He's not bidding; he's clearing the market."

The MC stammered out a new record for a privately held ceremonial standard, and Worthington gave a polite nod, as if scoring a table at a crowded restaurant.

The bidding hit fever pitch at Lot Eight: a fragment of an ancient feather cape, the red and yellow still vibrant under glass. The catalog note called it most likely cut from one of the lost King Kamehameha capes, a line that made Leilani's stomach turn.

"Estimated at two hundred thousand," the MC announced. "Do I hear two-fifty?"

Worthington didn't hesitate. "Three hundred," he said, not raising his voice.

The next few minutes were a blur: Worthington against a consortium of mainland investors, Worthington against the bishop's niece, Worthington against a mystery bidder who signaled with a lacquered nail from the third row. Each time, he pushed them into the stratosphere before he delivered the kill shot. Three-fifty. Four. Four-eighty.

By the time the gavel fell, the room was breathless, and the MC's hand shook as he logged the result.

Leilani tracked Worthington's body language. In the heat of the auction, his left hand kept a rhythmic tattoo on his thigh, fingers flexing when a bid hit a nerve. Twice, when the woman in lemon pressed him, a vein pulsed at his temple, and his lips went flat. He didn't like being challenged. He enjoyed winning.

Isaac sipped from the glass of sparkling water the

staff had brought him. "You see that?"

"I see everything," Leilani said. Her eyes were on Sam.

The next item—a wooden idol, 18th-century, grotesque in a way only missionaries could love—triggered a fresh round of paddles. This time, Worthington bided his time. When the number hit three hundred K, he entered late, one clean bid that doubled the last offer. The gallery gasped.

The MC swallowed and checked with the auction manager before accepting. "Six hundred thousand," he called, almost in disbelief. "Going once—"

Sam Worthington never looked up from his program.

The silence stretched until the hammer fell. Worthington signed the slip, folded it into his breast pocket, and sat back, owning the room.

"You think he's making a play for attention, or for the artifacts?" Isaac asked.

"Both," Leilani said. "He doesn't need either, so he's going to take them because he can."

The session unspooled in a rhythm: item, war, victory lap. By the end, Worthington had bagged five of the six crown lots and donated two to local museums, earning ovations and back-slaps from the elite row behind him. To anyone else, it looked like philanthropy; to Leilani, it looked like territory marking.

Intermission hit, and the room splintered into clusters: money talking to money, rivals licking wounds, press scrounging for soundbites. Worthington drifted to the foyer, instantly surrounded by a flock of acolytes.

Leilani leaned over to Isaac. "What do you bet he's got an agenda for every piece?"

Isaac grinned. "I bet he's planning his next move right now."

They hung back and let Worthington play the room. Leilani scanned for his regular security—sure enough, one at the main door, one in the gallery, a third ghosting the balcony above. She caught their eyes, and they ignored her the way good professionals do: with respect, and with the knowledge they'd already run her file.

Isaac finished his water and set the glass down. "You want to make contact?"

"Not yet," Leilani said. "Let him make the first move."

On the other side of the foyer, the bishop's niece clung to a phone, eyes darting between Worthington and her screen. She looked from Isaac to Leilani, and back at the stage.

"She's working for someone," Leilani said.

"Or against Worthington," Isaac replied. "Either way, she's got something she wants us to see."

Leilani's phone buzzed, a text from Tommy. **Surveillance picked up a white van with covered plates near the back of the gallery, unmarked delivery at 20:30.** "Bingo," she muttered.

"Trouble?" Isaac asked, reading over her shoulder.

"Possible," she said. "If the white van is tied to the artifact job, they could smuggle out the genuine pieces and swap in fakes right now."

He grinned. "So classic it's almost boring."

She smiled and watched as Worthington cut through the crowd, zeroing in on them like a barracuda with a fresh scent.

"Detectives," he said, inclining his head with cool grandeur. "Enjoying the show?"

Leilani played it casually. "It's a hell of a show, Mr. Worthington."

He scanned her body up and down and gave a predatory smile, not showing any teeth. "I try to support the local economy. And the local artists. My mother always said. Never let the art get away from you."

Isaac held out a hand, which Worthington shook, fast and dry. "You're building quite the collection," Isaac said.

"It's not a collection," Worthington replied. "It's a legacy. I want my children to inherit something with weight. If the museums want it, they're welcome to ask. But they have to outbid me." He let that hang before he flicked a glance at Leilani. "Some people think I'm buying up the island. I'm not. I'm keeping it from people who don't care."

"You always donate what you win?" Leilani asked, not quite curious, not quite accusing.

Worthington shrugged. "Most of it. But the truly important pieces—I keep those close. Heritage is like currency, Detective. If you let it devalue, you're left with nothing."

Isaac laughed. "Sounds like you ran a hedge fund."

Worthington's eyes crinkled. "Tech, actually. But the game's the same."

The auction manager pinged a glass, signaling a return to the gallery. Worthington tipped a finger at them. "Enjoy the evening," he said. He ran his eyes down Leilani's body, not trying to hide his leering. He looked at Isaac. "If you see anything you want, don't be afraid to fight for it."

He winked and drifted away, absorbing a fresh wave of sycophants as he reentered the auction hall.

Isaac let out a breath. "He's worse in person."

Leilani kept her eyes on Worthington's retreating back. "He's a pig, and he's hiding something. I need to see the shipping manifests after the sale."

Isaac grinned. "I'll get Tommy on it."

The second half of the auction passed in a blur—there were knock-down fights over a set of mid-century paintings, a heated spat between two aging surfers over a handmade paddle, and at least one live wager called from the crowd for the rights to an 'ohe kapala with a royal crest. Worthington scored another lot, sat back with his arms folded; satisfied.

At the end, the crowd broke for champagne and small talk, the next phase of the food chain. Isaac headed for the bar, but Leilani made a loop, tracing the route to the rear of the gallery. She found the security office, read the nameplate, and knocked.

The guard inside—older, mustached, and suspicious—opened and blinked at her badge. "Problem, Detective?"

"I'm making the rounds," she said. "Any unusual deliveries tonight?"

The guard shrugged. "Only the usual. Catering, flower guy. A white van showed up half an hour ago. They said they were with one of the buyers and dropped off a crate."

She raised an eyebrow. "Which buyer?"

He hesitated. "Didn't say, but the delivery was headed to the Worthington suite. Third floor, east wing."

Leilani nodded. "Thanks. If you see anything else, call me directly."

He grunted and shut the door.

She found Isaac by the sushi display, double-fisting mochi balls and already texting Tommy. "He'll get the delivery list from the back dock," Isaac said, voice muffled. "Wants to know if you want surveillance overnight."

"Tell him yes," Leilani said. "I'll swing by first thing. Worthington's not letting this one go without a show."

The lights in the main hall dimmed, signaling the end of the second round and the start of the real negotiations. Leilani watched as the guests peeled away in flurries, some giddy, some gutted. Worthington lingered by the exit, phone pressed to his ear, eyes locked on nothing.

As the crowd thinned, Leilani sensed a tremor of anticipation. Tomorrow, they'd start pulling the strings. For now, she took one last look at the empty displays where the auction items had been and promised herself she'd figure out what was going on. Even if she had to bid her whole life to win it back.

The auction house let the crowd bleed onto the patio, where champagne, smoke, and whispered gossip curled under the gas lamps. Leilani lingered at the edge, eyes following Worthington as he peeled away from his admirers and made for the bar. He moved with the loose confidence of someone born to dominate any room—no sidelong glances, no wasted steps.

Isaac nursed a whiskey and stayed a few paces behind. Close enough to hear Worthington's voice as he flagged the auction house manager to his side. The manager—balding, owl-eyed, sweat already haloing his collar—looked like a man summoned for his own execution.

Worthington leaned in, voice dialed down to a low, surgical hum. Leilani couldn't make out the words, but she saw the effect: the manager shrank, nodding with robotic speed, lips pressed so thin they disappeared. Worthington pointed at the ledger in the manager's hand. With a casual flick, he gestured toward a service corridor near the back. They slipped away, two shadows disappearing behind a tapestry of flying fish and a sign that said, Authorized Personnel Only.

Isaac sidled up beside her. "You see that?"

"He's got the manager on a string," she said, tracking the empty hallway. "They're heading for the office, or maybe the secure vault."

"You want me to tail, or you?" Isaac said.

Leilani grinned. "Rock-paper-scissors for it?"

He shook his head. "Ladies first. I'll cover the floor, see if anyone else is working a side angle."

She was gone before he finished his sentence. She slipped off her heels and set them in a corner, her feet soft on the marble, drifting past the crowd as if she belonged in every conversation. She took the long way around, using the glare of the patio lights to stay invisible, before she ducked into the service hall. It was cool and silent; all the heat and light bled out through thick drywall and money.

Halfway down, she paused. She heard voices ahead.

"Understand, Sam, this is not standard protocol. The provenance—"

"I'm not interested in provenance; I'm interested in results. If I'm paying six figures for a fragment, I want to know it's real."

A click from a lighter or a pen cap.

The manager said, "Our appraisers—"

"Are irrelevant," Worthington interrupted. "I have my own. Listen, I don't need you to do anything illegal. I need you to be discreet. The feather cape fragment and the idol are priorities, but I want the Koa paddle moved tonight. The Bishop Museum will make me an offer in the morning, but I have someone who will outbid them significantly."

Leilani peered around the corner. Worthington was in profile, posture coiled, eyes fixed on the manager with predatory stillness. The manager wiped sweat from his brow, hands shaking as he fumbled for his phone.

"We can arrange a private courier," he whispered, "but the chain of custody—"

"You'll take care of it. If you don't, I'll find someone who will." Worthington's smile flicked on, pure performance. "I'd hate for there to be… confusion about your position, after such a successful event."

The manager's laugh was airless. "No confusion at all, Mr. Worthington. I'll call a secure courier right away."

Worthington clapped him on the shoulder. He let go so fast the man nearly toppled. "Excellent. Go clean up; you look like you've run a marathon."

The manager ducked down a side stairwell, muttering apologies to the air. Worthington waited until he was gone, then checked his own phone, thumb dancing across the screen as he walked back toward the main hall.

Leilani slipped into the corridor and stood where the two men had conferred moments before. She clocked the security camera above the vault door, the digital keypad and the stack of fresh shipping labels by the manager's desk. The top label was addressed to a private air cargo firm out of Singapore.

She grinned, pocketed her phone, and headed for the stairs. The manager was at the landing, phone still glued to his ear, but he paused when he saw her.

"Detective," he said, trying for composure and missing by a mile. "Can I help you?"

She turned on the charm. "I'm checking on tonight's security. My boss wanted to be sure no one walks off with a million-dollar paddle."

The manager blanched. "We have excellent security. Truly. Every item's GPS-tagged, and nothing moves without triple sign-off." He dabbed at his brow with a handkerchief; the back of his neck mottled red.

"Good," Leilani said. "Is there a secure staging area? I'd love a look so I can see how the high rollers do it."

He hesitated. "It's really not—"

She let her badge show. "I'm sure it's all by the book. But people have a way of getting creative once the lights go down."

He wilted. "Of course. Right this way."

He led her past the security office, through a pair of locked doors, and into a room colder than a morgue. On a stainless-steel table, the feather cape fragment rested in a vacuum-sealed case. The idol sat next to it, grinning with its painted teeth, eyes glinting under the fluorescent lights.

"They'll stay here until shipment tomorrow morning," the manager said. "We never move valuables at night; it's policy."

Leilani studied the cases, noting shipping addresses. She pointed to the paperwork on the desk. "Everything accounted for?"

"Absolutely," the manager said. "I'll print a manifest for your review, if you like."

"That'd be great," she said. "We're trying to keep the collectors honest."

He smiled, but his eyes were wet and jittery. "Collectors are never the problem, Detective. It's the middleman."

She kept her poker face. "If you hear anything strange tonight, you have my number."

He nodded, grateful to be dismissed, and scurried off toward his office.

Leilani lingered, checking the inventory tags, the camera sightlines, and the layout of the exit corridors. The pieces were safe for now. Worthington would have to get a little more creative if he wanted to pull off a switch. She made a mental note to have patrol cruise the block every thirty minutes, if for no other reason but to make it harder.

When she returned to the main gallery, she slipped on her heels. Worthington was at the head table, laughing big and loud for the benefit of three donors and the governor's brother. The auction manager had recovered enough to return to the stage, but his hand shook as he gaveled the crowd into silence for the last few lots.

Leilani caught Isaac's eye across the floor. He gave her a subtle thumbs-up. "Later."

The evening rolled on, and the alcohol flowed as the bids stalled. Worthington didn't bid again, but he didn't have to. He'd already won. The others were catching up. As the night drew to a close, the crowd thinned, drifting out to their cars and drivers. Leilani stepped into the street, letting the cool air burn off the night's perfume.

Isaac joined her a minute later, hands in his pockets. "Did you get what you needed?"

She nodded. "The manager is afraid of his own shadow, and Worthington's running a side hustle. I'm betting he tries to move the artifacts before sunrise."

Isaac looked back at the glass-walled foyer, where Worthington held court with the governor's brother and a blonde with too-perfect teeth. "We tail the courier?"

Leilani smiled. "We tail the courier."

Above them, the chandeliers glimmered, emptying the last of their light onto the wet pavement. The game would move before morning, but tonight, they were in control.

The auction house had emptied to a trickle, with only the staff and the most stubborn socialites left clinging to their gin and gossip. The hallways had that scraped-clean, post-glamor quiet, like a casino floor at 3 a.m.. Leilani and Isaac didn't need to talk as they made their way to the manager's office—they were already synced, working the angles in parallel.

The office was little more than a shoebox behind a glass wall, with a too-large desk wedged inside, giving the whole thing the appearance of a stage prop for a play about paperwork and regret. The manager was already there, tie loosened, collar damp, the smile on his face as hollow as an empty vault.

He saw them coming and tried to conjure a smile. "Detectives. I trust you found the evening's proceedings satisfactory?"

Leilani flashed him her best smile. "We had some follow-up questions, if you don't mind."

The manager motioned for them to sit, but there was only one guest chair. Isaac took it, stretching out like he owned the place. Leilani leaned on the desk, close enough to make the manager sweat.

She started softly. "We're looking into the chain of custody for a few of the more significant items—especially the feather cape fragment and the Kamehameha-era idol. Do you have full provenance for both?"

The manager busied his hands with a sheaf of shipping manifests. "Of course. It's our policy to verify every acquisition, and—" he slid a folder across, but not quite within reach. "You understand, with pieces of this magnitude, there's always… sensitivity."

"Especially with the market being what it is," Isaac said. "Lots of big money from the mainland. Hard to keep track of where things are supposed to be."

The manager's lips twitched. "I assure you, everything we move is strictly legitimate. We have working relationships with all the major museums and—"

"But sometimes things slip through," Leilani said, finishing his sentence for him.

The man's eyes flinched. He cleared his throat. "Occasionally, there are… gaps. Old records, incomplete paperwork from previous custodians, but nothing that would compromise the legitimacy of a sale."

Leilani thumbed through the manifest. She jabbed a finger at one line. "This item—artifact 8117, listed as private transfer from benefactor via Singapore. That's not standard, is it?"

The manager folded his hands and fixed his eyes on the desktop. "Sometimes, for discretion, a client will prefer an offshore clearinghouse. It's legal, I assure you."

"But not transparent," Isaac said.

The manager bristled. "We take client privacy seriously. If we didn't, people would buy their treasures on eBay."

Leilani smiled, all teeth. "Who was the benefactor?"

He hesitated and shrugged in surrender. "The names are always redacted in these deals. But I can tell you it's not the first time we've handled a purchase this way for Mr. Worthington."

Isaac cocked an eyebrow. "He likes to use Singapore."

"He likes efficiency," the manager said.

Leilani closed the manifest. "And no paper trail.

Where do these items go after Singapore?"

"To wherever the client specifies," the manager replied, voice going brittle. "Sometimes it's a museum, sometimes a private home. I can only tell you where the item is until it leaves our custody."

Isaac shifted in the chair. "Any chance you get a look at where they're shipped after?"

The manager shook his head. "We never see the final destination. Sometimes I wonder if they'll make it past the warehouse."

Leilani let the silence grow, let the discomfort ferment. The manager started fiddling with a pen, clicking it in uneven bursts.

She pressed. "Can you get us a copy of the shipping log for the last six months? Only for the Hawaiian artifact category?"

The manager paled and nodded. "It will take some time, but—yes. I can do that."

Isaac stood, slow and deliberate. "Thank you. We appreciate the cooperation."

The manager gave them a watery smile. "Anything to help the investigation."

They walked out together until they hit the outer lobby. Leilani exhaled.

"He's terrified," Isaac said, half-smiling.

"He's not the only one who should be," she answered.

The night outside was sticky and humming with city

life. The parking lot was a parade of black cars and town cars, drivers holding doors, well-heeled guests fading into the darkness like ghosts of old money.

They walked together to Leilani's car, neither of them eager to break the bubble of adrenaline and shared suspicion.

"So, what's your take?" Isaac asked as he leaned against the passenger side.

Leilani shrugged. "Worthington's got the money, the muscle and the motive. If he's not laundering artifacts, he's laundering the history. And I don't like the sound of Singapore as a transit point."

"He could be clean," Isaac said. "He might really be what he says—a collector, an idealist. Or he's smarter than the rest."

Leilani laughed. "Nobody spends that much on local artifacts unless they want something nobody else has. My bet—he's the buyer and the fence. He'll donate a few pieces to look legit, and siphon off the rest to the highest bidder."

Isaac looked out over the lot, as if expecting to see Worthington's limo waiting with its lights on. "He's clever enough to play both sides. Maybe too clever."

"You want to run an op tomorrow?" she asked, already knowing the answer.

"Absolutely," Isaac said. "I'll have Tommy camp at the air cargo terminal and see if the shipment really moves."

Leilani pulled her keys from her purse, savoring the click as she unlocked the car. "He's either the most generous art patron in the state," she said, "or he's running the largest cultural heist Hawaii's ever seen."

Isaac opened her door. "Could be both. That's the scary part."

They stood in the muggy quiet, neither wanting to give up the game yet.

"See you in the morning?" she asked.

He nodded. "Don't stay up all night reading shipping manifests."

"No promises," she said, and meant it.

Isaac walked to his car, slid in, started the engine and the car peeled off into the darkness. Leilani sat in her driver's seat, letting the engine idle and the air cool her skin. In her lap, the folder from the manager's office seemed heavier than paper should.

She looked up at the auction house, the chandeliers now dead, the windows blank as the eyes of the carved idol she'd seen earlier. She wondered how many people in the city would ever know what it took to keep the past from being rewritten, auctioned off, or erased.

She put the car in gear and pulled out onto the avenue, headed home. The city was alive, and tomorrow would bring more secrets, more ghosts, and if she was lucky, a chance to reclaim something that belonged to all of them.

She drove into the night, thinking about all the ways history could be stolen, and how much harder it was to bring it home. Tomorrow, she would try anyway.

# Chapter Seven

## Kai's Discovery

Kai woke before sunrise, his internal clock set by the quiet fizzing of anxiety and anticipation. The house was a crypt at this hour—no neighbors' radios, no cats yowling at the trash cans, and not the soft, rhythmic snores that usually drifted from his mom's room after her late-night shifts. Only the blue glow of the kitchen overheads, and a kitchen table transformed into a war zone.

Posterboard, colored pencils, and Sharpies in hues that vibrated in low light. Three spiral notebooks, each bristling with sticky flags and cryptic marginalia. A digital voice recorder, already loaded with ten minutes of practice interview, sat wedged between his elbow and a pile of index cards, each one a scribbled question or bullet point. And, most important, his timeline—a six-foot epic of butcher paper that unspooled across the table, anchored with two cans of spam at one end and a rice cooker at the other.

He had spent hours straightening the lines, curving arrows from decade to decade, annotating every bubble with the date, location, and sometimes, a cartoon of the principal involved. He'd used the gel pens for the Stolen but Returned column, and the effect was electric. The only things missing were the last two interviews he had scheduled for today.

His eyes drifted to the clock: 5:00 AM. He had two and a half hours before school, and probably an hour before the world caught up.

Kai pulled his tablet over and tapped open his document. He cross-checked the interview prompts for the third time, making sure the order was tight and the questions non-repetitive. He knew his teacher would grill him about the difference between research and stories, so he was ready with a preamble.

"My project is to show how Hawaiian history survives when people try to take it away. I interviewed three kupuna about their experiences with artifacts, thefts, and how families pass down knowledge if the government or museums lose track. I hope this helps people realize the past is not only old stuff but living stories, and it helps get the lost stuff back."

He rehearsed it under his breath, running a thumb along the poster board for the hundredth time.

From the hallway came the unmistakable sound of his mom's bedroom door opening—the soft click, followed by a quick shuffle of socked feet across tile. She appeared in the kitchen, wrapped in a robe with a wild print of orange flowers, hair escaping in every direction, and dark circles visible in the dimness. But her eyes were alert, and her expression sharpened when she took in the mess on the table.

"Early start?" she rasped, pawing at the coffeemaker with muscle memory.

"Needed to run through the questions again," Kai said, doing his best to look responsible and adult.

She grunted approval, but the twitch at her mouth was the first sign of a smile. "Who are you interviewing first?"

"Aunty Kalani. She says if I show up late, she'll tell me only the tourist version."

Leilani poured two mugs of black coffee and slid into the chair opposite him. Her robe slipped, revealing a constellation of old hula bruises on her shin. She scanned the table, picking up a pen and clicking it reflexively.

"So, what's your angle, Sherlock?" she asked.

Kai flicked through his cards, showing her the question at the top. "I would like to know why people keep stealing artifacts if they know it's wrong? And why the police never found any of the artifacts, when they had fingerprints and stuff?"

She nodded, reading the index card. "That's good. But don't make it an interrogation. These people, some of whom lived through bad times, lost a lot."

Kai rolled his eyes in the practiced way of children everywhere. "Mom. I'm not dumb."

She snorted, but the laughter was all pride. "I didn't say you were. But remember, you get more with ears than with mouth."

He mimed zipping his lips but undid the motion. "Admit, though, some of this is like criminal mastermind stuff." He pointed to the timeline, where three thefts had happened in the same week during the 1970s. "No way it's a coincidence."

Leilani sipped her coffee and regarded her son with a strange softness. "You'd have made a good cop if you liked rules."

"I'm going to run the investigation unit someday," he said, grinning. "No rules, but I still get the badge."

"That's the spirit," she said, but her smile faded as she checked the clock. "Okay. I need you to be back by six-thirty. We have to leave for school by seven. That gives you," she squinted at the fridge clock, "an hour and a half to get the scoop, eat, and finish the summary."

He nodded. "I'll text if I'm running late. Promise."

She got up, drained the coffee in one motion, and grabbed her work shirt from the back of a chair. As she passed behind him, she ruffled his hair—an automatic, affectionate gesture she used less as he got older. He let it slide this time, too busy making sure the pencils were arranged by hardness and the voice recorder had fresh batteries.

"Respect the elders, ask before you record, and try not to talk over them when they get on a roll," she said, heading for the bathroom.

"Roger," Kai called after her, and turned his attention to his timeline. He scanned it for gaps, the places where the history didn't quite link up, and penciled in ASK ABOUT POLICE INVESTIGATIONS next to the red X in 1974.

With the last swig of cold milk, he packed everything into his backpack. The project was due next week, but he knew the burn in his stomach, like something important was about to happen, and he didn't want to miss it. He wondered if his mom ever felt that on the mornings she had a big case. Maybe it ran in the family.

He stood, shouldered the bag, and gave the kitchen one last glance. The timeline still taped to the table looked like the aftermath of a battle. He smiled at his creation, his obsession, and whispered a promise to himself:

"Gonna get the real story. Even if nobody else cares."

He checked the voice recorder again, double-checked the questions, and, with one last look at the clock, slipped out the door.

The day had barely begun, and already, Kai was in the hunt.

Kai pedaled the rusted cruiser along the strip of broken asphalt that skirted the water, his backpack thunking a steady rhythm against the seat post. He veered onto the sand-packed side lane and coasted to a halt in front of Aunty Kalani's house—a rectangle of sun-faded stucco hugged by a barricade of monstera and ti plants. Plumeria petals littered the walk. The morning sun painted the clouds a fresh orange, and the ocean was close enough that every window pulsed with the sound of the surf.

He locked up the bike and wiped his palms on his shorts. He'd known Aunty Kalani since he was four, but the prospect of recording her—of getting her story right—made his pulse stutter. She was the oldest living link to his great-grandmother, and his mom treated her with the reverence reserved for saints and disaster survivors.

The screen door banged once, and there she was: a small woman in a faded muʻumuʻu, hair tied back with a red scrunchie, wrists decked in a riot of shell and seed bracelets. She leaned on the doorframe, gave him a shaka, and called, "Eh, Sherlock! You bring me donuts?"

Kai held up a white box, which he carried on the handlebars the whole way. "Chocolate-glazed. Your favorite, right?"

She smiled so wide her crow's feet could have held water. "You know it, boy."

He followed her around to the lanai, ducking under a string of origami cranes that guarded the doorway. The space was a greenhouse: every surface crowded with cuttings in jars, and the air sweet and alive. In the far corner, a folding table sagged under the weight of old photo albums, stacks of yellowed paper, and an ancient transistor radio playing Gabby Pahinui at half volume.

Kalani settled onto a woven mat with her legs folded flat, gesturing for Kai to sit. He crossed-legged down and pulled out his notebook, voice recorder and a second box of donut holes, which he set like a peace offering between them.

"So," she said, fixing him with a look as sharp as a paring knife. "What do you wanna know, my detective?"

Kai started the voice recorder, red light blinking. "I'd like to talk about the museum thefts. And the old temple raids. And about what it was like to grow up when everyone thought it was okay to take what they wanted."

Kalani let out a long, practiced sigh. "You come heavy for breakfast, boy. I like it. You ready to listen, though? Not only record, but really listen?"

He nodded, pen poised. "Yes, Aunty."

She set her hands on her knees, thin brown fingers mapped with veins and age spots. "The first time someone stole from our people, they didn't come with guns or police. They came with curiosity. They said, 'Oh, what a nice paddle! What a pretty feather cape! Let me borrow it for study; I'll give it back later.' But they never gave it back. They kept the artifacts for themselves, for their museum, or for their story."

She reached for an album, its leather cracked and opened to a page of black-and-white photos: a row of young girls in hula skirts, some smiling, some staring at the ground. "That's me, third from the left. I was eight. My tutu made that pa'u with her own hands, cooked the dye herself from kukui."

Kai leaned in, squinting. "Was that at the Bishop Museum?"

"No, no. This was at the church. But afterwards, the museum lady came and took it. Said it was for the display, to show how we used to live. My tutu was happy—she thought the world would see us, respect us. She never got it back. Years later, when I was older, I went to see the dress. It was there, but not her name, not our village. There was a small plaque that said, early Hawaiian, unknown maker. Like nobody ever lived those hours to make it. Only a thing in a glass box."

Kalani's hand trembled as she turned the page. She

pointed to a photo of a shattered display case, with police tape stretched across the background. "1976. This is the one that got everyone talking. Some thieves broke into the Bishop Museum, stole the ‘aumakua idols, a set of fishhooks, and a kapa fragment. They broke nothing else, took nothing else. The police said it was drugs or bad kids. But I knew differently."

"Why?" Kai whispered.

"Because," she said. "The thieves left behind the gold, the coins, and the missionary treasures. They wanted only things with mana. The kind that still had spirit left in them. They knew exactly what to take and how to hide it."

Kai's pen almost couldn't keep up. "Do you think it was local people?"

Kalani shrugged, her smile returning a little. "Sometimes yes, sometimes haole. Sometimes both. It doesn't matter. Once a thing is out, it never comes back the same."

She rifled through the stack of clippings, hands fast despite the arthritis, and held up a yellowing sheet from the Star-Bulletin: **THREE ARTIFACTS VANISH FROM THE BISHOP; MYSTERY BAFFLES POLICE**. The photo showed a young cop, nervous and standing in front of a bank of empty glass shelves. "My cousin worked security. He got fired after the robbery. They never solved it."

Kai's eyes darted over the page. "Did you ever hear what happened to the stolen things?"

Her mouth was tight, and she seemed to measure

her words. "Sometimes people would talk. They'd say, 'I saw it on the mainland, in a fancy house.' Or 'Someone bought it for their private museum in Japan.' Once, a man told me he saw the idol in a church, dressed up like a saint. But I don't know, really. Stories are like rivers, always changing."

Kai leaned closer. "If you could, would you want them back?"

She gave him a long, heavy look, as if weighing him on a scale. "Of course. But not in a museum, not for looking. I want the kids to touch history. To remember. To know where it came from. What good is a treasure if you keep it behind glass and forget the hands that made it?"

He swallowed, thinking of the rows of glass at Bishop, the solemn faces of kids on school trips staring at things they could never own, never used, or never understand.

Kalani reached for the donut box, fished out a chocolate one, and popped it whole into her mouth. She grinned, chocolate forming on her lip. "You gonna eat, or take notes all day?"

Kai laughed; the tension broke, and he took a donut hole. "Did you ever think about stealing them back?" he asked, only half joking.

Kalani cackled. "Plenty of people did. But you know what happens if you get caught? You don't lose your job. You lose your family name. Nobody wants to be that kind of hero."

He wrote that down, underlining it twice.

She leaned back, glancing at the horizon, where the sun had climbed high enough to bleach the sky. "One more thing, boy. When you finish your project, don't forget the most important piece."

He looked up, expectant.

She tapped her temple. "Memory. The genuine artifact is not the stuff; it's the story. You remember that, okay?"

Kai nodded, but he already knew he would never forget.

He thanked her, packed the recorder, and made a mental list of follow-ups. As he walked out, Kalani called after him. "Don't believe every story you hear. But don't forget them, either."

He turned, smiled, and promised he wouldn't.

By the time he hit the sidewalk, his hands were shaking, and his head buzzed with the new shape of the puzzle. Not only who took the artifacts, but why, and what it meant for all the people who remembered what it was like to lose something sacred.

He checked the time and grinned. There was plenty left to find before school.

Kai's second stop was Uncle Makoa's house. He lived up the hill in a cottage wedged between a crooked mango tree and the narrow drive that led to the church playground. Makoa wasn't related, not by blood, but he and Kai's grandfather had grown up in the same village, so the term "Uncle" was enforced by unspoken law.

The door was open, as always. Kai knocked

anyway, and Makoa boomed, "Eh! Enter if you dare," his voice echoing through the cluttered living room.

Makoa was a retired shop teacher with bigger biceps than most people's thighs, a beard the color of wet sand, and a wardrobe of ancient aloha shirts worn to translucence. He was hunched over a workbench by the window, squinting through a jeweler's loupe at the innards of a broken clock.

"Detective Kealoha," he intoned, dropping the loupe with a flourish and holding out a massive paw for a handshake. "To what do I owe this honor?"

Kai had always loved the way Makoa made every visit sound like the start of an adventure.

"I'm interviewing kupuna about lost artifacts for my history project," Kai said, producing the recorder. "I want to hear about the old drum—your family's one, the one that got stolen."

Makoa's face softened, the bravado fading into a kind of prideful sadness. He plucked a battered shoebox from a shelf and thumped it onto the table. "You got time for a story?" he asked, not waiting for an answer as he opened the box and began laying out a series of yellow photographs.

Kai set the recorder between them and leaned in. The first photo showed a row of men in white shirts and malo, each with a hand on the shoulder of the next. Dead center: a drum almost as tall as Kai was now, its body smooth as river stone, head stretched tight as a trampoline.

"The pahu," Makoa said reverently. "It was old

when my tutu was young. Carved from a single Koa log, the skin from a shark my uncle caught when he was twelve. The sound could shake your teeth loose. It sat in our hale for a hundred years. Every ceremony, every funeral, every time someone needed to call the ancestors, that drum spoke first."

He ran a finger along the photo, tracing the outline of the drum. "In the summer of 1978, some idiots broke in and took it. They left the TV, the silver, and the war medals. Grabbed the pahu and ran. My father said it was like a death in the family."

Kai was already scribbling notes. "Did anyone ever find out what happened?"

Makoa laughed, a single sharp bark. "The cops made a report. They sent detectives from the mainland, but nothing. Some years later, a rumor: someone saw it in a private house on Maui, being used as a planter for orchids. I tried to get there, but by then, the house was sold, and the drum was gone. Now? In a warehouse or burned for firewood. Nobody knows."

He flipped to the next photo: the same room, the same line of men, but with a space where the pahu had been. Makoa jabbed a finger at the gap. "That's how fast things can vanish. You blink, and the world shifts. But you remember what you lost."

He sat back and studied Kai. "You gonna put this in your report?"

"Yeah," Kai said. "But it's important to know why they took only the drum, when there's other stuff that's worth money?"

Makoa grinned. "Have you ever heard of mana? That's why. People think that if you own the thing, you own its power. But it doesn't work like that. If you steal it, it haunts you."

Kai wrote that down.

Uncle Makoa leaned in, voice dropping. "Let me give you advice, boy. If you ever see a pahu, you tell me first. We make sure it comes home. Some things aren't meant to be behind glass or under lock. They've got to be where they belong."

Kai nodded, sensing the significance of the promise. He thanked Makoa, pocketed the recorder, and biked off with a mind full of sharkskin and phantom sound.

The third interview was with Aunty Palani, who lived three blocks inland in a duplex surrounded by the clucks of feral chickens and the metallic ping of neighbor kids smacking rocks with sticks. Palani was only in her seventies, but decades of sun and sea had written deep creases into her face. She sat on the stoop, feet bare and brown, swirling sand in a plastic tray with a popsicle stick as she waited for Kai.

"You made good time," she said, smiling. "Come, sit. You like juice?"

Kai shook his head, clicking on the recorder. "Can you tell me about the petroglyph tablets?"

Aunty Palani nodded. She drew a spiral in the sand with her stick. "My first job was at the university museum. I wasn't a professor or anything — sweep floors, help in the office. But I liked the basement, where they kept all the old rocks. My favorite was a set of tablets with petroglyphs, some as big as my hand."

She shaped a circle in the sand and marked it with hash lines, mimicking the tablet's marks. "They were found up at Kaena Point. Nobody knew what they said, but some thought it was a map or a list of chiefs. They put them in a glass case and told us to dust them once a week. At one in the morning in '74, the case was empty. No break, no alarm. Gone."

"Who do you think took them?" Kai asked, caught up.

She shrugged. "Could be anyone. A Professor, a student, or someone on a dare. It could be someone wanted to put them back where they belonged. Or sell them to a rich collector. But you know what? I hope they're hidden somewhere safe, and that someone is still tracing the lines with their fingers."

Kai watched her hands as she drew patterns in the sand. They moved slowly. She was reciting the old story, but with her body.

"Did the police ever find anything?" Kai asked.

Palani smiled, with no bitterness in it. "Police have better things to do than hunt rocks. And besides, the story is still here." She wiped her palm across the tray, erasing everything. "And here." She tapped her head.

Kai grinned. "That's what I want my project to be about. How people remember when the thing is gone."

Palani laughed, a rusty giggle. "That's the Hawaiian way. You lose the drum; you beat your chest. You lose the stone; you scratch it in the sand. But you never stop telling the story."

Kai glanced at his notepad, already two pages deep in red ink and exclamation points. He could see the pattern taking shape—the dates, the targets, the fact that money was never the point. It was about taking something that couldn't be replaced and hiding it away so no one else could have it, either.

He closed the recorder, thanked Aunty Palani, and promised to bring her a copy of the finished report.

On the ride home, Kai played the interviews back in his mind, snippets of memory looping over the hiss of wind and the click of his chain. He pictured a red line connecting each story, each theft, each ache left in the hollow space after the thing was gone.

By the time he hit his street, he already knew what the next step was. He was going to lay it all out, every missing piece, every year, every whisper, and rumor, and draw the lines that nobody else had bothered to draw.

His hands itched with excitement, and his legs pumped faster, because if he hurried, he could get a head start before the world caught up.

Kai skidded to a stop in his driveway, shouldered his bag, and sprinted inside, eager to assemble the case file that might change everything. But first, he had to get to school.

***

His excitement hadn't abated during the day, and he lost focus on what his teachers were saying as he thought more about his project. When the end of day bell rang, he grabbed his backpack and raced home. He had plenty of work to do to get the project finished by the due date.

By late afternoon, Kai's room looked like a bomb had gone off. The floor was a riot of paper: interview notes in messy columns, photocopied clippings that curled at the corners, stacks of index cards already battered by too much erasing. The centerpiece was a battered road atlas with its Oahu map spread open, page corners anchored with anything heavy—water bottle, stapler, half a geode he'd found in the yard. Over the last hour, he'd used a red Sharpie to mark every confirmed theft, cross-referencing dates with black lines that snaked between neighborhoods, museums and temples.

He moved with a single-mindedness usually reserved for finishing the last level of a video game or perfecting a pop shove-it at the skate park. Hands moving fast, and his tongue poking out from the corner of his mouth, Kai checked and double-checked his notes, drawing arrows and underlining the years in angry, deliberate sweeps. The pattern was obvious. Clearer than anything he'd seen in class, clearer than most of the detective shows he watched with his mom when she wasn't working overtime.

He worked his way from the bottom up. 1970s: the Bishop Museum, two schools, and three temples were hit in rapid succession. One or two items, but never the easy stuff, never anything insured. Sometimes the alarms were disabled, and there was no sign of forced entry at all.

1984: He wrote a side note. *Statue—nu'uanu*

*cemetery, gone w/out a trace.*

1992: University collection, stone idol taken. The news said it was an unprecedented theft, but the police gave up after two weeks. *No suspects*, the paper said. He circled the quote and drew a frowny face next to it.

1999: A priestess's feather lei vanished from a downtown church right before a festival. No sign of entry. According to the newspaper story, *the cameras were down for maintenance*. The coincidence burned a little.

He flipped to the present day, his hand tracing the last three red dots. The feather cape, the pahu drum, and the most recent—the paddle from the auction, which by now was probably on its way out of the state.

He shivered, not from cold but from the sense that he was finally on to something real. He imagined himself presenting the whole web to his teacher, who would have no choice but to give him an A. She might give him extra credit. If his mom looked closely, she'd see he had the detective gene after all.

His eyes hurt, and his fingers were stained red and blue from cheap markers. But he kept going, layering new lines and sticky notes on top of the old ones, narrating quietly as he worked.

"If you look at the timing, they always take a break for a few years after a big score. Once everyone's forgotten, they start again."

He jabbed a finger at the cluster in the 1970s. "It could be the same person. But that would make them super old, like a ninja grandma."

He grinned at the thought, but the idea seemed more like a copycat or a family legacy than random.

Kai leaned back on his heels, hands on his knees, and tried to see the pattern all at once. He pictured the route the thief (or thieves) would have to take, the neighborhoods they passed through, and the times of year they struck. Some were close to holidays, while some lined up with festivals or funerals.

He cross-checked the last date against his mother's work calendar — to make sure.

His phone buzzed, but he ignored it, lost in the sensation of the marker gliding on the paper, the sound of his own breathing, the taste of mystery on the tip of his tongue. Hours passed like nothing. The sun shifted, the light turned pink, and still he crouched there, filling in blank spaces and erasing what didn't fit.

At some point, he realized he was hungry, but the urge barely registered compared to the pulse in his ears. The more he wrote, the more the idea in his brain grew teeth. He knew he was getting close to something big.

He drew a line from the earliest theft to the most recent. From the place his grandma's pahu was stolen to the auction house where the paddle had vanished. The lines crossed right over downtown but veered into the warehouse district. Kai blinked, surprised—he'd expected the link to be about the items, not the places.

He pulled out a fresh index card and wrote: "I wonder if the stuff is still here or do they move it around but never really send it away."

He stared at it and said, "No way." But as soon as he did, the next thought tumbled after. "Unless it's someone local, someone who knows the city, who knows how to hide in plain sight."

He drew a circle around the thought and looked at the surrounding mess. He was a little dizzy, but the excitement was stronger. He started writing again. Notes to himself, reminders to check the city records for old houses, abandoned storage units, forgotten churches.

He was so deep in it he barely heard the call from down the hall. "Kai! Dinner!"

He flinched, almost dropped the pen, and glanced at the clock. He'd lost three hours without noticing.

"Coming, Grandma!" he yelled, his voice cracking.

He made one more pass over the map, underlining a spot that looked right—a hunch, but that's how detectives worked, right? He stuck a red pin on it, satisfied, and forced himself to stand.

As he walked into the hallway, he rehearsed what he would say to his mom when she got home, how he'd lay it all out for her, and she'd see he could be a real detective, too. The world outside his door seemed flat and dim compared to the case in his head. But he was ready, more ready than ever, to take the next step. He just hoped he wasn't the only one paying attention.

***

Leilani pushed into the house with a hip, closing the door behind her before the security latch could catch and rattle. Her arms ached, and her right temple throbbed from a day spent filling out statements, chasing down witnesses, and walking a line between hard-ass and negotiator for four hours straight. All she wanted was a hot shower, something not made in a microwave, and five minutes on the couch with her eyes closed before the next batch of call outs or paperwork.

Instead, she got a jungle of loose paper, red thread and Sharpie graffiti that stretched from her son's bedroom and spilled into the hallway. At first glance, it looked like the aftermath of a printer explosion, but she saw the pattern—everything radiated outward from Kai's bedroom like he'd set up camp at the center of a giant web.

"Kai?" she called, more out of habit than hope. He was always where the action was, even if the action was in his own imagination.

"Back here!" came the answer, muffled, like he'd barricaded himself behind a mountain of folders.

She dropped her bag at the door and tiptoed through the evidence. In the living room, an atlas lay open to Oahu, its spine permanently bent. A half-eaten musubi sat perched atop the remote. A sticky note labeled 1974 was tacked to the TV screen. She suppressed a smile. The mess was epic, even by her own standards.

Kai was on his knees in the middle of his room, surrounded by a fresh layer of index cards, strings, maps, and what looked suspiciously like her work notepad, pages torn out and repurposed. His eyes were locked on a spread of newsprint, lips pressed thin as he scanned each page. There was a fever to it, a restless energy that she recognized from every time she got close to the bones of a good case.

Leilani was too tired to ask. She stepped over a coil of red yarn and collapsed cross-legged next to him. "Show me."

He shuffled closer and shoved a pile of clippings into her hands. "When I talked to Aunty Kalani, Uncle Makoa and Aunty Palani, they all said the same thing—the thieves skipped the expensive stuff, went straight for the stuff with mana. The things that belonged to families, to the land."

Leilani nodded, thumbing through the notes. The evidence was messy, but there was an order to it. Every artifact loss lined up almost perfectly with something in the last few months. Her own case, the stolen pahu, was marked with a bright red star. Two other stars— one at the Bishop, and one at the auction house.

Kai leaned forward, all business. "Look at the pattern," he whispered, pointing to a cluster of dots on the map. "They're hitting the same neighborhoods every time. Always close to the freeway or the bus line. And they always break in during a holiday or festival, when nobody's home."

She stared. It was so obvious; she felt dumb for not seeing it before. The cases that looked random, the things that didn't fit—here, they connected. A perfect string from past to present.

Her professional brain caught up, and she started piecing it together. "That would mean it's someone local. Or at least someone who's been here a long time. Not any collector, but someone who knows the city."

Kai nodded. "Sometimes, they put the stuff back. After a couple of years, some things show up in a different museum. Or a private person donates it. But they never return it to the original owner."

He picked up a card and waved it. "It's like they're trying to play a game. Take, hide, move, return, but only when they're ready."

Kai hesitated, looking up at her with a strange, half-shy smile. "Is this…do you think it matters? I mean, is it something you guys could use?"

Leilani leaned forward, put her hand on his shoulder, and squeezed. "It's not only good. It's the break that makes the difference." She caught herself, saw the pride blooming in Kai's eyes, and hugged him.

She pulled back, glancing at the map again. "You know, we might have to make you an honorary member of the SIU."

Kai laughed, all the tension falling away at once. "Only if I get a badge. And like, two days off from school?"

Leilani grinned. "Don't push it."

She stood, eyes sharper now, mind already ticking through the next steps—who to call, what records to pull, how to run down the theory before the next theft hit. She sensed the exhaustion drop away, replaced by something older, a need to move, to act, to chase the story wherever it led.

She reached for her jacket and her phone and turned to Kai. "You want to ride with me on the next round?"

He blinked, surprised. "Yeah," he said.

She ruffled his hair and watched him glow.

As she dialed Isaac, ready to share the lead, she glanced back at the sprawl of maps and notes. The red lines, the careful stars, the evidence of a day's worth of obsessive work. Sometimes, she thought, it took a kid to see what everyone else missed, and it took family to finish what history started.

As she waited for Isaac to pick up, Leilani watched her son—already pulling out a fresh index card, already working the next angle—and realized she'd never been prouder.

"Isaac," she said when the line clicked on, her voice steady and urgent, "I've got something. No, my son has something. Meet me at the office in thirty. You're going to want to see this."

She hung up, grabbed her keys, and flashed a wink at Kai. "Ready for another case, Detective?"

He saluted her with the marker, and everything in the world made perfect sense. They moved as a unit, side by side, out the door and into the night—two story catchers, chasing the red thread wherever it led.

# Chapter Eight

## Federal Interference

Police headquarters had its own soundtrack after midnight. Air vents sighing like distant surf, muffled curses from the bullpen's night shift, the unbroken staccato of ancient, and yellowing fluorescent tubes. Most of the detectives had cleared out hours ago, leaving only the hard cases and the diehards. Leilani belonged to both categories.

She was working her own brand of therapy: pinning the day's forensics reports to a corkboard so riddled with holes it looked like it had survived an execution. She marked the key lines with sticky flags and rearranged the artifacts' photos. She glared at her coffee cup—half full, skin cooled to a rubbery sheen, but she drank it anyway. There were still puzzle pieces missing. She hated unfinished puzzles.

Somewhere on the far side of the squad room, Isaac wrapped up his paperwork. He logged off his computer with a care that said he didn't want to leave a trail, but spent longer than necessary lining up the pens on his desk. That got her attention. Isaac was neat, but this seemed to be to the extreme.

She glanced and caught him watching her before he looked away and started towards the elevator. His steps had that restless bounce she recognized from fieldwork, not the lazy roll of someone going home for the night. Leilani watched him slip on his jacket, check his phone, and disappear into the elevator. He hadn't said goodbye. He always said goodbye.

She let ten seconds pass. She packed up her folders, swept the loose sticky flags into her purse, and headed for the stairwell, letting the heavy doors close softly behind her. On the second-floor landing, she peered out, caught sight of Isaac striding across the parking garage, his head down and his pace set to urgent, but not too urgent.

She shadowed him, keeping three rows of parked cars between them, her Nikes nearly silent on the concrete. Isaac cut through the exit lane, got in his new all-electric Mustang, and sat there with the power off, scanning the mirrors. Leilani kept her own reflection out of sight by slinking behind the blocky shadow of a city truck.

A moment later, Isaac rolled out with the lights off and coasted down the ramp to King Street. Leilani waited three ticks and jogged to her Explorer with the windows tinted so dark it was nearly its own night. She rolled out after him, keeping several car lengths behind and watching for tails.

This wasn't her first surveillance, but it was the first time she'd tailed a man she'd let kiss her, once, well, twice.

They traveled north towards the marina. At this hour, the traffic was a hush of cabs and mopeds. Isaac's Mustang hugged the median like it feared getting noticed. He didn't speed, didn't roll stops, didn't do anything a cop wouldn't do. The only tell was the way he checked his mirrors—every three blocks, as regular as a metronome.

He turned off at the Sand Island Access Road and let the car idle at the gate. The marina offices were dead—only one light on at the fuel dock, a sodium bulb painting everything in the same shade of migraine orange. Isaac pulled past the chain link, coasted to a stop near the last row of loading bays, and turned off the motor.

Leilani killed her headlights three hundred yards out, rolled silently, and tucked her Explorer behind a line of storage containers. She crouched, shoes off now, toes prickling on the cold pavement. From here, she could make out Isaac's silhouette in the pool of streetlamp glow, hands in his pockets and his head on a swivel. He looked like someone who expected trouble.

Ten minutes passed. The city's background noise was distant and feral. Enough to give cover to the squawk of a lone tern circling overhead. Leilani checked her watch twice. If this were a dead drop, it was the slowest one in Honolulu history.

The unmarked black car with the Federal license plates came silently, headlights off. It glided up next to Isaac, engine humming so softly it could have run on battery. It was a car that never got pulled over because nobody dared ask who was driving it.

A woman stepped out. Not tall, but she moved like she owned the space, shoulders squared and her stride fast and unshowy. Her pantsuit was steel-gray, tailored in a way that made her look like she could draw a gun or a lawsuit without wrinkling. The only concession to the island was her hair, a jet-black bob that stayed dead straight in the humidity.

He didn't bother with pleasantries. "Agent Chen, you're late."

Chen tried for a smile. "You're early, and you know as well as I do that Feds liked to make an entrance."

Chen handed him a folder. "Everything you need to turn over the investigation to us, including the paperwork for your girlfriend's investigation." She lingered on the last word, let it curdle.

Isaac opened the folder and thumbed through the pages. "You could have emailed it."

"This isn't an email job," Chen said. "The Bureau wants a hard copy trail, nothing digital. There's a copy of a federal subpoena inside. Signed and sealed."

Leilani shifted closer, using a row of empty coolers as cover. She wished she had a phone handy, but the battery had died during her last web search for red Koa lacquer techniques. Instead, she took mental notes. She could hear every word, and the way Chen's voice worked—low, certain, and with no interest in being liked.

"What's the Bureau's angle on this?" Isaac asked. "I thought we were running point for Honolulu."

Chen leaned in, her face barely visible in the lamplight. "You were. But now it's interstate. The shipment out of the auction house? It's headed for L.A., and possibly the black market in Hong Kong. The scope's changed. You're local now, Torres. And this—" she jabbed a finger at the folder "—is your last favor. I should have gone straight to your chief, but I'm showing you a little professional courtesy."

Isaac's jaw ticked, the way it always did when he was clamping down on his temper. "That's not how the SIU works. We're still in this."

"You're in it until the paperwork says you're not," Chen said. "Don't take it personally. You were a good agent. But the higher-ups don't want the Honolulu PD fucking up a federal operation. Not with the political heat on the line."

Isaac closed the folder with a sharp snap. "You think the chief will let this slide?"

Chen shrugged. "That's her problem. Ours is making sure nobody gets hurt and the chain of evidence doesn't get contaminated. We are too close to shut this ring down, and we can't afford to have a bunch of local yokels get in the way and screw that up."

He paced in a small circle, folder clamped in one hand, the other running over his scalp like he could press the thoughts deeper inside his skull. "Our team has good leads. Better than what you've got from the mainland. We can help."

"Detective Kealoha and her team are not our concern anymore," Chen said. "In fact, the less you talk to her about this, the better for everyone. If we have to, we'll issue a gag order first thing tomorrow. Don't make me take that step."

Isaac stopped moving. "That's not possible."

Chen stepped closer, her heels a quiet percussion on the dock. "It is. And it's for your own good."

Isaac's laugh was abrupt and not at all amused. "I

remember when you were the junior agent who broke all the rules."

"That was before I learned which rules matter," Chen replied, not missing a beat. "The order in the envelope directs you to turn over all your evidence to the U.S. Attorney's office by noon tomorrow. If you fail to follow the order, I'll come get it, and I'll bring a team of agents with me. You don't want that kind of scene."

She turned, crisp as a blade, and got in her car. The engine purred to life and faded as she pulled away; the taillights flickering before disappearing down the causeway.

Isaac stood alone, the folder held like a brick. He sat down on the loading dock, kicked at a pebble, and finally dropped his head into his hands. He sat like that, hunched and silent, for so long that Leilani almost lost patience.

She watched as he stood, squared his shoulders, and walked back to his car, never looking behind him. He drove away slower this time, headlights on but dim, blending back into the city like another sad ghost at closing time.

Leilani waited until the silence had grown thick again. She padded to her Explorer, her heart pounding like she'd run a sprint.

She started the car, let the A/C blast, and tried to work out what to do with what she'd seen. Isaac had secrets. The feds were taking over. And her case—their case—was about to get ripped out from under them.

She tapped the wheel twice, thinking hard. If the Bureau wanted her team off the case, they were going to have to work a hell of a lot harder.

The night outside was already healing over the footprints. The sodium lamps made it look like nothing had ever happened at the dock, like every secret stayed buried a little longer. But Leilani knew better. And tomorrow, she'd make damn sure everyone else did too.

The next morning, the tunnel under the precinct was colder than usual—a trick of the wind or the leftover chill from the night before. Leilani waited in the dim archway, hands jammed in her jacket, foot tapping a nerve-frayed tempo against the painted concrete. She could smell motor oil, damp from last week's rain, and the faint tang of the janitor's lemon bleach, sharp enough to cut through any lie.

Isaac came down the steps from the main building, head low, eyes fixed on his phone. He wasn't wearing his badge, which meant he was distracted or trying not to be noticed—both of which made her pulse jump a gear. She stepped in his path, letting her shadow cut across the yellow lines like a tripwire.

"You gonna look me in the eye, or you gonna keep walking?" she said, her voice already halfway to a growl.

Isaac flinched, but recovered, switching off the phone and slipping it into his pocket. He tried for a smile, but it died on the way up. "Morning, Lei."

Her jaw locked. "Was that your plan? Meet with the Bureau behind my back and hope I wouldn't notice?"

His whole body stiffened like a dog noticing a larger, meaner animal. He looked at the floor, and finally at her. "You followed me."

"I had to," she said. "Because you weren't going to tell me." She shifted her weight, crowding him enough that he couldn't pass without shoving her aside. "What else are you hiding?"

Isaac's nostrils flared. "It's not what you think. The Bureau's been—"

She didn't let him finish. "The Bureau has been building a case for months. The Bureau thinks they own us, own the case, and own you. That's what I saw last night."

He shook his head. "They're trying to keep the operation clean. You know how federal task forces work."

"I know bullshit when I hear it," she snapped. "You stood and talked to Chen for fifteen minutes, and not once did you think to text me, call, or loop me in. After everything?"

He leaned back against the wall, folding his arms. It made him look smaller. "It wasn't my call, Lei. They handed me a subpoena. They told me to keep it quiet. They know how passionate you get and thought it would be easier if I smoothed the way."

She pulled a hand from her jacket and pointed it right at his chest. "You're keeping evidence from me now? Is that how this works?"

He pulled the manila folder from inside his jacket slowly, as if producing a weapon. "You want to see it?

Fine. There." He held it out.

She snatched it, tore open the clasp. The top page was a federal subpoena, U.S. Attorney letterhead. Below that, a mountain of grainy photographs—artifact close-ups, some tagged with blue latex-gloved fingers, some with a ruler for scale. At the bottom, a typed summary of "Hawaiian Artifacts—Interstate Trafficking Evidence, Torres/Kealoha SIU."

Her hands shook. "They're taking the case."

Isaac's voice went flat, all the usual music stripped out. "They're taking it because they don't trust the locals not to screw up the prosecution. They think we're too close. Chen wants the win for herself."

Leilani shot him a look that could have scored glass. "Or maybe because you gave it to them. Those locals are us, or did you forget that?"

He winced. "That's not fair."

She pressed, voice echoing off the low ceiling. "Isn't it? How did they get our evidence photos? Did you forget what team you're on, Isaac? Or do you like being the guy with two bosses?"

He paced, two steps forward, three back. "This is my job, Lei. Navigating both worlds, keeping everyone from stepping on each other's feet."

She barked a humorless laugh. "Bullshit. You left the Bureau. Your job is working for me. You ever think you're the one doing all the stepping?"

They were shouting now. Their voices bounced off the walls and down the length of the tunnel to where two uniforms were pretending to check their tire pressure, doing anything but look at the drama playing out by the exit.

Isaac saw the audience and dropped his tone, low and desperate. "Don't do this here."

"Why not?" she said, refusing to drop hers. "Are you embarrassed? Or are you afraid of what happens when people figure out you're working both sides of the case?"

He bristled, took a step closer, but she didn't back up. "You think I enjoy having to play cop for the Bureau after the way they treated me? You know what it was like when I left the FBI, Lei. They're not my friends. They're not my family."

"You're not acting like it," she shot back.

He ran both hands through his hair and let them drop to his sides. "This isn't about you and me. This is about getting the job done. About making sure the evidence holds up, that the people we put away stay put."

"So, why does it seem like it's always about you? We're doing the job. We're getting results, and your friend Chen wouldn't have anything if it weren't for us." she said, softer but sharper. The hurt leaking through, even if she didn't want it to.

They looked at each other. The wind at the tunnel mouth carried in a whiff of burning rubber, and something else—like the metallic taste right before rain.

She pushed the folder against his chest. "You want to be the Bureau's guy, you do that. But don't come home to my team and pretend you're with us."

He clutched the folder, the motion involuntary. "Lei—"

She cut him off, final and cold. "Pick a side, Isaac. Because you can't serve two masters."

He opened his mouth, but no words came out.

Leilani didn't give him the chance. She turned on her heel and walked away, never breaking stride, not when she passed the uniforms, who suddenly found their shoes extremely interesting.

She sensed a sting in her chest as she rounded the corner. She kept walking until the noise faded, until the world outside was so bright it made her eyes water.

Behind her, in the tunnel, Isaac stood alone, the folder crushed in his hands, his shadow split by the slanting light from the curb. She wondered if he'd follow, if he'd try to catch up, and if he'd know what to say if he did. But Leilani wasn't looking back. She'd made her choice. She had a case to solve, and this time, she was doing it her way.

# Chapter Nine

## The Cultural Center Facade

Leilani found Isaac exactly where she expected him: out beyond the perimeter of the cultural center's construction site, pacing the gravel with the tension of a dog on a leash. She waited until he turned, caught his shadow in the dust, and she called his name, sharp and low, like a warning shot.

He faced her, hands pocketed, mouth set in a line. "Morning, Detective."

She closed the gap with three strides, letting the click of her boots on loose rock fill the silence. "You told me there was nothing to hide with Agent Chen. So why was your badge out last night, Isaac?"

He didn't flinch. "I'm doing my job, Leilani. You chose not to ask the right questions."

She stepped until they were nearly shoulder to shoulder, the haze of morning humidity already condensing on her arms. "I asked what I needed to. You didn't answer."

He glanced past her, over the chain-link fence, toward the chaos of canopies and folding chairs where staffers were rushing to finish the setup for Worthington's grand opening. The event had already drawn a scrum of local media—every tripod and boom mic jostling for the best angle on the rising glass facade and its banner, white with bold navy: MOKULUA

HERITAGE CENTER—OPENING CEREMONY.

"Can we not do this here?" Isaac asked, nodding at a couple of security volunteers with laminated badges. "You want to chew my ass, wait until we're not surrounded by a hundred people with cameras."

She shot him a look, measured and cool. "You're the one who dragged the Bureau back into this. Not me."

"Worthington's got connections on the mainland," he replied, keeping his tone low. "If we don't play it smart, this is going to get snatched away by every alphabet agency in the book."

A voice—warm, musical—interrupted them from behind: "Leilani! You came early."

Leilani turned, already bracing for the switch. Naalei's silhouette was framed by a burst of sunlight, hair coiled into a loose plait, her hibiscus-print mu'umu'u radiant against the event's white-and-navy scheme. She glided over, arms open, and drew both Leilani and Isaac into a quick, fragrant hug.

"Ma," Leilani said, half-laughing. "You're going to outshine the entire event."

Naalei winked. "That's my job, baby." She flicked her eyes to Isaac, and he stiffened, surprised by the intensity of her smile.

"Are you good, Detective?" Naalei asked, her tone suggesting she could see right through him.

He cleared his throat. "Yes, ma'am. Happy to be on the guest list."

Naalei laughed, big and unselfconscious. She looped her arm through Leilani's. "Come with me. We have the best seats for the ceremony, right up front." She whispered, "Your uncle would be so mad if we sat anywhere else."

They walked together through the staged chaos of opening day. Volunteers arranged trays of cut fruit and trays of mini Spam musubi on every table. Lei makers, hands moving quickly, wove orchid strands at a pop-up booth near the stage. Three local newscasters preened in the reflected glare of a rented spotlight, mouthing weather updates into their iPhones.

At the ceremonial platform, the other kupuna had gathered, wearing an assortment of fresh leis and their best formal prints. Several nodded at Leilani, all of them eying Isaac with the practiced scrutiny of people who'd seen law enforcement come and go over the years.

The main event, however, was Sam Worthington. He stood on the stage, suit pressed so sharp it looked like it might break, a crisp white pocket square peeking from his lapel. He was already in story mode, a ring of photographers around him as he gestured at the sleek curves of the center's front entry. When he saw the approach of Naalei and her entourage, he excused himself from the press and cut directly toward them.

"Mrs. Kealoha," he said, taking Naalei's hand in both of his and bowing ever so slightly. "You are a vision. And your counsel on Hawaiian blessings has made all of this possible."

She flashed him a practiced smile. "It's a privilege

to be here, Mr. Worthington. The ancestors are watching.”

Leilani noticed the way his eyes lingered on her mother—hungry and calculating. She held his gaze as he offered his hand, but she did not take it.

“Detective Kealoha,” he said, softer, with the faintest flicker of amusement. “You must be very proud.”

Leilani didn’t smile. “We’ll see how the day goes.”

Sam’s grin didn’t falter, but she saw the way his right cheek tensed for a micro-spasm. “I trust you’ll be part of the security detail for the ribbon cutting? There’s always a risk of protesters. Last week, someone threatened to red paint the steps. I’d hate for that to stain such a beautiful day.”

Leilani tipped her head, noncommittal. “If anyone throws paint, I’ll make sure it’s only water based.”

Worthington laughed as if this were the funniest thing anyone had ever said to him. He turned to Naalei. “Can I steal your wisdom for a few minutes before the ceremony, Mrs. Kealoha? The university wants a photo for its alumni magazine.”

Naalei patted Leilani’s arm and followed him, pausing only to squeeze her daughter’s hand. Leilani watched the two of them walk off, Sam’s posture loose and practiced, Naalei regal as a queen with every step.

Isaac sidled closer, his whisper almost lost in the crowd noise. “He’s good. Knows how to work a room.”

“He’s working a lot more than that,” Leilani

muttered.

The first round of speeches was a blur of officialdom: local councilors praising "the new dawn of cultural revitalization," school superintendents exclaiming over educational outreach. Leilani nodded and clapped in the right places, her eyes never straying far from Naalei and Sam, who seemed to be in their own world at the side of the stage.

As the lineup shifted, Sam Worthington took the microphone. He held it with a confidence that bordered on arrogance, sweeping the crowd with eyes that missed nothing.

"Thank you, everyone, for being here. This is not only a building; it's a promise. A promise to the people of Hawaii that their culture, their artifacts and their stories will never be lost to time or to the highest bidder. This center, built with local hands and international support, will return treasures to their rightful home. Not in a warehouse, not behind closed doors, but in the open, where everyone can see and learn."

He paused for effect, letting the press cameras get a clear shot of the light haloed around his silver hair. "I could never have accomplished this without the guidance of Mrs. Kealoha and the wisdom of so many local families. The artifacts you see today have traveled a long way to return to their roots. Let's honor them, and each other, with gratitude."

He stepped back as the crowd murmured their approval and motioned to the row of kupuna for the ribbon cutting. Naalei, beaming, accepted the oversize scissors and posed for photos with the other elders. At the last moment, Worthington drew close enough to rest his hand lightly on her shoulder—enough for the camera to capture, and to make Leilani want to throw something heavy.

Isaac leaned in, voice dry: "He's got good taste, I'll give him that."

"Shut up, Torres."

As the ribbon fell and the crowd surged forward to the exhibit preview, Leilani spotted Worthington's project manager—the same nervous man from the auction, with a neck too thin for his tailored collar and a sweat mustache already forming under the heat lamps. The manager hovered at the entry, eyes darting from the VIPs to the security team to the artifact cases inside.

"Look at him," she said to Isaac, nodding toward the manager. "He's more worried than Worthington. You think he knows something's up?"

"He knows he's in over his head," Isaac replied. "Guy probably never thought he'd have to wrangle local police, the FBI, and whatever the hell you are all in one week."

Leilani suppressed a smile. "You're not off the hook. I want every detail of what Chen said last night. Not when you feel like it. Now."

He hesitated, then shrugged. "She thinks the case is getting bigger. Maybe organized theft, not just one-off jobs. She wanted me to keep you on a short leash."

"Good luck with that," Leilani said. She started

towards one of the side exhibit halls, Isaac falling into step beside her.

Inside, the hall was a shadowy hush compared to the morning's glare. Cases of polished glass lined the main corridor, each containing artifacts so beautiful and strange they looked like props from a film set. There was a paddle carved from black Koa, its blade scored with double-helix motifs; a fragment of feathered cloak, red and yellow as lava and sunrise; a row of shark-tooth daggers so wicked they seemed to hum with old violence.

A docent in a navy polo explained provenance to a knot of local reporters, but Leilani ignored him. She moved slowly from case to case, checking the labels against the list she'd memorized: five stolen from the Bishop, two from private homes, and three on loan from the British Museum that looked suspiciously like repatriated goods.

The last artifact in the row was a set of drum carvings—three small pahu, surfaces inked with bold, geometric designs. Leilani leaned closer, tracing the shape with her eyes. She recognized the iwi kūpuna motif immediately: the ancestor bones, lined up like vertebrae along the drum's edge. Her throat went dry.

"That's my grandmother's old pahu," she said, voice barely a whisper. Her scalp prickled. "That's not a museum copy," she said.

Isaac gave her a look. "The real thing?"

"It's the only one of its kind. That's the Kealoha line. My line."

She stood so still she barely breathed. At her side, Isaac's posture softened, almost apologetic.

She wanted to reach out, to test the drum with her fingers, to prove it belonged here more than anyone in the room did. Instead, she lifted her phone and snapped a picture, ignoring the flash.

A stir behind them—a gentle clearing of the throat—and Sam Worthington's voice, polished and syrupy. Now free of press obligations, he moved towards them with the loose stride of a man who already owns everything in the room. He paused in front of the drum, gave it a respectful once-over. He turned to Leilani and Isaac.

"Detective Kealoha. Can I ask your professional opinion of these drums?"

She faced him. He held a glass of sparkling water in one hand, the other perched on his hip, as if preparing to lecture a group of interns.

Leilani kept her own hands still. "They're impressive. Who did your provenance work?"

Worthington smiled slyly. "Most came through the London museums. A few from private collectors—estates on the mainland. I'll admit the drums were a surprise. My project manager, Dan, tracked them down in a gallery in San Jose."

Leilani flicked her eyes toward the display's label. "That's odd. These marks here"—she tapped the glass, above the bone motif—"are unique."

"Beautiful piece, isn't it?" he said, as if he were offering them a taste of some rare fruit.

Leilani held his eyes. "Do you know where it's from?"

He smiled slowly and deliberately. "I only know what my curator tells me. It came from a private sale somewhere on the Big Island and passed through several hands before landing in my collection. Do you recognize it?"

She allowed the question to hang, then smiled back, teeth bared. "It's the exact pattern my great-grandmother used for her halau. I haven't seen that design anywhere else."

Sam's eyes flicked to the side like he'd been caught with his hand in the cookie jar. "Your family, you say. How wonderful that it's been found and returned to the people. You must be very proud."

"I'd be prouder if I knew how it got here."

Sam quickly changed the subject.

"Isn't it amazing," said Sam, "how these traditions can travel so far? I've seen Maori tikis in New York, Samoan headrests in Paris—these cultures are all Polynesian cousins, after all."

Isaac's mouth twitched, but he said nothing.

Leilani didn't blink. "Maori and Hawaiian drums are nothing alike. If you want these stories to last, you might want to learn the difference."

Sam looked like he had been exposed. It was subtle—his eyes went flat, the line of his mouth tightened, the drink in his hand paused halfway to his lips. He laughed, brushing it off with a practiced shake of the head.

"You know your stuff, Detective. I wish every exhibit could have you as a fact checker." He leaned in, dropping his voice. "The real prize is coming next year: a full set of aliʻi regalia, including a helmet. The National Museum wants it, but I'm bringing it home."

She didn't smile. "Just make sure it actually belongs here when you do."

He raised a hand as if in surrender. "We can get the records for you, Detective. Full provenance. I want everything to be legitimate." He flicked a look at Isaac. "And if there's anything you need to discuss with the FBI, I'm sure Agent Chen will be happy to work with you. She's an old friend of mine, you know."

Sam spotted someone in the distance, excused himself and walked away.

Isaac checked the label. "On loan from the Worthington Foundation, previously attributed to an anonymous collector." He shot her a look. "Could be a coincidence."

She glared at him. "There's no such thing."

Leilani's phone buzzed—an incoming text from Tommy. **Worthington's office just received a shipment from Singapore, courier says it's artifacts for the grand opening. Want me to intercept?**

She typed back. **Stand by. Eyes only. Don't move until I say.**

Isaac saw the message over her shoulder. "He's not trying to hide it."

"He doesn't need to. He's already bought his way in."

They moved through the exhibit, making mental notes, before stepping past the entrance. The crowd had thinned, but the street was jammed with cars and news vans. At the curb, Naalei and Worthington were deep in conversation, her posture open and easy, his careful and intent.

Leilani watched them for a beat. "Let's keep moving," she said to Isaac.

The air in the main exhibition hall was sharp with a mix of new carpet, air conditioning and the silent tension of too many people pretending not to watch each other. Leilani strode through the wide aisle, Isaac half a step behind her, both with their hands near their pockets and eyes everywhere but directly ahead.

"Don't go chasing Chen's leads when we're here," she murmured, above the hush of the crowd. She was still raw from last night's argument—less an open wound than a tight, splintered scar.

Isaac shrugged. "I'm right where I need to be."

They moved through small clusters of guests. Leilani studied each artifact in the row of glass display cubes. The first was the Koa paddle—same as the missing one from the auction house, she was sure— with its blade edge worked into an intricate double-helix that shimmered when the light hit it. She took three pictures: one close, one at an angle, and one of the security seal.

Isaac tilted his head to see her phone. "Is that for the file?"

"That's for Kai," she whispered. "He'll get a kick

out of it."

Next was the feather cloak fragment, a streak of crimson and gold. Leilani recognized the bird species from childhood lessons, the bright feathers of the 'i'iwi and 'ō'ō. She snapped two more pictures, one with a hand in the frame for scale. An older man in an aloha shirt caught her eye and grinned.

"Excellent craftsmanship?" he said, his voice raspy from too much cigar smoke.

Leilani nodded, matching his smile. "Almost as good as the ones at the Bishop, but this has a better story."

He leaned in, lowering his voice. "They say a royal guard died protecting that cape."

Isaac interjected, "Stories last longer than stone."

The man winked and moved on.

Leilani looked towards the entrance and watched as Sam and Naalei returned to the lobby. A group of reporters formed around them. Sam seemed to take a back seat as Naalei spoke about some of the exhibits.

Sam left Naalei standing in a crowd of local reporters and moved along the exhibits. He glanced over and spotted Leilani looking at the paddle. He saluted her with the glass and drifted on to the next VIP knot, his project manager trailing after like a nervous shadow. Sam barely looked back, but when he did, his eyes met hers—calculating, a little desperate, and entirely unamused.

Isaac exhaled. "That was fun. What's your read?"

"He's scared," she said. "And he's lying about the drums."

Isaac nodded. "So, we check where the shipping really came from."

"Already on it." She snapped one last picture, this time of the project manager, turned on her heel, and left the building, sunlight washing the color from the world outside.

***

The conference room was empty except for the buzz of fluorescent tubes and the old air conditioner that vibrated with the slow, relentless urgency of a migraine. Leilani dropped her backpack on the nearest counter and slammed a stack of evidence folders down hard enough to rattle the racks of fingerprint kits. Isaac followed, silent, letting the echo settle before he spoke.

"You still mad?" he asked, voice low.

Leilani spun in her chair, eyes hot. "I don't have time for federal games, Isaac. I want every detail of your Bureau contacts—past and present—before we do another thing."

He set his own bag down and leaned back against the table, arms folded. "You want the truth? I'm only talking to Chen because we're outnumbered. You know that. I thought you'd rather have eyes on the Bureau than the other way around."

She was pissed. "That's not how partnerships work. You never told me about the subpoena."

"You never told me about your mother's involvement in this case." He looked her up and down, the old warmth gone. "You sidelined me, Lei. I got tired of pretending it didn't matter."

The only sound was the high-pitched whine of the overhead lights.

She wanted to bite back, but the energy had shifted. She was too tired for another round of shouting.

"Fine," she said, flipping open her laptop. "Let's actually work."

They sat at the table, the screen between them. She loaded the folder of photos from the exhibition, each shot tagged by time and location. She started with the paddle—the double-helix blade—and compared it to the inventory list from the Bishop Museum theft three weeks earlier. The two images matched down to the knot of sapwood near the grip.

Isaac murmured, "That's the missing one. No way there's another with the same grain."

She dragged the next file: the feather cloak fragment, its edge frayed but unmistakable. A click through the museum's lost-item database showed the same dimensions, same repair seam, same red dye pattern.

"This is the cloak fragment he bought at the auction," she said.

The third item was the pahu: ancestor drum, black with age, the lines of her grandmother's halau carved in neat rows along the rim. She brought out an old photo from the family album, zoomed in on the identical motifs.

Her hands trembled on the keys.

Isaac touched her wrist. "Sorry."

She pulled away and reached for her coffee, squeezing the Styrofoam cup until it bent.

"They're not pretending to be careful," she said, voice bitter.

Isaac nodded. "He's laundering the artifacts, Lei. Bringing them back, but not to the right people. To himself."

Leilani started a new document, listing the artifacts with their real provenance next to Worthington's exhibit labels. "He's disguising theft as philanthropy," she said. "And the whole city's buying it."

They worked for an hour without speaking. The evidence mounted: three more artifacts, all presumed missing or sold overseas, now suddenly donated by Worthington's foundation and displayed under new names.

Leilani checked her phone—two missed calls from Naalei, one unread text from Kai about going to the next-door neighbor's house for dinner. She typed a reply with her left thumb while clicking through the next batch of shipping records.

She found it on the third try: incoming manifest for the MOKULUA Heritage Center, air-shipped from Singapore, labeled as Polynesian Cultural Items. There were no serial numbers, only a packing list in bland legalese and a digital signature from the project manager.

Isaac cleared his throat. "Lei. I know I messed up. I know I should have trusted you with everything, but."

He stopped, words catching on his tongue.

She waited.

He tried again. "You're the best partner I've ever had. Including when you drive me crazy."

She didn't answer, but she didn't get up either. The old anger still thrummed in her, but it seemed smaller now, less a bonfire and more a stubborn coal that would never quite die.

They finished the evidence review, printing out the last sheet for the Chief's inbox. As they stood to go, Leilani let her hand rest on the pahu, her palm flat against the photo. She closed her eyes for half a second, and when she opened them, Isaac was watching—not with pity, but with a kind of fierce pride.

She picked up the printout and handed it to him. "We'll figure it out tomorrow," she said.

He nodded.

They left the conference room together, neither leading nor following, their steps in sync as they walked into the gathering dusk. The mission was clear.

As the headquarters' doors swung shut behind them, Leilani felt the old ache in her chest, but this time she didn't let it slow her down. There was too much left to do, and too many stories waiting to be returned.

# Chapter Ten

## Naalei's Revelation

It was after eight when Leilani pulled into the hula halau's gravel lot. The day's sweat still clung to her, dried by hours of AC and adrenaline and revived by the muggy night air as she killed the engine. The building was low and long, made of cinder block and old wood, and at this hour looked less like a cultural institution and more like a place someone might break into just to sleep on the cool floor. Through the small windows, the only light was gold and trembling—a handful of oil lamps, so dim they barely held back the darkness. It had always been that way. Halau weren't supposed to look like gyms or rec centers, and this one sure as hell never would.

Inside, it was quieter. The lamps hung in pairs along the north wall, glass chimneys fogged by age, their glow barely enough to map the perimeter. Shadows moved and pooled as she walked, creeping up the high mirrors and coiling around the painted murals. In the center of the floor, her mother, Naalei, was down on one knee, arranging a line of feathered gourds by height.

"Ma," Leilani said, not trying to keep her voice low.

Without turning, Naalei replied, "You're late." The words floated weightless, no trace of rebuke—a fact, as inevitable as gravity.

Leilani shut the door behind her. "Had to wrap something at the station."

Now her mother stood, brushing imaginary dust off her mu'umu'u, and turned to look at her daughter. The lamplight hooked through her gray braid, glinted off the silver at her wrist, and made her shadow loom huge across the opposite wall. Her face was all lines—some laugh, some worry and tonight, more than the usual share of the second. She studied Leilani's stance, the set of her jaw, and it was like the air between them thickened and shrank at the same time.

"You look like someone's been chasing you." Naalei's lips pursed. "Or you've been chasing ghosts again."

Leilani managed a weak laugh. "Bit of both." She peeled off her jacket and slung it onto a folding chair, letting her eyes adjust. The place looked the same as always: trophies and award plaques clustered near the door, the rank charts hung with colored sashes, a huge photo of Naalei's own teacher smiling down on all comers.

Against the wall, where the most important pahu drum in the room should have been, was an empty shelf. She forced herself not to keep glancing at it, the way you don't touch a scab or count a missing tooth with your tongue.

Naalei followed her gaze, lips tightening further. "I still look every time I walk in," she whispered. "That drum belonged here more than I ever did."

"I know," Leilani replied. The ache in her mother's voice was a familiar one. The kind you never quite grow out of when you move away, or when you become a cop and run headlong into pain as a matter of routine.

Naalei shook herself, turned brisk, and busied her hands straightening the skirt bundles and feather leis. "You eat yet?"

Leilani rolled her eyes. "I had a granola bar. I'm fine."

Naalei made a noise between a snort and a sigh. "I have poke. Sit before you fall down."

She pointed to the corner behind a folding screen patterned with bamboo and birds. The floor there was layered with woven lauhala mats, the kind you could sit on for hours without noticing the bite of wood underneath. Off to one side, a low table waited, two chipped bowls set out with care.

Leilani didn't argue. She slipped off her shoes and padded to the mats, settling with a creak in her knees. For a second, she let herself sink into the feeling— childhood, mixed with the grown-up realization that every time she came here, she was a visitor now.

"Ma—listen. The drums at the new cultural center." Leilani hesitated, but pressed on anyway, her voice pitched low and sharp. "The set of five pahu and the 'ulī'ulī with the worn red feathers. I recognized the engravings. They're old, before annexation. They had the shark tooth and starburst designs. That's from your grandmother's halau, yeah? From the Hilo side. The one that supposedly disappeared in the forties. And now Worthington's got it as an exhibit, with a plaque that says that they came from a private collection, but with no provenance, nothing. Did you know? Did you have any idea where it was all this time?"

She heard herself pushing too hard, but it was like the words were rocks tumbling out of her mouth, too many years of not asking the questions that mattered. She'd come here looking for comfort and instead found the past walking around in the present, barefoot and hungry.

Naalei's hands paused in mid-fold, the fabric of the lauhala skirt rippling between her fingers. She seemed to shrink before she set down the skirt carefully, as if it might break. Her lips pressed together; Leilani could see the muscles working behind the skin, the way they did when her mother was angry but refusing to show it.

"I didn't want to believe it," Naalei said quietly. "When I saw them on display, the aunties in the alumni group, they all said no way. Not after so long. If it was the same design, how could it still exist?"

"It's the same one, Ma. I know it. I checked the base for the old chisel marks you talked about. The repair with the Koa patch—" Leilani stopped, suddenly aware of the old ache in her chest, the one that throbbed whenever she stared at family photos, everyone smiling except for the space where her father used to be. "It's not only a drum. It's part of what's missing."

Naalei exhaled, a sound that was half breath and half memory. "Those drums were hidden during the war. My tutu said they'd be confiscated or burned if the wrong people found them. So, they hid them in the old spring tunnel, near the sugar mill. But after the war, the entrance collapsed. Everyone assumed they were gone."

"So, how the hell did a billionaire from Connecticut end up with them?" Leilani's voice was a blade, but she softened it at the last instant. "You think Worthington's people found them by chance?"

Her mother's gaze flicked up, sharp and luminous in the lamplight. "He didn't find them," she said, the words stretched thin by regret. "I asked him. I didn't tell him they were from our family. Someone sold them. Someone who knew the family or the island's stories. That's how these things always go."

Leilani thought of stolen art, of artifacts looted from places that barely made the news. She wondered how much of her life was shaped by people selling things that didn't belong to them. Perhaps this was why she kept returning to the halau, after she'd outgrown all the costumes and the dances and the sense that here, at least, was something nobody could take away.

"I want it back, Ma," she said. "Not for the case. For us."

"I know," her mother replied, her face crumpling in a way that made Leilani want to look away and never stop looking at the same time.

Her mother kneeled beside her, pouring tea from a battered thermos. For a minute, they sat, the silence made gentle by the sound of the oil lamps ticking and the faint slap of the breeze against the louvered windows. Only after she'd placed the tea in Leilani's hand did Naalei speak again, her voice pitched so low it almost disappeared in the dark.

"There's something I should have told you long ago," Naalei said, eyes fixed not on her daughter, but on the blank wall where the drum had once presided. "Something about our family that changes everything about these thefts."

Leilani blinked, confused by the sudden shift, and straightened her spine. "What do you mean? I thought you said—"

Her mother held up a hand. "Not the stuff I told you about Kumu Lani, or your tutu's activism in the seventies. This is older. Deeper."

Naalei reached for a wrapped bundle beneath the low table and set it between them, hands reverent as she peeled back the tapa. The bundle looked heavy, but when the cloth fell away, what it revealed was nothing but an old wooden chest, the kind you might keep keepsakes or recipes in. The sides were carved with patterns—shark's teeth, zigzags and a line of interlocked triangles. Leilani traced them with her eyes, suddenly aware of a tightness in her neck she hadn't known she was carrying.

Naalei popped the lid and set it aside. Inside, the contents were simple: a few yellowed pages, the ends curled and brown; a small, blunt wooden figure with eyes rubbed nearly smooth; a length of cord knotted at intervals, each knot marked with red or blue thread.

"Your great-grandmother was more than a hula teacher," Naalei said, her voice a ghost's breath above the rain falling outside. "Our line was kahu, back before the missionaries or the sugar lords or any of the new names for authority. Guardians—not only of knowledge, but of real things. Things people wanted to erase, or steal, or destroy."

Leilani exhaled slowly, letting the words seep in. The case files, interviews, and surveillance logs faded, replaced by the thought that she was twelve years old again and about to hear a story too wild to repeat at school.

She reached for the wooden figure and turned it over in her palm. It was warm from the box; the grain burnished by a century of fingers. "You're saying Tutu was hiding things?"

"I'm saying she was the one who figured out how to hide them," Naalei replied. "She and the other families. When the American laws made old gods and old ways illegal, someone had to decide what to lose and what to keep. They invented tricks—songs, stories, codes in the carving and in the dance. Sometimes they hid a thing in plain sight and let the police or priests think they'd broken the chain, but the chain was only sleeping, never lost."

Naalei slid the documents across the mat. The script was spidery, a mix of English and pidgin and something older, all interlaced. "You know how many times people tried to get this halau closed? How many times our pahu vanished and came back again, like a ghost?"

Leilani let her eyes drift to the empty place against the wall and felt her breath go tight.

"Tell me what you mean about the drum," she said, her own voice smaller than she wanted.

Naalei's eyes glittered in the dim light. "The drum that was stolen—your Tutu made that with her teacher. The skin, the wood, and the way it was painted meant something. It was a story and a map. A map of everything our family ever hid, or saved, or brought back from the dead. They called it the Ku'uipo pahu, after the secret lover of the ancestors. The person who took it knew what it was."

Leilani's world shrank to the size of the mat. For a long time, she said nothing, letting her mind catch up to the fact that the puzzle she'd thought was about evidence and suspects and jurisdiction had always been something else. Something that ran all the way back through her own blood.

Outside, the rain had picked up, and the wind shook the window slats. The lamplight shadows leaned and flickered on the walls. For the first time since the case began, Leilani wondered if she wasn't chasing a thief, but someone trying to finish a job started centuries ago.

Her mother watched her carefully, the way you watched a storm forming on the horizon.

"Do you believe me?" Naalei asked.

Leilani answered without thinking. "Yeah," she said. "I do."

And as she looked down at the old wooden figure in her hand, she felt the chain tug—a real thing, not lost, only waiting.

The chest sat between them, small enough to cradle in both arms but somehow dense, as if it contained a personal gravity. For a few moments, neither woman spoke. Leilani's fingers tapped the lauhala mat, and her brain skipped restlessly between the puzzle of the thefts and the unreality of her mother opening a treasure box like a fairy tale.

"Ma," Leilani said, voice breaking the spell, "how long have you been keeping that thing under the floor?"

Naalei smiled a little, and it was a strange smile—regret, pride, mischief, all together. "Since your Tutu's last birthday. Before that, it was always in her room, up high where I couldn't reach it." She paused. "I was a snoop, you know. Got in trouble more times than I can count."

Leilani nodded, rubbing at her neck, already falling into the childhood rhythm of wanting her mother's stories to last longer than her patience. "What's in the papers?"

Her mother picked out a folded page, the corner torn, and the surface gone soft with time. "This is the first chant I ever memorized," she said, laying it flat. The words wavered, the pencil barely visible: a tangle of Hawaiian, English, and a private code. "My kumu called it the hiding song, mele huna. Not meant for performance. Only to teach you how to remember without writing anything down."

She smoothed it with her palm and slid it toward Leilani, who bent closer and traced a line of script. With her training, the writing was still hard to follow—some words were spelled phonetically, others crossed out and replaced with doodled stars or sharks.

"You see here?" Naalei tapped the margin. "She told me that if I ever lost the way, this would lead me home."

Leilani read the line again, slower. "Is that literal, or are you screwing with me?"

Her mother shrugged, her face deadpan. "In this family, it's always both."

They laughed; the release of tension was physical. Naalei leaned in, her voice lowering. "But it's not just song and story. Look." She picked up the ki'i: the little wooden man, naked but for a faint red line across its midsection, the bottom rounded and smooth. At first it seemed crude, but the more Leilani stared, the more it seemed like the kind of thing you could hide in a pocket or bury in a jar. Something meant to travel.

"He's missing an arm," Leilani said, lifting the figure. The right side ended in a blunt stub, smooth from handling. "You ever ask why?"

"Tutu used to say it was so he could pass through the bars," Naalei answered, half-laughing. "So, he could escape when they locked him up."

Leilani grinned, and could see her grandmother, tiny and fierce, making up stories to keep her grandkids from being afraid of ghosts or cops or both.

There was also a photograph in the chest, faded almost to nothing. Four women in mu'umu'u stood in front of a high altar, all of them serious, hands folded at their waists. The only way Leilani could pick out Tutu was the sharp chin and the stubbornness of the eyes. She passed a finger over the faces, feeling a chill as she did. "Is that her? Kumu Lani?"

The pride in her mother's face was unmistakable. "Yes. She taught me every word I know, but she had secrets. This." She pointed at the chest. "It was only ever opened when things got bad. Or when there was a threat. I don't remember her ever showing it to anyone else, including my father."

Leilani let that settle and set the ki'i down with more care than she meant to. "So, the drum. You said it was a map."

"Yes. Or the first piece of one." Naalei's fingers hovered over the yellowed sheet. "When the missionaries came, they wanted to take away the old ways. The ali'i hid what they could, but the kahu—my line, and others like us—found ways to move things. Sometimes from church to church, sometimes into caves, sometimes disguised as something nobody would steal."

She gestured toward the practice hall. "Here, we have hiding places. None so good as the old ones, but enough to make them look twice."

Leilani sensed herself floating, the way she sometimes did at the edge of sleep or when staring too long at the ocean. "So that drum—our drum—there's more to it than being an heirloom."

"There's a pattern on the skin," her mother said, and now she was all business, kumu mode. "Red paint, made from 'alaea clay and a kind of resin I can't get anymore. Tutu said you could read it if you knew the right story. But she only told me the first half, and she said I'd learn the second part when I needed to."

Leilani braced her elbows on her knees, completely drawn in. "Do you remember what the pattern looked like?"

Naalei closed her eyes, searching. "Diamond in the middle, four triangles around it, and a circle with three dots off to the side. The edges had lines—some straight, some jagged. It was a code, I think. Numbers, or something else." She smiled, a little sheepish. "I never paid attention to that part, because I never thought anyone would take it."

Leilani rocked back and sprang to her feet. "Ma. The drum at the Bishop Museum had a similar pattern. The curator told me it was strange, almost like a tattoo instead of regular decoration."

Her mother's eyes widened. "It must be part of the set. Part of the map."

Leilani paced, all detective now, but with a different energy—like she was looking for the next step in a dance instead of the next place a perp might run. "If it's a code, whoever took it wanted the message, not just the history. They're looking for something hidden, something bigger."

Naalei nodded, catching up. "And if that's the case, the other stolen artifacts might be clues too. Connected somehow. Either way, that makes the drum at the Bishop Museum a target. If someone knows about the code."

A memory surfaced for Leilani, sharp as a needle: the first item stolen from the auction house had a feather lei twisted into a spiral, red and yellow, with an unfamiliar black border. She'd dismissed it as decorative, but now she wondered if there was a message, a code, something woven into the tradition that would go unnoticed by outsiders.

She stopped pacing and crouched beside the chest, staring hard at the ki'i. The missing arm, the red line, the rounded base—it all seemed random until she pictured it rolling, moving, escaping. She realized it might fit into something, maybe a cavity or a slot, or act as a key.

She grabbed her phone, opened a new note file, and started rapid-firing questions into it: "Possible artifact-based scavenger hunt? Pattern significance? Other items with hidden codes? Why now?"

Her mother watched with quiet amusement, but she didn't interrupt. Instead, she wrapped the tapa cloth back around the chest, hands steady. "You're thinking like Tutu," she whispered. "She'd be proud."

Leilani's chest swelled, the old guilt about not being Hawaiian enough or not being a good enough daughter dissolving under the strange pride of being part of a bigger, older story. She sat down, suddenly tired and sipped her tea. The sweetness of the dried ginger cut the bitterness of the bag, and she let herself be comforted by the simple taste.

"So, what do we do?" Leilani finally asked, her voice steady.

Naalei placed her hand on her daughter's. "We remember. We follow the trail. And if the map is leading somewhere, we go there first. Before they do."

Leilani nodded. "I'm going to need your help, Ma. You might have to be an expert witness. Or a... consultant."

Her mother grinned, all the old mischief returned.

"You think I'm gonna let you have all the fun? Detective, please."

They sat in silence, staring at the chest and all it represented. For Leilani, the puzzle had flipped upside down. But the next move was clear.

Leilani could only keep still for so long. After ten minutes on the mat, she was up and moving, boots in her hand, pacing the length of the halau's mirrored wall. The floorboards under her bare feet were smooth as glass, every step ringing faint and hollow in the old building. She liked it better this way; when she was in motion, her mind sorted through details without letting anyone's feelings get in the way.

Her mother didn't say a word. She watched, her eyes soft and hands folded over one knee, as if she'd expected this reaction. She knew Leilani needed space to metabolize emotion the way most people needed time to process a meal.

Finally, Leilani stopped near the space on the wall. The one she'd avoided looking at since she'd walked in. She pressed her palm to the wood where the drum should have stood. "You could've told me," she said, barely above a whisper. "About all this. About being kahu."

Naalei shrugged, her braid sliding off her shoulder. "Would it have made any difference?"

Leilani's first impulse was to answer yes, but she stopped herself. "I don't know. It might've helped me understand why you were always so…" She searched for the word but gave up. "Why does it hurt you so much to see the old stuff disappear?"

Her mother smiled, small but real. "You had to leave. I wanted you to see the world. If you'd grown up with that weight on your back, you'd have hated it. Hated me."

Leilani let her hand fall. "And now?"

"Now?" Naalei said, unfolding her legs and standing, the motion so smooth it made her seem younger. "Now you come back. You choose for yourself."

They met in the middle of the floor, mother and daughter, each holding on to more secrets than they could say out loud. Leilani forgot about the case, the paperwork, and the aches in her body. She was here, in this room with the only person who'd ever really understood her.

Leilani glanced at the chest and at her mother. "If the thefts are about building a map or finding something hidden, what happens if the thieves get all the pieces?"

Naalei looked serious. "Depends on who they are. Some want to sell. Some want to break the story so no one else can have it. Some," she paused, her eyes narrowing. "Might want to put it back together. But not for a good reason."

Leilani rubbed her temples, then straightened. "We need to see if any other artifacts went missing. Ones with patterns, markings, anything that matches what's in the drum code. Possibly from the other halau, or from churches or family shrines."

Naalei nodded. "Start with the old temples, too.

Your great-aunt used to say there were caches in the valley caves, places nobody ever mapped because they were too dangerous or too scared."

Leilani took out her phone and started making a list. "I'll need names. Dates. Any relatives who might know the old routes or chants. You said you memorized some—"

Her mother cut her off. "I'll do better. I'll come with you."

Leilani looked up, surprised. "That might be risky. The last time we tried to interview a kahu about missing items, it got ugly."

Naalei's lips twisted in wry amusement. "That's because you went in as a cop, not as family."

They both grinned, the same crooked angle.

Leilani sat back down, this time cross-legged, her nerves calmer. She reached for the ki'i in the chest and turned it over in her hands, running a thumb along the missing arm. "It seems heavier than it should," she said. "Like it's waiting to be used."

Naalei smiled, taking the figure and setting it between them on the mat. "That's the point. These things weren't made for show; they were made for moments. You carry it with you, but you don't use it unless you have to."

They fell silent again, the mood less tense now—almost gentle. Leilani scanned her notes. "If you're up for it, I want you to be our cultural consultant. Official. The Chief will hate it, but she can deal."

Her mother's face shone with something close to

pride, and she reached out to take both of Leilani's hands in her own. "I'd like that. It's time to stop pretending we're not part of the same story."

They sat that way for a while, palms pressed together, the past and future running through their veins. Without breaking contact, Naalei hummed—a low, rhythmic song that Leilani hadn't heard since childhood, but which seemed to rise from the floorboards themselves. The tune was simple, a series of repeating notes, but layered in it was a sense of being grounded, held. Protected.

After a minute, Naalei drew Leilani to her feet. "Follow me," she said, and guided her daughter through the first steps of a hula kahiko, the ancient style. Nothing elaborate—a sway, a step, a shift of the hands from heart to horizon, as if sharing the burden with the air itself.

At first, Leilani felt foolish. She was out of practice, her movements stiff. But as her mother's hands shaped the motion, she found her feet, let the song take over, and forgot the world outside. Together, they danced a circle on the mat, their shadows crossing and recrossing in the lamplight. It was a ritual not of protection, but of trust—a silent promise that whatever happened next, they would face it as a team.

When they stopped, both were breathless, but smiling. Leilani brushed a loose strand of hair from her face and grinned. "You always make me look bad," she said.

Naalei shrugged, eyes sparkling. "You always catch up."

As the lamps burned low, and the last echoes of their chant faded, Leilani let the old doubts fall away. She was not chasing ghosts or solving someone else's mystery. She was home, in her own story. And this time, she was ready to follow the map, wherever it led.

# Chapter Eleven

## Undercover Operation

Leilani stood in front of her bedroom mirror and weighed herself like evidence: the facts, the body, the story it had to tell tonight. The lighting was brutally honest, the low-watt bulb exposing every freckle, every place her tan had lapsed. She'd gone through five wardrobe changes already—linen slacks (too PTA), a black sheath (too funeral), a pantsuit that looked like it would call the cops on its own daughter. Each one hung limp now in the closet like evidence bags on a drying rack.

On her bed, the last option glinted: a blue sequined cocktail dress she'd never worn, tags still biting the lining, a clearance gamble from the Ala Moana Bloomingdale's. She picked it up, held it to her ribcage, and squinted at the effect. The dress said, "aloha, I'm fun," but the mirror said, "auditioning for a bad reality show." She put it on anyway, sliding the fabric over shoulders carved from ten years of deadlifts and police academy calisthenics. The hem clung to her thighs, stopping halfway to decency. In the reflection, her legs looked longer than she remembered, and she felt something unfamiliar: the sharp-toothed thrill of not blending in.

She could already hear Isaac's voice in her head, low and grinning. "Damn, Lei. Trying to catch a billionaire or give him a heart attack?"

She snorted, tied her hair into a knot, but re-did it

twice until the part looked both accidental and perfect. The makeup was next—a sweep of powder to kill the shine, eyeliner so tight it could draw a blood sample. Last came the lipstick, a color called Queen's Kiss that her mother would have called brave and most men would have called a warning. She pressed her lips, checked for smears, sucked in her cheeks, and watched the mask settle over her bones.

In the silence, her phone vibrated on the dresser. A message from Naalei, as expected.

"Remember, keep your head. Don't let them walk you into a trap. I love you."

Leilani thumbed a reply. "Don't worry, Ma. This is surveillance in high heels."

She set the phone down; her smile faded as soon as she read her own words. She glanced at the clock. She'd have to leave in fifteen minutes or risk the mortification of being late to a shakedown for the super-rich.

She moved to her jewelry box, half expecting to find it empty. But there, next to the shell necklace she'd won in a childhood hula competition, lay the quarter-sized GPS tracker that Tommy had delivered that morning. She palmed it, feeling its coin-weight, and tucked it into a seam in her purse. Just in case Worthington's private collection lived up to the rumors.

Her clutch was laughably small—barely big enough for a phone, lipstick, and one credit card. She opened it, paused, and weighed the SIG in its Kydex holster on the bed. It was an old ritual: load, chamber check, and mentally plot the best place to hide the bulk.

Not tonight, she thought. Not with Worthington's metal detectors and hired security. She locked the SIG in the gun safe in her closet.

Instead, she picked up her badge, slipped it into a silk pocket in the clutch, and checked the backup: a tiny canister of pepper spray, the legal kind, disguised as a lipstick tube. She double-checked the tracker battery, checked her phone for spare juice, zipped up the clutch and set it on top of the dresser.

Her final prep was to run a finger along the inside hem of the dress, searching for the hidden stitches she'd made earlier with a sliver of carbon fiber— enough to slice through packing tape or, if it came to that, a zip tie.

She eyed the result. Not half bad. She looked like someone who belonged at a high-roller's party, or at least someone the bouncer would let in without a second glance. It was a mask, but masks were part of the job.

She heard Kai's voice echoing from the kitchen:

"You look like a secret agent."

She laughed, shaking her head. "Nice try, bug. You're staying home tonight. Mrs. Kaliki will be here any minute?"

He appeared in her doorway; his eyebrows raised at the dress. "Is Grandma going too?"

"She's the star. I'm the bodyguard."

Kai nodded, grabbed a bottle of water from the

fridge and popped it open. "Don't get shot."

"That's the plan," she replied

She felt his eyes on her as she checked her purse again—tracker, phone, badge, lipstick and her own face in the mirror. She almost believed she could pass for one of Worthington's elites. She remembered the plan: walk in, listen, watch, plant the bug, get out. Simple.

She exhaled, checked her teeth one last time, and let her face relax into the careful blankness she wore at every crime scene. It was time.

She met Mrs. Kaliki on the steps. "He has some homework to do before TV, and he can stay up until ten." Mrs. Kaliki nodded and entered the house. Leilani locked the door and walked to her Explorer, her heels ticking against the cracked driveway. With each step, she was less herself and more like the person she'd trained to be: invisible, in plain sight. She started the engine, put the car in gear and headed for her mother's house.

Leilani rolled up to the Worthington estate in near silence, the engine humming beneath Leilani's heartbeat. The mansion wasn't big—it was the kind of place that bent the surrounding air. From the road, you saw a hedge, a wall, and the glass-and-coral sweep of the building rising out of the dark like a glacier on fire. Every window reflected torches, pool lights and the last curl of sunset over the ocean. The driveway was freshly power-washed and lined with SUVs, each one bigger than her house. Her battered Explorer didn't fit in. She caught her own reflection in the rearview: her eyes wary, her lips already pulling into the smile she used for city council fundraisers and the chief's annual BBQ.

The front door was not so much a door as an event—a slab of carved ohia wood set into a frame of fossilized coral, with a security panel disguised as a bronze mail slot. Before she could reach for the knocker, it swung open and a uniformed staffer with cheekbones like an afterthought greeted her. "Aloha, Ms. Kealoha. May I take your bag?"

Leilani gripped her clutch like a live grenade. "It's fine, thanks."

From behind her, Naalei stepped forward, resplendent in a crimson mu'umu'u patterned with subtle gold. Her hair was up, secured with a trio of feather combs, and the effect was both matriarch and movie star. The staffer's eyes flicked over Naalei's outfit, then lingered a microsecond too long on the tattoo spiraling up her forearm.

"This way, ladies." He led them through an entryway floored in black lava tile and up two shallow steps into the heart of the house.

Inside, the mansion was a fever dream of architecture: floor-to-ceiling glass walls, tiki wood beams angled like the ribs of a beached whale, and— everywhere—art. Real art. On one side, a massive oil of three hula dancers, bodies elongated and luminous against a storm-colored sea. On another, a four-panel kapa collage mounted behind anti-reflective glass. Everywhere else, artifacts: shark-tooth daggers, feathered cloaks in vacuum frames, a canoe paddle inscribed with names that made Leilani's stomach lurch in recognition. The whole place reeked of money and the restless need to prove something with it.

The staffer deposited them into the main room and vanished. Inside, half a dozen clusters of people orbited low tables spread with poke, caviar and little towers of mochi in pastel colors. The crowd was a predictable blend of local politicians and their plus-ones, three men Leilani recognized from various art consortium boards, and one woman she was sure had run an anti-tourism PAC last year. They all wore the same glazed look—pride, greed and a dash of unease.

Leilani scanned the perimeter, copping a quick count of security cams (four), bodyguards disguised as pool boys (two), and exits (everywhere, if you weren't afraid of a three-story drop). Along one wall, two servers in matching sarongs set up an open bar, the glassware sparkling like diamonds.

She turned to Naalei, who surveyed the crowd with the gentle amusement of someone watching a middle school play. "Nervous?" Leilani asked.

Naalei smiled. "Only for them."

The room stilled as the host emerged, hair backlit by the recessed LEDs that followed him like a personal halo. Sam Worthington cut through the crowd, pausing for air kisses and shoulder squeezes, but his eyes were fixed on Naalei like a predator tracking a rare bird.

"Mrs. Kealoha!" he called out. "You are more beautiful away from your halau. I hope the drive wasn't too terrible."

He took her hand in both of his, squeezing it a shade too long. He turned to Leilani with a smile that could win a Senate race. "Detective. I'm honored you could join us."

"Thanks for having us," Leilani said, letting her tone hover between warm and neutral.

Worthington's gaze slid over Naalei's outfit and shoes, returning to her face. "Stunning dress," he said, "and a more stunning daughter. You must be so proud."

"Every day," Naalei said, voice soft and final.

The crowd exhaled, and conversation restarted, but now every other guest found a reason to check out the Kealohas. Some nodded discreetly; one man openly raised his glass in a silent toast. Leilani registered every glance, each one filed into its mental folder: who to watch, who would talk, who would sell a secret for a favor.

Sam steered them to a corner with a prime ocean view, the sun bleeding out over the horizon; the tide hammering the rocks beyond the lawn. "We're so lucky to have you here tonight. Mrs. Kealoha, since your knowledge of traditional practices is legendary. I hope you'll help me correct anything we got wrong in the exhibit."

He leaned in. "Since this is my home, it matters to me that this isn't another vanity project. I want it to be real."

Leilani watched his eyes, saw the moment when the host act slipped and something sharper flashed behind the blue. He was selling, but to her mother, not the crowd. She could smell an agenda but couldn't quite pin it down yet.

Naalei put a hand on his sleeve, a brief, motherly touch. "Culture isn't a checklist, Sam. If you respect the people, they'll show you the right way."

Worthington grinned, let his eyes linger on her face a second longer than etiquette required. "That's why I need you, Naalei." The informality of the first name was deliberate, and the tiny wince on her mother's face said she'd caught it.

Leilani stepped in. "I hear you have pieces here in your home that have never been shown in Hawaii. Is that true?"

Sam turned to her, shifting gears with almost supernatural ease. "Absolutely. It took years of negotiation—private collections, international loans, and a few diplomatic cables. If you're curious, I'd love to give you a tour myself. After dinner."

He smiled, but his body had already pivoted back towards her mother, drawing her further into the warmth of his attention.

Guests filtered through, offering their congratulations, sometimes dropping compliments Leilani was sure were designed to be repeated later like sound bites on the nightly news. She took a glass of water from a passing server, ignoring the more lethal stuff. She wanted her head clear, every sense dialed up.

She watched as Worthington drew Naalei into a huddle of collectors, all of them hungry for the Kumu's approval, laughing at her jokes, nodding like devout students. Her mother's face was a mask of courtesy, but now she flicked her eyes toward Leilani—a tiny signal, "I'm okay, but keep watching."

Leilani moved through the party, not only observing but mapping the room. Each guest had a role to play, and she played hers: gracious, a touch exotic, professional but not too professional. A man in a pale linen suit tried to chat her up, but she let him monologue about Polynesian ancestry until he ran out of facts. She caught snippets of deal talk—grants, endowments, leveraged art loans—and the current rumor that a piece stolen from the British Museum had surfaced in an East Coast collection.

When she passed the open patio doors, she caught sight of two young men whispering into their phones, backs to the crowd. The longer she watched, the more obvious it was: private security, ex-military or ex-cop. She logged their faces and checked the perimeter for less obvious threats.

The evening unspooled in a blur of toasts, introductions and photo ops. The sky went from orange to black; the sound of the surf traded for the babble of inside jokes and professional gossip. Worthington never let her mother out of his sight, and the guests followed his lead. It was a court, and he was the king.

By the time the last round of drinks was passed, Leilani was bored stiff and itching for movement. She perused her phone—two texts from Kai, both memes, and one from Tommy. **Update?** She replied. **Deep in enemy territory**. All good. She put the phone away.

She glanced at her mother, who gave a tiny, reassuring nod. But when Worthington caught Leilani's eye, his smile looked genuine this time, almost grateful. "Detective," he called. "Care to see the collection?"

He didn't wait for an answer; instead, he motioned for Naalei and Leilani to follow. They wound through the house, past the showpieces and out to a private gallery near the pool. The door was painted with a spiral design, black on white. As they entered, a small panel blinked blue—motion sensor, or something more.

Inside, the temperature dropped. The lighting was perfect, the air crisp as a morgue. In the center under glass, lay the new acquisitions: a row of feathered god images, three stone implements, and at the far end, the pahu drum from the halau's story. Leilani's skin prickled. The markings were exactly as her mother described—red, geometric, old.

Sam's voice lowered, intimate now. "I know there's controversy. Some people say these should stay where they were found. But I think it's more important that they survive, don't you?"

He looked straight at Naalei; the mask was gone. "Otherwise, they'll be lost. Or worse, destroyed."

Naalei stared at the drum, looking at the rows of ancestral images. Her face was inscrutable. "You can't own this history, Sam. It's not for sale."

He reached for her hand, then stopped, as if reconsidering the gesture. "Tell me how to do it right," he said.

Leilani watched it all, catching the echoes of every stolen artifact case she'd ever worked, every family heirloom pawned for a lie. She wondered what it cost to build a fortress of memories you could never really keep.

She stepped closer to the drum, running her eyes over the code of lines and dots, the puzzle left by her ancestors. The narrative—her narrative—was struggling to emerge. Behind her, Worthington and her mother spoke in low, urgent voices, oblivious to anything else. She took a slow breath, memorized every detail of the gallery, and prepared for the next move.

Worthington led them past the first row of display cases, his hands clasped behind his back like a tour guide who also owned the museum and everyone in it. Under low LEDs, every artifact threw a shadow ten times its size onto the cream-colored walls.

He started with a carved idol, its face stark and angular, obsidian eyes bulging beneath a woven crown. "Lapulapu," he announced, savoring the syllables. "Acquired in Manila. Tracked to the 1830s." He looked to Naalei. "You ever seen one this pristine?"

Naalei walked closer, her hands respectfully folded at her waist. "Not since I was a child. That kind of finish only comes from years of oiling. It wasn't for display—it was alive in someone's house." She didn't touch the glass, but she leaned close enough that Leilani could smell her mother's perfume—pikake and old sandalwood.

Worthington's smile widened, pleased. "Exactly. I

like to think of these pieces as living history. Not only relics." He angled his chin at Leilani. "Your daughter has the same energy, Mrs. Kealoha. She never lets a case go cold."

Leilani kept her face blank but mentally logged the comment. Sam was trying too hard—overlapping the personal and professional, waiting for her to slip. She studied every case, every object and every camera tucked out of sight. The display cabinets were lined with a soft blue that matched certain hallways in the FBI field office; the lighting was polarized, not for aesthetics, but to screw with standard video capture.

They moved to a wall of shark-tooth weapons—paddles, knuckles, a dagger she'd seen in a textbook once but never up close. Sam lifted one from the rack (no alarm, instead a click as the latch released) and handed it to Naalei with the care of a man passing a Faberge egg. Naalei accepted the blade and rolled it in her hands, weighing the balance. "You know what these were for?" she asked Sam, cocking an eyebrow.

He took a beat too long to answer. "Ceremony. Or so the literature says."

Naalei smiled but didn't correct him. "If it's a true shark's jaw, it was for protection. But the ones with metal insets—those were made after contact. They're for show."

Leilani caught the faintest tremor in Worthington's hand as he set the next artifact on the table. He enjoyed sparring but also learning in real time. "You're enjoying consulting on the heritage center project?" he said, turning his full attention to Naalei.

She paused, weighing her words like stones. "You've made it a respectful process. Most donors don't ask before displaying."

Sam gave her a look that was part gratitude, part hungry. "You'd be surprised how often people try to sell me fakes. Or pressure me to take items they stole from their own families."

He was signaling something, but Leilani couldn't figure out if it was a confession or the world's worst attempt at flirting.

They turned to a case with three wooden drums—each one blackened with age, bands of red pigment spiraling the bodies. "These are from your line, yes?" he asked, voice dropping to a reverent hush. "We went to significant trouble to verify the markings. I wanted to be sure before putting it in the permanent collection."

Naalei looked pained but nodded. "You did your research. That's my grandmother's work, down to the pigment. I could almost hear her yelling at me for tracking dust on the floor."

Worthington let his hand rest on Naalei's elbow—but Leilani clocked the moment her mother tensed, then forced herself to relax. "You've done more to preserve these traditions than anyone in the state, Mrs. Kealoha," Sam said. "It's an honor to have you here."

"The honor comes with a bunch of paperwork," Naalei replied.

He laughed, charmed and a little unnerved. "You don't mind helping with the exhibits? The cultural center will have a dedicated space for local families, with your oversight."

Leilani watched the hand linger, watched the way Sam angled his body to close the space between them. She wanted to step in, to interrupt the little courtship, but her cop's brain screamed: You're getting played.

Instead, she drifted to the gallery, letting the reflection in the glass show her both the artifact labels and the angles of approach. If she needed to bail her mother out, she'd have two seconds to get from the exit to the center case—and maybe four more before Worthington's security descended.

She logged all of it: the weight of the glass, the security panel's green "unlocked" light, the code pads tucked next to the track lighting. A less seasoned cop might have missed the false wall behind the center case. She caught the outline—a hairline seam where a storage alcove or safe room could be concealed. That was where you hid the stuff you didn't want on tour.

She took a surreptitious photo with her phone, hiding the action in a yawn.

At the other end of the gallery, Worthington was still working his angle. "The Council is coming for a tour next week," he said. "Would you consider coming by to give a talk? We'll pay the honorarium, of course."

Naalei's answer was gentle but evasive. "We'll see. The ancestors have a say, too."

He laughed, squeezing her arm a bit too tight. "I can't argue with that." Then he looked at Leilani, farther down the gallery, as if remembering she was there. "Detective, you haven't said much. You don't approve?"

She kept her expression mild; her hands folded in front of her. "I'm here to learn, Mr. Worthington. So far, you've exceeded expectations."

He liked that—she could see it. He enjoyed being measured and told he'd won.

He turned back to Naalei, lowering his voice. "If you see anything you want back—anything you think belongs to your family—tell me. I can make it happen. Quietly."

Naalei's face didn't move, but Leilani saw the tension ripple through her shoulders.

It was time to change the subject. "Can I use the restroom?" Leilani asked, already halfway to the door. Worthington nodded, distracted by his captive audience.

She walked the corridor slowly, making a show of searching for the powder room, but she was scanning for what Worthington didn't show off: the hidden doors, the security layout, the cross-wires of control in his palace. She passed a bank of closed doors, each with a card reader or numeric pad. Every third light fixture had a pinhole lens; every hallway had a small, green-lit panel with its own pulse. On the way back, she peeked out onto a side terrace and counted three more "pool boys" in navy polos, whispering into their sleeves.

By the time she returned to the gallery, Worthington

and her mother were at the center display, heads bent close over a roll of ancient kapa. The moment she entered, he stepped back, resetting the social distance, as if nothing had happened.

She glanced at her mother, who gave her the tiniest nod: Yes, I'm fine. Yes, I've got it.

Worthington, now host again, gestured toward a small cart of sparkling wine and stemless glasses. "Shall we toast?" he said.

Leilani accepted the drink, letting the bubbles chill her mouth. She watched Sam refill her mother's glass, watched him watch her mother.

He was obsessed, but not only in the collector's way.

She wondered if he was about to slip, and if so, whether she'd catch him in the act or in the aftermath.

They sipped and admired, and in the ritual silence that followed, Leilani sensed the room lock itself around them. Three people, three stories, and a whole gallery full of ghosts waiting to see who blinked first.

Worthington was in full seduction mode, except the target wasn't her mother, or the audience, or the ghosts in the gallery. He wanted something only Naalei could give—a blessing, or an unspoken permission to keep playing king of the island. And Naalei, who had learned long ago how to hold a man's gaze without giving an inch, let him talk, let him work, let him believe he was almost there.

For Leilani, this was the gap in coverage—the moment in every con or heist when the mark got cocky, thought the grift was working, and stopped looking for a cop in a cocktail dress. She faked a laugh at Sam's next anecdote, checked her phone like she'd gotten a message, and excused herself for a work call.

She walked out into the hallway, her steps casual and her eyes everywhere. The blue velvet runner muffled her heels, but the wall lights threw her shadow ten feet ahead. She listened for voices and went right, past the powder room, through a half-open door into a paneled library that smelled of old money and cedar. No one was inside, but she caught the reflection of a surveillance dome in the window. She ducked, made it to the inner corridor, and counted the cameras: two, both were pointed at the main hallway, with a dead zone just before the double doors marked Private— Staff Only.

The gallery layout echoed in her mind—the fake wall, the storage behind it, the security panel with its dull green light. She checked her clutch, let the tracker thrum against her palm, and kept moving.

Past the double doors, the house changed. The floors changed from velvet runner to concrete, the walls from painted coral to raw cinder block. She ducked into a service alcove and listened: a distant hum of refrigerators and the low chuckle of a dishwasher on rinse cycle. She moved fast but silently, careful not to scuff the floor or set off a motion sensor. At the end of the hallway, another locked door, this one with a fingerprint reader.

She smiled. Sometimes, rich people made it too easy.

Next to the reader was an antique brass keyhole—a backup for when tech failed or the staff's hands were full of canapes. She bent, checked the seam, and found the tiniest scratch marks. Someone opened this door a lot, probably for after-hours tours or to impress the donors who liked to see the real back-of-house. She slid a fingernail between the casing and the panel, and the catch gave. The door swung inward enough for her to slip through sideways.

Inside, it was arctic and dry. The hum of the air system was louder, and the lights flicked on low—infrared to preserve what was in the room. It was a vault, or maybe a prep lab. The walls were lined with industrial shelving, every row stacked with foam-packed crates, some stenciled with museum codes, others plain and rough, like they'd been dragged out of a shipping container the hour before.

No display cases here. No plaques. Only the goods, raw and waiting.

The door snicked shut behind her, and she moved down the first aisle. Her fingers drifted over the packing lists, reading the spidery handwriting: HAWAII—COLL. #17 / Provenance: Bishop Estate / AUTHENTICATED 2019. The next crate: Aotearoa / Private Loan / Transit Only. The smell of old lauhala and burlap tickled her memory.

She found the crate she wanted. It was heavier, newer, stamped with the logo of the same East Coast auction house that had laundered two of the items stolen in last year's theft ring. She took a photo of the tag, then traced the seam with her fingertip. It wasn't locked but sealed with packing tape. Worthington trusted his perimeter and probably didn't expect a cop with a magenta manicure to break the chain of custody.

She peeled the tape carefully. Inside were layers of acid-free tissue and a nest of sand. In the center was a collection of small stone idols with no tags and no catalog numbers. There was a handwritten note on high-end stationery. **For Review, HOLD until further notice.** The return address was a Swiss security company.

She set the tracker in the corner of the crate, pressing it into the foam where it would transmit but not rattle. She closed the box, smoothed the tape, and backed away, careful to reset every detail. She took three more pictures—one of the shelf, one of the space, and one of the emergency exit sign in the ceiling, in case she needed to get out fast.

On the way to the door, she heard footsteps: slow, deliberate, and male. Not Worthington, as he would have called out and made it an entrance. This was staff, or private muscle. She flattened against the wall and watched through the crack as a young guy in a navy polo carried a tray of glassware to the end of the corridor. He stopped, set the tray down, and scanned the hall—probably bored, but trained to look for trouble.

She waited until he moved back the way he came.

Leilani counted to five and slipped out, letting the cold air erase her scent. She moved back through the service corridor, past the library, and out onto the main floor, where the sound of laughter and music spilled in from the patio. She examined herself in the mirror: no smudges, no visible panic. Good.

She walked back into the gallery to find Worthington still holding court, her mother still the undisputed center. Naalei shot her a look—a flicker of worry, or relief—and Leilani relaxed, as if the work call had been nothing.

She glimpsed herself in the reflection next to the pahu display: sequined dress, hair up, eyes sharp. Still there. Still watching.

She made a mental note of every exit. The next step was out of her hands—she'd planted the tracker. Now, it was time to see what the billionaire and her mother would do when no one was left but the two of them, and all the secrets in the world.

The last toast fizzled before ten. Most of the collectors and politicos drifted out early, eager to lock up their gossip before the morning's headlines. The hardiest of the party crowd found themselves thinned out, wine-warmed and moving in slow spirals to the door. Only Sam, Naalei and Leilani remained in the gallery, the three of them lit by the icy blue of security LEDs and the refracted glow off the polished stone idols.

Worthington leaned in, close but not quite touching Naalei. "Your perspective ensures we honor the true spirit of Hawaiian traditions," he said. His voice was rawer than before; the performance faded. "I need to do this right. For the island, and for you."

He placed his hand on her shoulder, soft and deliberate, as if waiting for permission. "I'd like to discuss your continued involvement in the cultural center further. Maybe over dinner, just us. Next week?" The room was silent enough to hear the whir of the air vents.

Naalei didn't answer right away. She glanced at Leilani, read the air, and moved back to Sam. "We'll see," she whispered. "The ancestors are always watching."

Worthington exhaled, a little less of the king now, a little more the orphan kid who'd spent a lifetime clawing for the thing he couldn't name. He let his hand fall. "Thank you, Naalei. Really."

The moment hung there, but broke when Leilani coughed and stepped forward. "We should get going, Ma. Long drive."

Naalei nodded, slipped her arm through Leilani's, and let herself be guided out of the gallery. Worthington watched them, his face unreadable, as the door eased shut behind them.

They crossed the main hall, past the dead-eyed tiki and the silent rows of trophies. Outside, the ocean made its own music—the hush and suck of the tide on the rocks, and the buzz of insects in the salt air.

Leilani slid behind the wheel, started the engine, and let it idle as her mother pulled her hair loose and closed her eyes. The night had drained something from both.

"He's very interested in you," Leilani said, careful not to sound too amused.

Naalei made a face, halfway between a smile and a wince. "Yes, but not in the way he thinks. There's sadness in him. Like he's afraid the story ends if he lets go." She opened her eyes, bright again. "What about you? Did you find what you needed?"

Leilani's hands tightened on the wheel. "You saw?"

"I always see," her mother said matter-of-factly. "Did you get it done?"

Leilani nodded. "The tracker's live. He's holding artifacts off the books, and he's hiding at least one in transit from a blacklisted auction house. I got pictures. We'll get a court order if we have to, but I need to see where it goes."

Naalei reached over, touched her daughter's cheek. "Good work, baby."

Leilani smiled a little. "You were amazing in there. He respects you. I think he's scared of you, too."

"He should be," Naalei said, her laughter tired but true.

They drove in silence for a few blocks, the glow of the house shrinking behind them. The hills were black. The only light was the thin line of streetlamps following the curve of the coast.

"Do you think he's dangerous?" Naalei asked, voice low.

Leilani mulled it. "I think he's desperate. That's sometimes worse." She shot a look at her mother. "You okay with me using you as bait?"

Naalei snorted. "I raised you, didn't I?"

They laughed together, and the tension melted. Leilani felt like herself again—not the badge, nor the muscle, but the whole mess of hopes and nerves that came from being her mother's daughter and her father's stubborn shadow.

At a stoplight, she opened her phone: the tracker's icon blinked, live and pulsing. She dialed Isaac, who picked up on the first ring.

"The bait is in the water," she said. "Get ready to track."

Isaac's voice came back, tight and awake. "Already watching the ping. You need backup?"

"Not yet. Stay sharp. He'll make his move soon."

She ended the call, then turned to her mother. "Want to get breakfast on the way home?"

Naalei smiled, tired but alive. "Only if you promise not to arrest the server this time."

Leilani laughed, and they took the next curve fast, the lights of the Worthington mansion vanishing behind the ridge.

Ahead, the city sprawled in silence, every streetlight a waypoint. The work wasn't done—would never be done—but tonight, she had her mother at her side, and the hunt was only beginning.

# Chapter Twelve

## The Informant's Warning

Isaac sat cross-legged on his futon, the only light in the apartment being the sullen blue cast of his laptop screen. The hour was late, and the neighborhood outside his window had collapsed into the silence that bred confessions and fever. On the coffee table, a field of old manila folders and Polaroids fought for territory with half-eaten Chinese takeout and the empty red shells of beer cans. He could see his own shadow on the wall, stretched and angular, the face that stared back a stranger's—gray around the eyes, leaner than he remembered.

The laptop keys clattered beneath his hands. It was an ugly night for data entry. He'd been at it for hours, running the latest data dump from the information Leilani could get from Worthington's personal collection.

He wiped his eyes, blinked away the itch, and leaned closer. The permits for the artifacts were all in order, as were the shipping manifests. He sat back and scratched his chin.

"Could we be wrong about Worthington?" he asked himself. "Everything in his personal collection checks out. It's possible he's not a crooked collector." He stopped and looked at his image on the laptop screen and laughed. "Jesus, Torres. You need to get out more. You're talking to yourself and answering your own questions."

He clicked out of the document, turned off the desk lamp, and leaned back in the chair. He was shutting down when his phone chimed with an incoming message. He picked up his phone and looked at the time. "Shit." He opened his text app, spotted the new message from an unknown number, and clicked on it.

**Got news. Time critical. Danger close. Meet me at the beach luau in twenty.**

Isaac's heartbeat spiked, a physical punch he sensed in his molars and wrists. He knew the sender. Timo was a ghost in everything bad that happened on the island. He was also a confidential informant. Timo had provided Isaac with some valuable information while he was with the FBI, and this was his initial contact since Isaac had joined the HPD. He knew instinctively that the information would be good.

He didn't hesitate, not this time. He fished his phone out of the rubble on the table and dialed Leilani. The display lit up her contact: "Kealoha, Lei." He noted the name as it rang, let his thumb tap the phone in the rhythm of a bad habit.

On the fourth ring, she answered, her voice rough with exhaustion but still edged with suspicion. "Torres. This better be good."

"I got a text from one of my CIs. I reached out to him for information about the Bishop Museum robbery. He wants to meet at the beach luau in twenty minutes. His information has always been solid."

The silence on the line was sharp. He heard her draw breath, caught the faint click as she shifted the phone to her other ear.

"You sure this isn't a setup?" she said.

He raked his hand over his scalp, fighting the urge to snap. "He said the info is time sensitive. He said that danger was close. Not sure what that means, but I need to follow up."

"Okay," she said. "You want me there or not?"

He didn't answer but let the question hang. Isaac was a reactionary person. He was very methodical, but he knew Timo might be in danger.

"I need backup, Lei," he said, lowering his voice. "This feels wrong. The way he wrote the message—he's not himself."

She was quiet again, but this time it was a different silence—calculating, measuring risk against reward.

"I'll be there in fifteen," she said. "If you're early, sit tight and don't make contact until I get there."

He exhaled, the tension in his gut easing enough to let the panic in.

"Copy that," he said.

She hung up without saying goodbye. He set the phone down, watched the screen fade, and stared at his own reflection in the window. The street below was dead, but his nerves jumped like a wire in a rainstorm.

Isaac stood and moved through the apartment, stepping around the detritus of a week spent chasing shadows. He shrugged on his jacket, a faded black thing with a holster stitched into the lining. The SIG sat heavy against his ribs. He checked the magazine, racked the slide, and did it again for the comfort of routine. Old Bureau habits die hard.

He grabbed his badge, a battered leather wallet, and the last fortune cookie from the carton on the table. He cracked it open, read the slip—*Your patience will be tested, but your loyalty will be rewarded*—and tossed it onto the pile.

He gave the place a last look, checked that the laptop screen was dark, turned off the light, and locked the door behind him.

The hallway outside was institutional and bland, the kind of corridor where every footstep echoed for a lifetime. He took the stairs down, skipping the elevator and hit the street level in under a minute. The night air was wet and cold, the sodium lights making everything look like crime scene photography.

As he walked to the car, his phone buzzed again—another message, same unknown sender:

**I'll wait 5 minutes, then I'm gone. Come alone.**

He viewed the text as the old Bureau training snapped to life and let the city's darkness settle around him.

He got in the car, started the engine, and pulled out slowly, scanning the mirrors for the telltale blip of a tail. The luau was seven minutes away, all surface streets and zero traffic. He killed his lights a block early, rolled into a parking spot, and found a spot near the walkway to the beach. The weather was beautiful, and the luau was in full swing and crowded.

He checked his phone. The twenty-minute timer on Timo's message was down to two minutes.

Isaac settled into his seat, put one hand on the SIG, and waited, counting each breath. He thought of the promise he'd made himself: don't get attached, don't make it personal, don't call for help unless you want to owe someone forever.

The phone buzzed again, once. He read the message and smiled. The smile that came from knowing you were walking straight into the heart of a storm.

**Walk down the ramp to the beer tent. Turn left.**

He glanced at the clock. Time to find out what was going on.

The luau was a weekly event put on by the Chamber of Commerce, and it usually drew a crowd. It was the perfect place for a clandestine meeting.

Leilani had parked across the street and killed the headlights. She walked along the beach until she spotted Isaac coming from the street. She could feel Isaac's presence before she saw him: the faint tension in the air, the whisper of his jacket when he moved. He waited at the base of the ramp, hand loose but not empty. A silhouette set against the flames from the huge fire pit.

"Took you long enough," she whispered as she slid up beside him.

"I was early," he replied. "He's already here."

They walked towards the beer tent. She nodded and scanned the area. There at the far edge, hunched in the shadow of a refrigerated truck, was Timo. He wore a windbreaker three sizes too big, the hood up, and his head ducked low. Every few seconds, he peeked out from behind the beer truck and scanned the lot, like he expected every person on the beach to turn into a hired gun.

Isaac nodded toward him. "You want to do the honors?"

Leilani rolled her shoulders, stepped out, keeping her hands where Timo could see them. "Nice night for a jog, Timo," she called softly.

Timo jumped, eyes wild, but once he clocked her and Isaac together, he seemed to deflate. "I said come alone," he hissed, voice cracking.

"We are alone," said Isaac. "No one here but us and a thousand tourists. You have something for us?"

Timo hesitated and looked past them down at his shoes. His hands shook. His watch—a Patek, real and probably worth more than Isaac's car—glinted in the strip light, but the rest of him was thrift store panic.

"So, what's up, Timo?" Leilani asked, keeping her tone businesslike. "Why the rush?"

Timo licked his lips, his eyes darting. "Because you're not the only ones looking. Someone else… they know about the Worthington play. It's tomorrow night, midnight. A crew, all ex-military, local with a mainlander. But they're getting into the new cultural center after hours. You need to be there before they are."

Isaac said, "Why tip us off?"

Timo shook his head, mouth trembling. "Because Worthington's playing both sides. He wants to look like the victim to get you guys off his back. He's moving several stolen artifacts off the island, but he wants to look like a hero when they turn up again. He hired his own thieves. Said to make it look like an outside job. In three months, the stuff will miraculously reappear—but it will be fake. The genuine stuff is heading for Asia."

Leilani stepped closer, dropping her voice. "And what do you get, Timo?"

"Out," he whispered. "I want out. My cut's nothing compared to what they promised the hitters. But I know too much now. They said they'd take care of me if I played it straight, but you hear things." He rubbed his wrist, not noticing the watch anymore. "Like I'm already dead. They're waiting for the paperwork to catch up."

Isaac reached for his phone, thumb hovering. "You got names? Entry points? Anything we can use?"

Timo shrank back. "If I give you the names, I'm done."

"You already are," said Leilani, voice flat. "They'll know you talked the second it blows up. Give us the list, and we'll take you to a safe house. We'll arrange for a new ID. I've done it before."

Timo's teeth chattered, a pathetic sound in the silent garage. "I have a number. The head guy, he calls himself Tex, but he's not from Texas. I swear. Accent's more like North Dakota. He's ex-military, with scars up the right arm. Drives a black SUV, rental plates, glass tint so dark it looks like a hearse."

Isaac glanced at Leilani. "Sounds familiar."

She nodded. "We've seen that SUV outside Worthington's house. Last week."

Timo looked from one to the other, and hope flickered. "So, you'll help me?"

Timo spotted something that spooked him, and he turned without saying a word and raced up the hill towards the sidewalk. Leilani and Isaac looked at each other and raced after him.

"Timo, stop," yelled Leilani

Timo's reply was drowned out by a screech—a tire catching hard on asphalt, the roar as a vehicle surged towards Timo. Isaac was already moving, arm out to yank her behind the vending machine. The SUV came into view, windows down, lights off, engine snarling. The muzzle flashes were blinding.

The first round hit the side of the back of the beer truck, a plume of metal and dust spraying over their heads. Timo tried to run, but the second volley caught him in the shoulder and spun him sideways. He shrieked and collapsed behind a trash can. Leilani rolled out, SIG drawn, and put three shots through the SUV's windshield. Isaac followed with two more, which shattered the rear window.

The crowd ran in every direction to find cover as more shots rang out.

The SUV swerved, clipped the curb, and ricocheted off the streetlight, glass raining onto the ground. A door flew open, a man in all black tumbled out, weapon up. Leilani glimpsed him—big, ugly tattoo across the throat.

He spotted Timo behind a trash can, fired a three-shot blast from a short rifle, and Timo jerked. He dove back into the SUV as Leilani fired three rounds. She thought one of her rounds hit pay dirt as the guy pulled the door shut. She dropped her clip, reloaded, and fired five more rounds at the SUV as it sped down the street, side-swiped a car stopped at the light, and fishtailed around the corner.

Isaac was the first to reach Timo. Blood covered his jacket. "

Timo made a noise, half sob, and half curse, but his eyes rolled white. "You promised," he croaked, and went limp.

Leilani's hands trembled as she checked Timo. The informant was bleeding badly, with froth at the corner of his mouth. "We need EMS," she shouted at Isaac, but he was already on the radio, barking codes and coordinates.

She tried to staunch the wound, pressing down hard with both hands. Timo coughed, a spray of pink foam spattering her wrist. "Don't let them find me," he rasped. "Not in the open."

"We got you, Timo," she lied, hoping the dying couldn't smell a lie.

He choked, his eyes rolled up, and he was gone.

She sat back on her haunches, let her arms hang loose, and listened to the hiss of radiator coolant from the SUV and the distant, insistent pulse of approaching sirens.

Isaac paced, jaw clenched. He stared at her and then

at Timo, and the hole-riddled concrete all around. "Shit," he said, almost reverent.

Leilani nodded, wiped the blood on her jeans, and stood. "We kicked the hornet's nest."

She stared at Timo's body. "He was right, you know. Worthington's playing both sides. Now we've got a schedule, a crew, a playbook."

"Yeah," said Isaac, softly. "But we also have an all-out war. They'll hit tomorrow night, no question. But now they know we're coming."

Leilani felt the ache in her jaw and realized she'd been grinding her teeth. "Good. Maybe they'll make a mistake."

The sirens grew louder, the street brightening as the first black-and-whites pulled to a stop, blue and white lights painting the world in flickers. She holstered her gun, stood tall, and let herself be seen. In the chaos, someone shouted her name, but she stood and watched as the medics attended to Timo, and one stood and shook his head towards her. They unfolded a body bag and set it next to the body. He looked smaller now; all the life squeezed out of him.

Isaac came to her side, his presence a quiet, stubborn gravity. "You, okay?" he asked, voice almost gentle.

"Yeah," she said. "I'm mad."

They watched the scene spiral—uniforms taping off the area and crowds forming along the crime scene tape with cell phone cameras rolling. Leilani replayed the firefight in her mind, every shot, every breath, every microsecond. The rumbling in her gut wasn't fear—it was focus.

"I need to call the Chief," she said. "Tell her it's tomorrow, midnight. She's not going to be happy when I tell her that Worthington is playing us. He's invested huge money in the city, with a lot more to come. Any luck with the information I sent you from his private collection?"

He shook his head. "Every artifact in his private collection has been properly purchased and properly transported. He has the documentation for everything. On the surface, he looks like a legit collector."

"We missed something. I recognized the names of several auction houses around the world that are under investigation. He can't be legit."

Isaac glared at her. "So, you think I missed something, huh?"

Her mouth became a tight line. "I don't think you missed a thing; I said we missed something."

Isaac holstered his pistol and stepped away. She knew he was annoyed, but she also knew she wasn't accusing him of anything. She didn't have time to deal with his moods right now, so she let him walk away and sulk.

She remembered the blood on her hands and wiped it away again, harder this time.

As the cops drew chalk lines around Timo's body and snapped photos, Leilani looked down at Timo's shattered watch, the hands frozen at 2:13.

***

The beach didn't sleep. As the sky paled from black to several shades of orange, the place became its own kind of city. Mele's forensic team marked evidence with cones and sticky flags, while press stringers circled the crime scene tape with lenses hungry for a narrative. The ambulance sat waiting while the coroner's van idled under the low ceiling, its hazard lights reflecting off the concrete walls.

Leilani moved through the chaos with practiced authority, clipboard in hand, her badge visible, gun holstered. She wore the night's sweat and a line of dried blood across her left arm, but her stride was crisp, and she never flinched from the wreckage.

Timo's body lay by the beer truck, now zipped in a gray bag, but a dark fan of blood covered the sand. Mele was crouched at the scene, her white coat spattered with the unromantic side of forensics. She dusted the back of the truck for prints, bagging the shattered glass in quick, accurate scoops. The team worked in silence, the only music the tap and hum of evidence collection.

Isaac stood off to the side, near the stairwell, eyes locked on nothing. His shirt was ripped at the shoulder when he dove behind the trash can and caught an edge. He'd wrapped it tight with a strip of gauze from a paramedic kit. He looked at the ground, jaw clenched, and his face a mask.

Mele finished up, snapped off her gloves, and joined Leilani at the far edge of the scene.

"He bled out in under three minutes," Mele said, voice flat. "Entry, exit, pulped the lung. No way he could have talked much longer."

Leilani nodded, eyes tracking over the cones and the swirl of red and blue reflection on the concrete. "Did you get the shell casings from the SUV?"

"Two types of brass," Mele replied. "Both military grade, one stamped Federal, the other Winchester. They weren't worried about mixing their brands."

Leilani made a note. "Prints?"

"Nothing yet, but the shooters weren't wearing gloves. We'll look closer at the casing once we're back at the lab."

The siren split the morning stillness, and it faded as an unmarked Dodge Charger parked next to the scene. Sergeant Tano Pualani and Detective Espinoza jogged over, phone pressed to Tano's ear. His face was lined with exhaustion, but he didn't show it in his stride.

"Hey, boss," Tano said, sliding the phone into his pocket. "We got a break. A patrol unit found the hit SUV abandoned in a beach lot off Sand Island. One dead in the front seat, gunshot to the chest. No ID yet."

Leilani looked at the timeline on her clipboard, then at Tano. "When?"

"About fifteen minutes ago. Still warm," Tano replied. "Patrol's taping it off now."

She turned, scanned the scene for Tommy, who had walked over to the ambulance. She waved him over. "Tommy, you're with Tano. Bag and tag the SUV. Start with the dead guy. Call the ME and have them send a team and have Mele do the same. Get Mele photos before you touch anything."

Tommy nodded, eyes wide, and hustled to catch up with Tano as he jogged to the unmarked car.

Leilani exhaled and tucked the clipboard under her arm, noticing the sharp pain of an adrenaline crash. The press was gathering by the beach ramp, their chatter a low, persistent drone. She ignored them and headed over to Isaac.

He didn't look up until she was two feet away. When he did, she caught the red in his eyes, the effort it took for him to keep it together.

"You doing alright?" she asked, her voice softer than usual.

He shrugged. "Tired. And pissed off."

She glanced at the concrete, at the streaks of blood and the forensic powder that dusted everything in a faint haze. "Me too."

They stood there letting the noise of the garage wash over them. Isaac's fingers twitched, a nervous rhythm. "He was right," he said. "The ring's moving up the timeline. They were supposed to hit the center tomorrow, but now… who knows."

Leilani nodded. "We have to assume they know we're watching. They might move up the heist, or they could go quiet. Either way, the inside man's gone."

Isaac let his head drop, then straightened. "Timo was scared of Worthington, but more scared of whoever's bankrolling this. I don't think it's about artifacts anymore."

Leilani considered that as the weight settled into her chest. "There's more money, more risk. There could be a kill list."

He met her gaze, the tension in his jaw returning. "You think they'll try to take us out, too?"

"If they think we're in the way," she responded.

A uniformed officer jogged up, notepad in hand. "Detective Kealoha? The media wants a statement."

She walked to the tape, found the camera cluster, and leveled her best press face. "We're investigating a homicide connected to an ongoing investigation," she announced. "No public threat at this time, but we are asking for tips from the community."

A dozen microphones shivered as they caught every word, and the cameras clicked. The reporters jostled, looking for an angle, but Leilani had already turned away.

When she returned to the beer truck, Isaac had moved. She found him smoking a cigarette despite the sign on the post. He gazed at her, shrugged, and took another drag.

"Worthington's holding another charity event day after tomorrow," he whispered. "If the ring doesn't strike tonight, that's when they'll make their move."

She considered this. "We need to be ready. Full surveillance, double the guards, and run all background checks on event staff. Akira can vet the guest list."

Isaac grinned, faint but real. "Will Worthington be there?"

"He'll show," she said. "He likes the spotlight."

They stood together in silence; each lost in their own storm. Outside, the dawn had cracked open. The city was waking, but Leilani sensed the night's cold in her bones.

She turned to Isaac. "You could have handled Timo alone. Why call me?"

He flicked ash onto the step. "Because he was my responsibility. And I wanted to show you I'm on your side."

"You don't have to do that," she said.

He smiled again. "That's why I called."

They let the silence stretch.

The coroner's crew loaded Timo's bagged body into the van. The wheels squeaked on the ramp. Leilani watched it disappear into the orange light of morning.

Mele walked up, evidence bags in hand. "For what it's worth, we'll get something out of this mess. Possibly enough to finish the job."

Leilani took the bag, glanced inside, and nodded. "You're the best, Mele."

Mele shrugged, a ghost of a smile crossing her lips. "That's what they pay me for."

She left, dialing her next call. The garage echoed with her footsteps.

Leilani lingered, watching the sunlight chase away the shadows on the deck. Isaac finished his cigarette, flicking the butt into a rusted coffee can.

"We have a chance," he said.

"We have one shot," she corrected.

He nodded. "Let's not miss it."

They walked out into the morning as the city awoke. Leilani took a breath slowly.

The job was never finished. But the case was no longer a puzzle. It was a war.

At the edge of the beach, she paused. The coroner's van idled, waiting for a break in the traffic. Leilani watched as it rolled away, taillights vanishing into the waking city.

"See you at the briefing?" asked Isaac.

She smiled, all teeth. "Try and stop me."

He laughed, and the sound echoed—real and sharp—through the hollow belly of the garage. They parted ways, each lost in their own chain of thought, but bound together, not by rules or badges, but by blood. And by the promise of more to come.

# Chapter Thirteen

## The Auction House Raids

The elevator rattled like a cheap amusement ride as it dragged Leilani up the Honolulu PD's concrete tower. It was barely past seven in the morning, but the building pulsed with more light and caffeine than most office parks managed by noon. Every floor stank of recycled air and stress, but none more than the SIU's home on the fourth floor. The war room at the end of the hall was full before she walked in.

They called it a "multi-use conference room," but it was a closet with chairs. The whiteboard took up the entire far wall, the metal tray underneath buckling from years of dry-erase abuse. Today, every inch of the board was layered with evidence photos, shipping manifests, and satellite shots of Oahu's industrial ring. Three auction houses had their own mug shots, each underlined in red and taped beside glamor headshots of their respective owners. It looked less like a task force briefing and more like the inside of a conspiracy theorist's minivan.

Leilani set her coffee down and waited for the chatter to die. There was no need to call order—these were the people who'd followed her through shit storms before, who read her mood before she ever spoke. Isaac was at the end of the table, distributing thick manila folders down both sides. Each envelope landed with a thump and a slap: names, warrant forms and assignments. He was the last to sit, never making a show, but always marking the tempo of the room.

The team looked exhausted. They had split surveillance duties during the past four nights at the cultural center, but the robbery Timo had told them about before he died never happened. They didn't know whether the shootout in the garage made them change their minds or not, but after four exhausting nights, Leilani called an end to the surveillance and sent everyone home. It was during that short sleep period that Isaac kept working at his home office. He compiled all the evidence they had accumulated on several of the bigger and most prestigious auction houses and galleries, and after a final review, he knew he was ready to present the evidence.

Leilani, who was still in the office writing up the surveillance reports, met him in the conference room along with their liaison from the DA's office. Their review of the evidence, followed by time to write up the search and arrest warrant affidavits, took most of the night, and at 5 a.m., the deputy DA woke up a judge and raced out of the office. At 6 a.m., having received word that the warrants were signed, Leilani called in her team and coordinated the raids with the patrol division.

Sergeant Tano Pualani started the briefing. His hair was still wet, a trace of salt on his collar—he'd clearly paddled out for a quick set before work, but nothing in his posture betrayed a single wasted second. "Hit times are synchronized. Kaimana Gallery is primary—Lei, you've got that. Tommy, you'll take Pacific Rim Collectibles. Torres, you and I have the Aloha Auction House. Warrants are clean and signed, no wiggle room. Entry's legal, but expect friction."

He paused, looked at Leilani, and yielded the floor without a word.

She stood and tapped her pen against the whiteboard, eyes sweeping the table. "We're here for digital records, not the merchandise. Every single file, every provenance certificate, every trace of payment is evidence. The artifacts are only half the job. Unless we can prove the intent, these places get a slap on the wrist and go right back to business."

She pointed to the headshots. "None of these owners are going to roll over. Don't expect gratitude. Each of these people is wired into city politics, the business community, or," she smirked, "the art world, which is worse. That means cameras, lawyers, and probably their own press. Don't let it rattle you. Do your jobs and document everything."

Tommy Espinoza raised his hand. "What about the fancy glass cases? Can we finally kick down some doors, or is this another be respectful to the cultural steward's moment?"

That got a snort from the folks in the room, and even Leilani couldn't keep the smile off her lips. "Do what you have to, Espinoza. Don't get your face on TikTok unless it's for something good."

Tommy did a little air fist-pump. "I'll practice my camera angle."

Isaac leaned in, his voice steady. "Secondary targets are the back offices. That's where they'll run if anything goes wrong, and that's where the off- the - books stuff is hidden. If you see an office staffer sweating, follow them. Don't wait for the go-ahead, move."

Tano took back the baton. "Our threshold is probable cause, but these places know how to dance around it. If they give you access, take it all. If they stonewall, radio in, and we'll escalate. No cowboys today. We go in by the book."

Leilani circled three words on the whiteboard with a squeak of the marker: Provenance, Payments, Exports.

"These are the lifeblood of the operation," she said. "Every document, every forged certificate, every cash payment to a third party—bag it and tag it. Do not let a single artifact out of your sight until the evidence team has signed off. And check the serial numbers against what Mele's already flagged. We know at least four items match prior thefts from the Bishop and several private estates. This is not a drill. Every piece we recover is a story stolen from a family or the state. Treat them that way."

The energy in the room was sharp, the pregame hum before a big match. Tommy bounced a little in his seat, clearly trying not to look as amped as he was. The older detectives leaned forward, hungry for the work that mattered.

Leilani let her eyes drift to Isaac. He was working the table quietly, making eye contact with every person, and sealing each brief with a nod or a point. He looked up at her, and she saw the old connection—the trust that got people through the worst moments, the faith that if the world caught fire, the person at your side would have your back.

He gave her a tiny nod, barely a muscle twitch, but it said everything. It was the first time in weeks she'd noticed the weight of the case lift.

She took a breath. "One more thing. These places look clean. They look legit. Their owners throw charity balls, fund public works and donate to school bands. But make no mistake—they're trafficking our heritage. They are stealing history and laundering it for profit. They're not getting away with it on our watch."

There was silence as every officer in the room let that land.

Tano glanced at his watch and handed out radios. "Suit up. Vests under plain clothes. Keep your weapon out of sight unless you expect a fight. These places open at nine. We'll hit them at oh-eight-thirty to avoid pedestrian involvement. No civilian injuries, no press leaks. We run this clean."

The team scattered to gear up, voices low, adrenaline high. Tommy got to the coffee urn first, pouring two sugar packets in before the brewing stopped. "You ready for this, boss?" he asked Leilani, slinging his evidence kit over one shoulder.

She grinned. "I was born ready. It's the paperwork that scares me."

Tommy laughed, and for once the sound didn't seem out of place in the department.

Leilani found herself alone at the whiteboard, the ghosts of the last twenty-four hours flickering behind her eyes. She scanned the headshots again, the smiling faces, the perfect hair, the untouchable confidence of people who never thought the law would darken their door.

Isaac came up beside her, quiet as a shadow. "You didn't have to go that hard on the speech," he said.

She kept her gaze on the board. "If they don't believe it matters, it doesn't."

He nodded, letting the silence do its work. After a minute, he said, "I can go with your team if you would prefer."

"You're with Tano," she said. "He needs you to keep him from going full surfer-bro when the press shows."

Isaac chuckled. "He hates the cameras more than anyone I've ever met."

"All the more reason," she said. She grabbed her own folder, double-checked the radio, and started for the door.

He stopped her with a hand on her arm—not possessive, an anchor. "We're good, right?"

She looked him dead in the eye. "Yeah. We're good." She didn't smile.

He held her gaze a second longer, his hand dropping away.

In the corridor, the teams lined up, each detective and patrol officer running a last check on their vest and holster. Tano looked like a coiled rope, calm but unbreakable. Tommy did a little side shuffle, tapping his foot, barely hiding his excitement. The junior officers carried themselves with a kind of borrowed gravitas, knowing this was a career-making morning.

Leilani took point, leading the squad to the elevators. As the doors slid shut, she felt the old surge: nerves, yes, but more than that—the certainty that today, they'd hit back. This time, the story would end with something saved, not stolen.

The elevator hummed to life, and as it descended, Isaac met her eyes in the mirrored wall. A wordless nod, a promise: no matter what waited on the other side, they were in it together.

On the ground floor, the doors opened into sunlight and the first cut of morning breeze. The teams separated, each to its own mission, each exactly where they needed to be. The last words Leilani wrote on the whiteboard hanging in the air.

**Don't let them win.**

Leilani squared her shoulders, moved into the light, and headed for her Explorer.

Carl Tanaka had just entered the detective bullpen when he spotted Leilani and her team heading for the elevators. They were all wearing raid gear. He set his coffee on his desk and walked to the conference room, but the shades were closed, and the door was locked. He asked a couple of the other detectives what was going on, but no one had any real information. All anyone knew was that there was a raid happening somewhere.

Tanaka pulled out his phone and typed a quick text to the number in his contact list. He waited for a response.

His phone chimed. **Worthless info. Do better, or your kid won't make it out alive.**

He set the phone down, and his hands shook as he reached for his coffee, which spilled on his desk. He didn't notice as tears filled his eyes.

***

Kaimana Gallery was all glass and air, a place where the floor looked expensive. Leilani's team swept in at eight-thirty sharp, the city getting ready for another day outside, but inside—pandemonium. The employees preparing for the customers froze as the plainclothes officers advanced, badges out, voices measured and calm. A woman in black slacks and a waterfall of silver hair dropped her latte mid-scream. Two security guards reached for their earpieces and stopped, hands up, when they realized how badly they were outclassed.

"Honolulu PD, search warrant!" Leilani said, loud enough to cut through the shattering nerves of the gallery staff. The doors slammed behind her squad as they filled the space, with Mele's forensics unit only a step behind.

The owner, Ms. Kaimana, no first name, but the brand, tried to step in. She had that polished confidence people paid to acquire, but the quiver in her voice betrayed the panic. "You can't—this is a place of business; I have appointments."

"Your appointment is with me," Leilani said, sliding the search warrant across the reception desk like a poker chip. "Please step aside, or we'll have to detain you."

Kaimana stared, eyes small and sharp, shrugged as if she'd already decided to let the lawyers fix it. She reached for her phone, but Leilani was faster, gently pinning her hand to the counter and nodding to the officer behind her to cuff her. "Only until we clear the building, ma'am. No hard feelings."

The staff were gathered in the main room, some openly gaping, others too stunned to move. Leilani made a quick headcount—six employees, no VIP guests—and split the squad, half to sweep the main floor, half to hit the back offices.

The gallery was a maze of glass panels and ambient lighting. Every step risked a collision with a priceless artifact or a freshly installed art piece, but Leilani's team moved like cats, never touching anything they didn't intend to. Mele's forensics team snapped pictures of every room, every computer screen, every trash bin. Within minutes, the gallery looked less like a showroom and more like a police procedural on fast-forward.

The comm crackled in Leilani's ear. "Aloha Auction, entry successful," said Tano's voice, calm as a weather forecast. "Owner's lawyer on site. No resistance, but they're running shredders in the back room."

"Copy," she replied. "We're clear on the floor. Back offices next."

Detective Mike Kilo met her at the staff hallway, breath tight but eyes dancing. "Found something fun in the copy room. You're gonna love it."

She followed, careful not to touch the artifacts

hanging on the wall. In the tiny back office, Mike pointed at a scanner feeding page after page into a file called "Temp_Discard." On the desk, a printed log listed outgoing shipments for the last six months. Each line was a perfect grid of artifact names, fake recipient addresses, and—most damning—codes matching the list from the Bishop theft.

Mele stepped in, already snapping shots. "They didn't bother hiding it. This is their master list."

Leilani's adrenaline ran cold. "Print a copy. Secure the hard drives and make sure Kaimana herself doesn't get near a trash can."

A yell from the showroom. She turned, heart climbing her throat. From the front window, one uniform waved her over, his face red.

"Boss! You need to see this."

She jogged up, Mike in tow, and saw the cause: through the side window, across the narrow back courtyard, a figure in a suit and sunglasses moved smoothly, and unmistakably. Sam Worthington. He didn't run but turned and walked to his car. He glanced over his shoulder and for a half-second, his eyes locked on Leilani's through the glass.

Leilani checked the appointment book on the counter. Sam had a 9 a.m. meeting with the owner. He slid into his car and pulled out of the parking lot.

Leilani's fist tightened around the door frame. "Should I have uniforms pursue?" asked Mike.

He was already moving, but she stopped him with a hand. "No. The primary scene comes first."

Mike scowled. "We can run him down. He's right there."

"This is what he wants," she said. "He'll be watching to see how we react." She forced herself to let go, although every muscle screamed to chase. "We don't have a warrant for him. We can't stop him from having a meeting with the owner of the auction gallery."

They turned and headed towards the office. It was time to inventory everything in the shop.

* * *

At the Aloha Auction House, things were less picturesque and more surgical. The outer offices were bland, a façade of low-rent minimalism, but the real action was in the back: a reinforced door, a wall of security cams, and a biometric lock that resisted every trick in the book until Isaac and Tano made the manager override it with the threat of an overnight stay in the holding tank.

Inside, it was a bunker. Shelves stacked with lacquered cases, each one labeled with a name, description, and an ID number. There was a leather-bound ledger on the desk—old-school, but with the same artifact codes found at Kaimana.

But the best part? The bookcase. It looked standard issue, but when Tano leaned on it, the whole thing rotated like a secret passage in a movie, opening a walk-in closet lined with what looked, at first glance, like cheap reproductions. But Isaac was no rookie—he picked up a ceremonial bowl and ran a fingernail along the base, exposing an original mainland museum tag, hastily blacked out.

Tano let out a low whistle. "They're not trying to be subtle."

Isaac radioed in. "Auction house locked down. Found a hidden room, significant haul. Starting inventory now."

He set the bowl aside, careful not to touch any more than he had to, and began photographing every item, every page, every Post-it note. He didn't let himself think about how many artifacts were missing, or how long it would take to get them home.

Tano swept the main floor with three plainclothes officers. They found the owner curled under the reception desk, thumb-typing frantic texts to an unlisted number. Tano confiscated the phone and bagged it. No drama, just business.

In the front window, press crews were already lining up, jostling with iPhones and voice recorders. Isaac ignored them, let the uniforms manage the spectacle. He'd done this before—more times than he liked to admit. The trick was to stay cool, focus on the case, and never let the vultures smell fear.

He listened as Leilani's voice buzzed in. "Status?"

"We're clear," he said. "The team is documenting everything, and we're boxing up all the documents we've found."

Isaac smiled, small and private, and got back to work.

* * *

Pacific Rim Collectibles was a gallery in name only—a converted auto body shop on the edge of Kalihi, with rusted metal roll-ups and the lingering smell of brake fluid. Tommy's squad hit it right after eight-forty-five, catching the two staffers loading a shipping container. They wore T-shirts and flip-flops, and the only sign they knew what they were moving was the care with which they handled the boxes.

Tommy called out, "Hey, fellas—mind if we check your paperwork?"

The staffers blanched and tried to shut the container, but it was too late. Two uniforms had them cuffed in seconds. The inside was a hoarder's heaven: stacks of sealed crates, hundreds of them, each tagged with destination ports in Singapore, Hong Kong, and Dubai.

Tommy worked fast. "Get Mele's unit back here. This is the big one."

He popped open the top crate, whistling low when he saw the contents. More than artifacts, there were rare books, navigational tools, and jewelry. All marked as "local crafts," but with a little shaking, the bottom layer turned up what he was after: the same forged provenance certificates that tied the ring to Kaimana and Aloha.

"Fucking jackpot," Tommy said, and radioed it in.

The next hours were a blur of logistics. The forensic techs shot hundreds of photos, bagged every artifact, and secured the phones and laptops of the warehouse crew. Tommy found a small office behind a tarp divider, with two tablets synced to a cloud server in Manila. One open chat read: "SW—shipment 13 on schedule. Releasing funds tonight. Good work, team."

Tommy attached it to the text and sent it to Leilani. **Thought you'd want to see this.**

She radioed back, cool as a cucumber: "Bag the tablet. We'll show the Chief."

"On it, boss."

As the dust settled and the officers started the long slog of inventory and transport, Tommy let himself breathe. It wasn't every day a detective got to blow open a multi-million-dollar operation before lunch.

He winked at one of the evidence techs, then cracked a Red Bull. "Next time, remind Lei she owes me a steak dinner. You know, for doing the heavy lifting."

The tech grinned, and the hard linoleum and humming fluorescent lights were almost celebratory.

* * *

Back at Kaimana, Leilani watched the press gathering on the street, every lens turned up like sunflowers to the first cop who'd step out and say a word. She hated the camera. She always had. But she knew the play: get ahead of the narrative, show control, and never let the city see you sweat.

Mike's voice broke in. "Warehouse is good. All the suspects are in custody. Mele's team is working the scene now."

"Solid work," she said. "Put the closed sign on the door. Let's keep the civilians outside for now. Tano— status?"

The reply was brisk. "Auction House is in the bag. The lawyer is still squawking, but we have the evidence."

"Copy," she said. "Now it's time for the paperwork."

She waited while the staff filed past, most of them too stunned or annoyed to care, then walked a final loop of the gallery. The white walls were bright and empty now, every case documented and tagged. In the office, she watched as Mele's team mirrored every computer drive, shrink-wrapping the evidence for chain-of-custody.

Isaac's voice sounded in her ear: "Lei, are you guys good?"

She nodded and realized he couldn't see her. "Yeah. We're good. We made the play. Now we see what the Chief says."

He let that hang a moment. "We'll get him, Lei. Worthington can't keep his hands clean forever."

She smiled, tired but real. "He'd better not. He still owes me an apology."

Mike walked in, holding two coffees and a box of Leonard's malasadas. "Hey, boss. You want sugar or more sugar?"

She took the donut, tore it in half, and handed the rest to Mele. "Both," she said. "We'll need it."

The evidence crew finished up, the uniforms started rolling out the suspects, and the sunlight through the gallery window shone cleaner than before. Leilani finished her coffee, wiped the sugar from her lips, and walked outside to face the day. It wasn't victory, not yet. But she could taste it.

***

The evidence room was supposed to be sterile, but this morning it vibrated with the messy energy of a used car lot in full swing. Desks overflowed with crates, laptops, hard drives, and the inert, low-key menace of a hundred cultural relics bagged and tagged for court. On one wall, a line of monitors ran live feeds from every holding cell, interview room, and evidence locker in the building. Most mornings, you could track the flow of paperwork by the steady drip of the coffee maker; today it couldn't keep up.

Leilani stood near the center table, surrounded by a group of techs, detectives, and the low hum of exhausted accomplishment. She watched Mele and her team catalog the artifacts with the focus of an ER nurse—meticulous, no motion wasted. Every piece went from plastic bag to numbered case, photographed, before being logged on a shared spreadsheet that already listed several million dollars in stolen heritage.

On the big screen, a map traced shipment after shipment out of Honolulu. Red lines arcing to Singapore, Hong Kong, and Dubai, each one matched with transaction receipts and manifests so perfect they'd fooled customs for years. But the further Mele's techs dug, the clearer the fraud became. Certificates of authenticity reused, the same signatures copied and pasted, chain-of-custody verifications all stamped by the same notary with a fake address in Pearl City.

"Boss, you need to see this," called Akira.

Leilani weaved through the mess and saw the tablet—last seen in the hands of the Pacific Rim warehouse manager—unlocked and open to a messaging app with enough encryption to make a defense contractor jealous. But Akira had a knack. She'd bypassed the screen lock, and now message after message scrolled past: codes, wire transfers, and digital receipts. In the most recent thread, a blunt message read, "Next payment only on delivery. Security risk otherwise."

Leilani leaned in, reading the thread twice. "That's Worthington, no question. He ran these people like a syndicate."

Akira nodded. "There's more. We found emails to a shell company in Jakarta, along with a different set to a bank in Abu Dhabi. Everything is routed through offshore accounts. It'll take a while, but this is a trail I can follow."

She flagged the most interesting messages and moved on. Leilani stepped back, watching the dance of crime scene tape, polygraph scheduling, and techs assembling a mountain of evidence for the DA.

Tommy rolled in, holding an entire carafe of coffee in one hand, a fistful of arrest reports in the other. He set both on the table and grinned. "Seven in custody. Three gallery owners, four runners. One of the muscle boys pissed himself and asked for a deal in the back of the patrol car." He poured coffee into a paper cup and added, "He gave up his VPN password. Merry Christmas."

Mele raised a hand from her workbench, not looking up. "This one's got a side order of humility, huh, Detective?"

Tommy snorted. "I'm glad to see them in real cuffs for once."

Leilani let herself smile, then turned as Tano strode in, face all business. "I checked on Worthington," he said. "FAA records suggest he took a charter from Hickam. Private jet. Last ping was two hundred miles west, headed for the international date line."

Tommy grimaced. "So, we missed him."

Tano shrugged. "Doesn't matter. His buyers are on ice, his money pipeline got cut, and we have enough evidence for ten extradition requests. He'll never set foot in Hawaii again unless it's in a jumpsuit."

Leilani watched the busy scene, her team working with a sense of purpose she hadn't seen in a long time. The mood was pride, sure, but there was a ragged edge of unfinished business.

Mele finished her round of evidence tags and beckoned Leilani over. She had a handful of provenance certificates, each bearing an identical signature. "See this? All the same pen, and all on the same day, all with different item numbers. They didn't stagger the dates. These people thought they were untouchable."

Leilani took one, felt the weight in her hand. "They always do. Until they're not."

A junior officer walked by with a box of Leonard's malasadas, the same as at the gallery. Tommy snagged one and handed another to Leilani. "Fuel up, boss. Gonna be a long day."

She took the pastry, shook the powdered sugar onto the floor, and bit in. "Thanks, Tommy. You did good today."

He grinned, wiped his hands on his jeans, and left the room whistling.

A little after four, the chaos settled. Most of the suspects were in holding; the first press conference had wrapped; the DA's office emailed thanking Leilani by name for preserving the chain of evidence. She snorted, knowing that her inbox would be flooded with subpoena requests by dinner.

She wandered to the far table, where Isaac sat alone, hunched over a computer with a half-eaten musubi at his elbow. He didn't look up as she approached.

"Hey," she said. "Do you mind if I crash the party?"

He slid the laptop toward her, the screen full of international wire transfers and a spreadsheet of artifacts with highlighted lot numbers. "Pull up a chair."

She did, and together they scrolled through the document, following the breadcrumbs as the ring laundered pieces from Oahu to Asia, and sometimes back again under new names and fake certificates. The heat of the monitors radiated on her face, as did everything they'd done to get here.

Isaac broke the silence first. "You ever think we'd actually get them all?"

She considered. "No. But I always wanted to.

You?"

He shrugged. "I thought we'd take out a couple low-level flunkies, close a case or two. I never figured we'd take out the whole damn industry."

She scanned the screen, her voice softer than she meant. "You ever think about leaving and taking this win to the FBI?"

He gave her a long look and shook his head. "Not unless you fire me."

She smiled, and it was a real one.

The door to the evidence room opened and Chief Mori walked in. She was wearing her dress uniform with sharp creases. She stepped up to Leilani and Isaac. She was aware of the extent of the operation, having been the department's spokesperson at the press conference. Now she wanted to see the evidence for herself. Leilani walked her through the shelves, showing her the lists of stolen items. She showed her the computer printouts and walked her through Isaac's maps and spreadsheets.

She walked around the room and shook hands with everyone who was still onsite, walked to where Isaac was sitting, and shook his hand.

"Well done, guys. Once you get the evidence squared away, give everyone on the team a couple of days off. They deserve it."

She turned to leave but stopped and faced Leilani. "Lei, walk with me."

Outside the evidence room, she stopped. "I've already had four calls from the FBI. It seems they think we crashed one of their long-running operations. Were you aware they had an op running?"

Leilani wasn't sure if her answer would lead to a reprimand, but she needed to be honest. "Yes, ma'am. A local agent, Chen, hit Isaac with a subpoena for us to turn over all our evidence. They wanted to grab our case. She thought Isaac would work with her for old times' sake, so she tried to go around me. Isaac brought it to my attention. We have three more days before we have to comply with the subpoena."

The chief was quiet for a few minutes, and Leilani waited for the bomb to drop. The chief smiled. "So, you and your team were able to complete our operation before the subpoena deadline?"

Leilani nodded.

"Well done, Detective. Let me know if there's any blowback." She laughed, turned, and walked away.

Leilani entered the evidence room and felt a little lighter.

For a while, they sat, the screens painting their faces in blue and white, the hum of the evidence room a gentle white noise. Mele's techs worked the background, and every few minutes, a fresh piece of evidence slid across the table to be logged.

Isaac pulled up a map of the Pacific. Red lines traced from Honolulu to a dozen port cities. "We've cut off his local network," he said. "Worthington can't move anything without these people. He's going to have to start from scratch."

Leilani tapped a finger on the table, eyes distant.

"But he's still out there. And he knows we're coming for him."

Isaac smiled, his usual crooked line. "Let him run. He's not the first, and he won't be the last. But we'll keep going."

She nodded, leaned back, and watched as the officers kept sorting, cataloging, and bagging history.

The evidence room buzzed on, a hive with a purpose, and the city outside caught up to the new day.

Somewhere, Sam Worthington was already laying his next line, plotting his next play. But for now, here, Leilani Kealoha and her team had the upper hand. It wasn't a victory, not really. But it was enough. And in this business, sometimes enough was everything.

# Chapter Fourteen

## Federal Friction

The conference room smelled of bleach and cold pizza. Under the flicker of the fluorescent lights, the evidence table sagged under its own weight. Battered legal folders, rows of clear evidence bags, and a junkyard of cell phones, laptops, and provenance certificates stacked three-deep. On the corkboard, the crime scene photos overlapped in a frenetic grid with each artifact circled in red, every suspect labeled, as if a simple visual diagram could ever explain how it all fit together.

Leilani stood at the head of the table, one palm braced on a sheaf of suspect interviews, the other hand flipping through a load of digital printouts. Isaac was at her elbow, going over the forensics summary for the third time, silent except for the occasional tap of his pen. Both looked like hell with bags under their eyes, shirts untucked, and sleeves rolled to the elbow in the universal language of a long-haul crisis. But the room buzzed with a kind of tired satisfaction. They'd done the impossible, cracked the ring, and the news would sing about it.

The moment shattered with the sound of heels hitting tile at a velocity short of violence. The conference room door flew open, ricocheting off the stopper, and FBI Special Agent Sarah Chen appeared in a tailored suit so sharp it could have opened a jugular. She didn't bother to flash her badge since everyone here knew who she was. Instead, she dropped a blue federal folder on the table, hard enough to rattle the plastic water bottles, and threw a piece of paper down after it like a gauntlet.

"For Christ's sake, Kealoha. Six months of federal investigation down the drain because you couldn't wait forty-eight hours," Chen said. Her voice was pure razor wire, more lethal for its low pitch.

Isaac's pen froze midair. He shot a glance at Leilani, whose jaw was already locked in its battle position. She lifted her eyes from the table and squared her shoulders-one cop to another, no quarter.

Leilani slid the subpoena towards herself with a single finger, then skimmed the header. "It's a subpoena, Isaac. Evidently, the Bureau's not sending a fruit basket," she said, not breaking eye contact with Chen.

Chen leaned forward, both hands braced on the back of a conference chair. "Don't get cute. You compromised an active multi-agency operation that extended across three continents, in case you missed the briefing. Every piece you seized last night was under federal observation. This is the second time you've fucked me on an important case, and I'll be damned if I'm going to let it happen again."

Isaac looked from Leilani to Chen. "What are you talking about?"

Chen looked at Leilani with fire in her eyes. "While you were on the mainland with your task force, your girlfriend here interfered with a major jewelry theft case I was running. We were within a day or two of arresting all the players when she swooped in and arrested them."

Isaac looked at Leilani. "Is that true?"

Leilani smiled. "She was dragging her feet. Tano got word that the team was preparing to leave the island, so we raided their hideout and busted them all."

"You went behind my back," yelled Chen. "Couldn't be bothered to let me know."

Tano stepped up to the table. "We did notify you," he said. "You were in a meeting and couldn't be disturbed, so we let Agent Fellows know, and he was going to fill you in. We waited as long as we could for you to get back to us, but we had to move."

Chen stammered but remained silent.

"So, you're mad at Leilani and her team because your guys failed to fill you in and you missed the bust," said Isaac.

"Her intrusion in my case," said Chen, "cost me a promotion and made the FBI look incompetent."

"And because of that," said Isaac. "You want to tear apart a solid investigation?"

"An investigation we were all over until she interfered again," said Chen. "We didn't need a briefing. You guys were well aware we were involved in the same case."

Leilani looked across the table at Chen.

"Actually, we did miss the briefing," said Leilani. "Since you went around me and asked Isaac to turn over our evidence to you. So yeah. I guess we missed the briefing. We had reason to believe the artifacts were going to be shipped overseas within twenty-four hours," Leilani replied. "You want me to stand down and let half of Hawaiian cultural history walk off the island in the back of a container truck?"

Chen scoffed, a sharp exhale that set the entire room on edge. "What you did was trigger every major player to scramble. You seized not only evidence, Detective. You scattered suspects into a dozen jurisdictions, all of whom were ready to roll on the real players once the shipments cleared customs."

Isaac stepped in, voice measured but urgent. "Sarah, we didn't have a choice. We got word from two sources that the stuff was being moved out through nonstandard channels. This wasn't a slow drip; it was a tidal wave. Someone was clearing inventory fast."

Chen cut him off with a palm. "I'm not talking to you, Torres. You're barely here." She flicked her gaze back to Leilani. "I know you think you're some kind of hero, but let me break this down for you in language you'll understand. You've made the Honolulu PD liable for obstruction, and I can all but guarantee you'll be facing internal review, if not formal charges. If you're lucky, you'll lose your badge if not your pension, and you will probably end up in jail."

Isaac's body tensed—caught between two worlds, the old and the new—and Leilani saw the way his knuckles whitened around the case folder. She didn't let herself blink.

"Would you like to know what's really happening, Agent Chen?" Leilani said, her voice rising a hair. "While you were busy building a textbook case, genuine artifacts and stories were getting laundered and lost forever. We didn't have the luxury of time. We had to act. If you'd bothered to clue us in, we could have coordinated."

Chen let go of the chair and paced the length of the table. Every so often, she jabbed a finger towards the evidence pile. "This isn't about your island pride or your mother's hula class, Detective. It's about organized crime—hundreds of millions of dollars, money that gets people killed in Dubai or Singapore or fucking New York. If you had waited one day, we could have taken down the biggest buyer on the West Coast. Now he's in the wind and every one of your suspects has a lawyer dialing in from out of state."

She reached the far end of the table, spun on a heel, and marched back. The other detectives in the bullpen, Tommy, Tano, and a couple of the admin staff, had all stopped working and were pretending to do paperwork so they could eavesdrop through the glass.

Leilani matched Chen's aggression, stepping around the table so they were two feet apart, separated only by the mess of evidence. "Let's call it what it is: you didn't want local PD touching your case because you thought we'd screw it up, and when we didn't, you got pissed because now you'll have to share credit."

Chen laughed, a cold thing. "You are so far out of your depth, Kealoha, it's almost cute."

Isaac's voice broke in, hard and brittle. "Sarah, you brought me in because you thought I'd smooth things over. But this was never about the Bureau or the HPD. It was about doing what was right for the case. These artifacts aren't only evidence; they're living heritage, and if we lose them."

She cut him down with a glance. "Stop. Don't play that card, Torres. You could have worked through channels. Instead, you went along with her and screwed us both."

The tension was a living thing, every word an escalation, every silence a fuse burning toward something atomic. Chen stared down Leilani, neither refusing to be the first to blink.

Leilani planted both hands on the table and leaned in. "You want my badge? Come ahead. But you better be prepared to explain to the press why the FBI sat on its hands while indigenous artifacts got ripped from their homeland."

Chen's nostrils flared. "You think the press gives a shit about your sob story? They're going to run with whatever I feed them. And right now, you and your partner are the story."

Isaac, voice lower, tried one more time. "Sarah. This isn't helping. We were after the same result. We got there before you. Had you bothered to inform us about what was happening on your end instead of trying to run roughshod over us, this might have worked out better for you."

Chen didn't look at him. She tapped the subpoena, still vibrating on the table, and spoke to Leilani as if nothing else existed. "You will comply. Full handover of all evidence by close of business today. If you so much as leak one more photo or artifact before then, I'll have you arrested for interfering in a federal case."

Leilani straightened, every muscle in her neck tight as a bowstring. "Actually, we won't be complying with your subpoena. We now have to be concerned with the chain of custody for all the evidence we have gathered, and I can't have that information falling into the wrong hands. I hope you like paperwork, Agent Chen."

"Wrong hands," Chen screamed. "Who the fuck do you think you're talking to? You realize you've left the HPD on the hook for a half-dozen counts of jurisdictional overreach?" Chen said, slapping her hand on the table. "Your officers stormed Kaimana Gallery while it was under live surveillance from federal assets. They tailed and detained a foreign national—on the diplomatic list, by the way—without notifying our task force. Did you read the list of what you blew up, or did you count the press hits?"

Leilani didn't move, didn't flinch, but her cheeks burned.

"We followed probable cause," Leilani said. "Everything in those affidavits was signed off by the DA. If you had intel to share, you should've shared it."

Chen leaned forward, knuckles pressing into the fake wood. "Don't start with the DA. He's in enough hot water for granting the warrants. It's like you people coordinated your actions so you could fuck up my investigation. You didn't break procedure; you set the entire timeline on fire. There's an international task force in Geneva waiting for these guys to slip, and now every target has gone to ground."

Leilani opened her mouth to argue, but Chen rolled right over her. "And let's talk about evidence. Half the artifacts you recovered were already tagged for an international sting. Your team unboxed them and staged a press conference. You might as well have sent them a warning letter and a fruit basket."

Isaac cleared his throat, his first sign of life in minutes. "Sarah, it was my call too. If there's an internal review, I'll take the heat. Lei only did what we agreed—"

"You don't get to play the shield, Torres," Chen snapped, never taking her eyes off Leilani. "You left the FBI for a reason. Don't screw your old team just to look like a hero."

He winced and took a half-step back, but Leilani's spine got taller. She matched Chen stare for stare, never blinking. "If the artifacts had left the island, they'd be lost for a generation. I wasn't going to risk that—not for anyone's career, especially yours."

"Spare me the melodrama," Chen said, pushing away from the table and beginning a slow, deliberate pace. She jabbed a finger at the corkboard, at the case files, and at Leilani's chest. "This wasn't some noble sacrifice, Kealoha. You gambled, and you lost. If this blows up, you're done here—and the next time you look over your shoulder, it'll be an internal affairs officer, not me, asking for your badge."

She let that land. An actual threat, and the whole bullpen could feel it. Tommy had stopped pretending to work—his eyes locked on the drama like a fan at a playoff game. Mele's lab crew had sidled closer to the glass, frozen mid-transfer with a handful of bagged laptops.

Leilani's hands were flat on the table now, all the way white at the fingertips. "We did the job you couldn't do. We have the evidence, and we made the arrests. You're pissed because we got the credit for doing in six weeks what you've been working on for a year. Do you really think I give a shit about some fat cat in Europe who's forging Van Goghs? Well, I don't. I care about the artifacts that your people have been stealing from these islands for decades. Well, yesterday we put a big hurt on that and took out some big players, and I will not apologize to you or any other stuffed shirt for doing our jobs. You want my badge? It's going to take more than idle threats and empty promises. "

Chen stared, her voice dropping low. "But you might want to start packing your desk anyway. And tell your team to enjoy their little victory lap, because when the Feds finish the review, there won't be a team left."

Isaac's patience snapped, but not loudly. He stepped between them, one hand on the table, the other up in a halting gesture. "That's enough, Sarah."

Chen paused. The silence in the room was so sharp you could hear a mouse piss on cotton.

Isaac held her gaze, his own eyes suddenly colder than the air conditioning. "Lei's my partner now. If you need to come after someone, come after me."

For a split second, everyone stood there, the three of them locked in a triangle of rage and loyalty and disappointment. Then Chen's lips twisted, the way you smirk when you realize the hill you've chosen is steeper than you thought.

"Fine," she said. "But don't expect me to go easy. This isn't over, not by a long shot."

The room was still humming when Chief Mori arrived. She didn't knock. She didn't have to. The sound of her heels—the real, old-school, nothing-sensible-about-them kind—made every cop on the fourth floor straighten like they'd been called to the principal's office.

She entered in full-dress uniform, though it was barely nine in the morning. Her hair was smooth and contained, her makeup almost invisible except for a glint at the cheekbone. When she walked into the conference room, the temperature dropped by ten degrees, and every eye in the bullpen pivoted to watch.

"Agent Chen," Mori said, her voice measured, "I understand you have concerns about the department's role in the Worthington artifact case."

Chen had returned to her predatory lean at the table, but she had the sense to rise when Mori came in. "Chief. Your officers compromised a long-term federal investigation—"

"Sit down," said Mori. It wasn't a suggestion.

Chen sat.

Mori surveyed the room in a single sweep: Leilani with her hands locked on the table, Isaac's face caught between pride and dread, the mess of evidence bags and printouts, and, in the center, the still-warm subpoena. Mori stepped around the end of the table, picked up the blue folder, and read the top page. She closed it with deliberate care, like she shut the lid on a bomb.

"I received a copy of this from the U.S. Attorney at six this morning," Mori said, setting the folder flat. "He expressed many of the same complaints you did. But unless I'm missing something, Agent Chen, federal law enforcement does not have exclusive jurisdiction over crimes committed within the city of Honolulu."

Chen bristled, the color climbing in her neck, but Mori held up a palm and continued. "Let me clarify our position. Every action taken by Detective Kealoha and her task force was authorized at the highest level, myself included. If you need documentation, I'll provide it. If you want a meeting, you can schedule one. But this department does not stand down for a jurisdictional pissing match."

The silence was a living thing. The forensic techs out in the hall went still, pretending not to listen. Isaac let out the smallest breath. Leilani's fingers loosened their death grip on the table a millimeter.

Mori focused her attention on Chen, her tone softening only a fraction. "I understand the urgency of your case. But my priority is and will always be the safety and dignity of the people who live here. Those artifacts you wanted us to sit on. They're not only evidence, Agent. They're family. They're home. You ask any person in this building if they would have let those crates leave Oahu and the answer will be no. Every time."

Chen opened her mouth to reply, but Mori wasn't finished. "That said, the city has no interest in making enemies of our federal partners. From here forward, you'll have full access to the evidence. If you want a liaison, I'll assign one. But don't mistake professionalism for subservience."

Chen's phone chimed, and she glanced at the number. She was about to press the red button. "You're going to want to answer that, Agent Chen," said Chief Mori.

Chen glared at her, picked her phone off the table and pushed the green button. "Yes, ma'am," she said as she stepped away from the table.

A flush spread along Chen's jawline, but her voice stayed controlled. "Thank you, ma'am."

She turned and faced the chief. "My apologies, Chief. I meant no disrespect. I had concerns about the chain of evidence; however, I understand I may have misunderstood the scope of your operation."

Mori cut in with a nod. "Thank you, Special Agent. You'll have access to every scrap of paperwork and video you need. Detective Kealoha's reports are more thorough than any I've seen from the Bureau in my tenure. If there's a flaw, we will address it. But I suggest you focus on the actual criminals, not the people who stopped them."

She slid the subpoena down the table to Chen, who caught it with both hands. The gesture was subtle, but the meaning was clear. This is our case.

Chen held Mori's gaze, but the fight was gone. "We'll coordinate," she said carefully, her voice holding the edge of defeat. "But don't expect this to be the end of the discussion."

Mori inclined her head, the closest thing to a bow she ever offered. "Of course not, Agent. But while you're discussing, we'll be working."

Chen rose, collected her folder and subpoena and left the room with her spine as straight as rebar. She didn't look back.

Mori waited until she'd disappeared down the hall and looked at Leilani and Isaac. "Your team did excellent work, but now the hard work begins. Expect every inch of the next steps to be under a microscope."

Isaac nodded, his relief so obvious it was almost embarrassing. "Understood, Chief."

Mori's gaze lingered on Leilani. Her voice lost its steel. "This isn't the first time we've had to defend ourselves from our own side. Don't let it stop you from doing what you know is right."

Leilani met her eyes and nodded once, a slow, deliberate movement. "I won't."

Mori let a rare smile slip, small and sharp. "That's what I'm counting on." Then, louder, to everyone in the room. "I'd like a briefing at ten. Bring coffee and a snack. We may be there for a while."

She walked out, leaving a hush behind.

The tension in the conference room unwound all at once. Tommy breathed again. Mele and her techs shuffled back to their bench, a little spring in their step. The overhead lights seemed to hum less angrily.

Akira looked up from her laptop. "What was that

call about? Chen sure changed her tune in a hurry.”

Isaac rolled his chair closer to Leilani. “You ever see a federal agent lose to local PD?” he whispered.

She cracked a smile, small but real. “I think our chief is not afraid to push buttons. Let’s get ready for the briefing. We will not let her down.”

Outside, the sun climbed another inch. The next battle was already waiting, but for now, they’d won the day.

# Chapter Fifteen

## Betrayal Unveiled

After hours, the SIU case room seemed different—like a mausoleum for every crime that ever touched the island. The only light came from the glow of the dual monitors, one for Leilani, one for Isaac, both hunched on opposite sides of the conference table. The long strip of LED ceiling bulbs had been off for hours, replaced by the grumble of the coffeepot in the break alcove and the steady rubber band snap of tension as one of them found a lead and lost it.

It was nearly 2 a.m. The world outside was black, the city's traffic nothing but a low hum through thick security glass. Leilani wore the same clothes she'd started in—her blouse from the morning already crusted with dried coffee and sugar from Tommy's get the day started malasada bribes. Isaac's jacket was off, sleeves rolled up, his left arm a patchwork of notes scrawled in blue Sharpie where he'd run out of Post-its. In the silence, every keyboard clack sounded like a hammer. Every sigh was as loud as a police siren.

They were looking for a ghost, but not the supernatural kind. Something in the logs—a string of access times, logins, calls placed after hours. They were following leaks, tracing lines of betrayal that had started as a trickle and were now a river with no headwaters. Three of the six suspects picked up at the auction house bust had already lawyered up with the city's best. Two had been released pending further evidence. The last one had gone missing right after being interviewed.

"It doesn't add up," Isaac said. His fingers rattled on the keyboard, flipping between CCTV feeds, personnel access logs, and old case reports. "The info had to come from inside. But not from us. We haven't said anything on open channels since Mori's directive."

Leilani looked at the screen until the text blurred into a block of white. She rubbed her eyes. "The leak is post-arrest. After the press conference. Looks like someone's pulling records to build a defense."

Isaac snorted. "Not unless they have admin clearance. You can't get to the sealed interviews from a normal terminal."

"Unless you use the LT's override," she replied. "Or the DA's."

"Neither of which we touched," Isaac said. "You see this?" He flicked a tab at her. "Here—3:11 a.m. Two days ago. Someone logged into the SIU shared drive, but with guest credentials. Downloaded the entire case report on Pacific Rim Collectibles."

Leilani leaned in. "Who was on shift?"

He pulled up the duty roster, traced a finger down the list. "Two uniforms, one admin, and—" He paused. "Tommy. He was logging evidence from the warehouse."

She squinted, trying to remember the morning after the raid. Tommy looked like hell, but he always did after a big bust. "You think he did it?"

Isaac's lips pressed into a thin line. "He's green, but

he knows the protocols. He'd have no reason to pull sealed files. And look." He pulled up another window. "Security footage from the evidence room, same night. That's him, all right. He goes in at 2:57, comes out at 3:20. Doesn't sign out a single item. But check this—he's got a cell phone in his left hand."

"Against policy," Leilani said.

"Way against." Isaac let the video run. Tommy paced the length of the storage racks and stopped at one of the high lockers, the B Section, where the high-priority cultural artifacts were locked down until final transfer. He stood there motionless and angled his phone for a good twenty seconds before tucking it away. When he left, he wiped his hands on his jeans, then looked straight at the camera, blank as a sandbag.

Leilani frowned. "Pull the badge log from that door. Let's see if it matches the time."

A few seconds of typing and Isaac had the data. "Yup. Opened with his card. No one else in or out for forty minutes."

She rocked back in her chair, every cell in her body buzzing. "He's been off the last three days. Said he was going to see family on the North Shore. Said his mother was sick." She swallowed. "He's never mentioned family before."

Isaac spoke, then stopped. Instead, he opened a personnel file, flicked through Tommy's HR history, and found…nothing. No home address on the North Shore, no local family listed, only a P.O. box downtown and the name of a landlord who doubled as a bail bondsman.

"He lied," Isaac said, almost to himself.

A cold rush swept through Leilani. She thought about Tommy, all the brief moments, the eager, wide-open questions, the Red Bull jokes, the way he always asked for extra responsibility. The way he sometimes parroted lines from her own briefings, but with enough slack to make it sound like it was his idea. She thought about how he'd been the first to find the hidden room at Pacific Rim, the one with the shadow records and fake shipping manifests. She thought about how proud he'd looked when he'd handed her the inventory report—so proud she'd never checked it herself.

"He's a leak," she said. "Our leak."

Isaac kept his eyes on the screen, but his hands trembled. "He's our friend," he said so softly she almost missed it.

Leilani closed her own laptop and stood, stretching the ache out of her neck. "Don't take it personally. That's what they count on. We need solid proof before we make a move."

She stepped to the whiteboard, yanked down the current case flow, and started writing on a blank square:

*03:11–Tommy logs into the drive*

*03:20–Evidence room access*

*03:21–Calls made*

She turned to Isaac. "Phone dump?"

He shook his head. "Not since he left town." He switched tracks, hammered out a subpoena request, and waited as the screen clicked and spat out a cell phone log for the last week. Dozens of numbers, but one called five times in a single night—a mainland cell with a masked area code.

He double-checked the call duration and hit up an FBI resource that could back-trace disposable numbers. Within thirty seconds, the reply came: Sam Worthington's travel secretary, a direct line to his Gulfstream, recently deactivated but rerouted to a virtual office in Geneva.

Leilani scanned the screen. "He's not a leaker. He's selling us to Worthington."

"Probably not only us," Isaac said. "The artifacts, too. Worthington's out of the country, but his crew's still here. They're paying Tommy for access and probably more."

The room felt colder. The ghost wasn't in their system—it had a face. A badge and a gun.

"So, we bait him," she said.

Isaac nodded. "We set a trap. Make it look like we're transferring the actual evidence and prep a decoy crate. Set up surveillance. If he takes the bait, we have him dead to rights."

"And if he's not alone?" she asked.

"Then we're ready," Isaac said.

They mapped out the plan, step by step. Tommy's next shift is tomorrow. He'd have to sign in at the duty desk. The decoy evidence transfer would hit the schedule at 11:30 p.m. Late enough to make him think no one else was around. Leilani would be on the floor,

Isaac watched the feed from the server room. Tano and two uniforms were hidden on standby.

"Still," Isaac said, turning off his monitor and staring into the afterglow, "he's one of us."

Leilani stepped closer, put a hand on his shoulder. "They count on that," she said. "We don't give them the satisfaction."

She left the room first, boots thudding on the linoleum. Isaac stayed a moment, watching the blue light fade from the monitors, then followed, sealing the door behind him. The SIU was quiet, but the hunt was on. The ghost had a name now, and by tomorrow night, it would have a face on the wall.

Carl Tanaka watched as Torres and Kealoha left the conference room. He knew something was going on, so he slipped into the room and looked at the whiteboard. There was a note for that Espinoza kid talking about moving the evidence to the feds. He slipped out of the conference room, pulled out his phone, stepped into the men's room, and picked an empty stall. He pulled out his phone and sent a text.

**Artifact evidence going to feds.**

The response was immediate.

**Make sure evidence is destroyed. Son depends on it.**

Carl walked to his desk, sat, and put a plan together. The times on the note on the whiteboard were specific, and he knew once everything was stacked and ready to go, no one would be watching it until the feds arrived for pickup. He knew when he would make his move.

He felt good that after tonight, his son's debts would be paid, and he'd be off the hook for any more dirty work.

*** 

The evidence vault after dark was a shrine to paranoia. Cinderblock walls, reinforced steel doors, every surface caged and coded with labels that meant everything and nothing. Leilani waited behind the far row of tall shelving units, in the dead air between the chemical stink of fingerprint powder and the copper tang of cleaning solvent. The hum of fluorescent lights overhead was the only sign the world was still turning. The security camera's red LED was as faint as a pulse, barely catching her silhouette among the racks.

She'd been there nearly three hours, sitting on a rolling step stool and staring at the caged bins where the Worthington haul was staged for tomorrow's transfer. Each box was banded with green evidence tape, a barcode, and chain-of-custody labels still pristine. The decoy crate, heavier than the others, sat dead center, topped with an orange folder marked OUTGOING: HPD HQ—INTAKE 0900. The bait.

The plan was simple. Tommy would come in for his scheduled night check, see the paperwork, and the note on the whiteboard—if he took the bait—he'd access the crate directly and remove key pieces of evidence. A signal from his keycard or a fresh biometric scan would trip the silent alarm and cue Tano's team in the annex. If Tommy were smart, he'd run a rehearsal first. Probably walk the floor and check for cameras or witnesses. If he were really smart, he'd bolt now and never look back.

But when the door cycled open at 11:37, it wasn't Tommy's mop of hair silhouetted by the hallway light. It was Senior Detective Carl Tanaka—homicide, old-school, and two months out from retirement. Tanaka had a face that always looked one hour past the edge of patience. Tonight, the lines on his cheeks were so deep they looked like they might split.

He stepped inside, a little hunched, glancing over his shoulder. No one else followed.

Leilani pressed back against the metal rack, staying low. Tanaka's steps were careful, measured, but he didn't waste time with the smaller bins. He made a beeline for the high-security lockers at the far end—B Section, the same one Tommy had cased in the footage. Tanaka didn't hesitate. He punched his keycard, twisted the deadbolt, and popped the locker like he'd done it a thousand times before.

She watched as he took out a thick three-ring binder. The label read: Supplemental—Confidential. S. Worthington / 2025. He didn't open it. Instead, he reached into his jacket and pulled out his phone, thumbed the camera, and took pictures of the rest of the evidence in the box. With a fast scan up and down the aisle, he put the cover on the box and picked up the binder.

He was good. Efficient. Too efficient. Leilani took a breath, stood, and moved into the aisle. "That's enough, Carl."

Tanaka's shoulders flinched, but he turned slowly, like he'd expected her. "Shit, Kealoha. You move quietly." His voice was even, but his eyes—usually a little sleepy—were jittering all over her, the room, the ceiling.

"Put the phone on the table," she said.

He did, hands open. "It's not what you think."

She kept her hands loose, but let her jacket fall open, badge, and SIG both visible. "I think you accessed evidence without a warrant or a sign-off. I think you've been in here before."

Tanaka's lips pursed, a nervous tic. "I'm not selling you out. Or the case. I had to—"

She closed the gap, stopping four feet away, just out of reach. "You had to do what, Carl? Cover for your kid who's in over his head? How many times have you bailed him out? Have they all been by stealing evidence?"

Tanaka shook his head hard enough that a lock of hair fell loose. "You don't understand. He's got leverage. The mainlanders—Worthington, his crew— they got to me months ago. Said if I didn't pass on anything that came through the SIU, they'd—" His mouth snapped shut.

She waited. "They'd what?"

He shook his head again. "Doesn't matter. It's not about me."

She held his gaze. "Why tonight?"

Tanaka's hands were balled into fists. "They said tonight, or the offer is off the table. That you'd be off the case. They wanted every record scrubbed before the morning transfer. Anything that connects the thefts to the new Councilman's campaign, anything that makes Worthington look dirty. I'm supposed to bag the files and leave them in the lot."

"You think that's going to make this disappear?" she asked.

He smiled. "I think I don't have a choice. Never did."

The air went still. She saw his left hand twitch once towards the holster under his jacket. She didn't draw, not yet. "You're not walking out of here with that binder, Carl."

There was tension in his voice. "Don't make me do this, Kealoha."

A noise in the hallway—a shuffle, or a cough—echoed in the steel vault. Leilani registered it without taking her eyes off Tanaka. She tapped the mic in her ear and said a single word: "Now."

The outer door banged open. Isaac's voice, strong: "Detective Tanaka. Step away from the evidence. Hands up."

Tanaka froze, and as fast as a trap snapping, he dove sideways, using the shelving as cover. He hurled the binder behind a row of boxes and reached for his sidearm.

Leilani drew but didn't fire. "Don't, Carl. Please don't."

Tanaka's eyes were wild. "He said he'd kill my son. Said there'd be enough money to clear all the charges against him."

Isaac moved to block the door. "You don't want to do this, Carl. Think of your son."

Tanaka, half-crouched behind a bin, glanced between them. He was shaking. "You're not listening," he said excitedly. "He owns everything. This is just insurance."

He lunged, crashing into a line of shelving, knocking two boxes down. The chaos gave him enough cover to raise his pistol and fire a wild shot toward the exit. Isaac grunted and dropped to his knees, a bloom of red staining his shirt sleeve.

Leilani didn't hesitate. She leaped the aisle, caught Tanaka around the wrist, and slammed his arm down against the steel shelving. He fired once more; the round pinging off a locker and ricocheting into the drywall. She twisted his arm until the gun clattered out of reach. Tanaka bucked and tried to throw her off, but she rode him down, driving a knee into the small of his back. He sobbed once, tried to roll, but she already had the cuffs out, locking one wrist, then the other.

He went limp, breath ragged.

Isaac crawled over, using his good arm to steady himself. Blood oozed down his forearm, but he kept the gun trained on Tanaka. "It's okay," he said, his voice shaky but calm. "It's over."

Leilani keyed her radio, voice steady as ever. "Officer down, evidence vault. Suspect in custody. Roll medical now."

She sat back, panting, and watched the old detective weep into the linoleum.

She looked up at Isaac, who managed a crooked grin through the pain. "I always figured the paperwork would be the death of me," he said.

She tried to smile back, but her hands were shaking. "You're not dying yet. I told you; the bad guys always go for the file cabinet."

Outside, the sound of boots and radios grew louder. The medics would be there in under a minute. She wanted to close her eyes, but couldn't. She watched as Tanaka shrank in on himself, smaller with every breath.

He looked up at her, eyes red. "Tell my son I'm sorry."

She nodded, unable to speak.

Isaac leaned in, his voice low. "You did good, Lei."

She nodded again, but the tears were coming now, silent and slow.

The medics poured into the vault, shouting and cutting away Isaac's shirt, patching him up with practiced hands. Tano's team scooped up Tanaka, now quiet, wrists cuffed behind him, and read him his rights as they dragged him out. The binder, scattered but intact, remained where it had landed, the only thing left out of place.

Leilani sat alone, watching the camera's red light blink at her, recording every second. She wiped her face, holstered her SIG, and stood. Her knees buckled for half a heartbeat but held. She walked out into the hallway, head high.

The evidence room would never feel safe again, and

somewhere, the man behind all this watched and waited for his next chance, but Leilani Kealoha would be ready.

***

The hospital room looked like every other box in the city—white walls, blue tile, a window angled at the right height to see the palm trees and not the parking lot. The air was thick with antiseptic and the metallic buzz of the ceiling vent. An IV bag hung over Isaac's bed, a slow drip feeding his good arm. The other was bandaged from his bicep to his wrist, so bulky it looked like he'd tried to arm-wrestle a cement mixer. He wore a disposable gown, hair pushed flat on one side, but his eyes were bright and clear.

Leilani sat in the visitor's chair, her knees up, chin resting on her folded arms. The cuffs of her pants were still streaked with Isaac's blood, and her shirt—she realized too late—had a brownish rust stain across the belly, right where she'd cradled his shoulder. She'd meant to go home and change, but she couldn't bring herself to leave. Not yet.

The monitor beeped, sharp and regular, echoing in the early morning quiet. Neither of them spoke for a while. Isaac finally broke the silence.

"Wanna sign my cast?"

She shot him a sideways glance, a smile lurking. "I'm saving it for your tombstone."

He grinned, winced, and let his head fall back. "Damn. Are you always this soft?"

She let her face drop into her hands. "Never." Her

voice when it came, was low and ragged. "You scared the hell out of me."

Isaac didn't reply, just watched her. "You're the one who took down Tanaka. I got shot for being a dumbass."

"Don't say that," she said, sharper than she meant.

He shrugged or tried to. The movement pulled at the wound, and he hissed. "You know, after all those years with the Bureau, I always thought if I got hit, it'd be some junkie on a bad day. Not another cop."

She let out a breath. "We were so sure it was Tommy."

Isaac nodded. "Still might have been if Tanaka hadn't shown up. Guess he figured you'd be easier to handle than Tano's crew."

A nurse slid in, checked the IV and the blood pressure, scribbled notes on a pad, and left. The silence returned.

Leilani found her voice again. "They debriefed Tanaka. He confessed to everything."

Isaac's eyes flicked over to her, curious. "How bad?"

"Worse than we thought," she said. "Worthington got to him through his son. Gambling debts. Threatened to go after his kid. Promised if he kept the records clean, the son's slate would be wiped." She paused. "He said he'd do it again to keep his family safe. He said that it was easy for someone on the outside to access the camera feeds and with some AI magic put Tommy in the frame. Akira spent the morning checking the feeds, and sure enough, we were hacked."

Isaac exhaled, a sound equal parts relief and regret. "We should've seen it."

She nodded. "We both missed it."

They sat with the monitor's beeps filling the gaps.

"Any news about Tommy?" he asked.

"Tano's interviewing him now," she said. "He's clean. Upset, but clean. He had no idea any of this was happening under his nose. He was on the North Shore. His mom is dying. The phone number belonged to his father. He hasn't spoken to them in years, but when the end is near." Leilani let her voice fall off.

Isaac closed his eyes. "I owe him an apology."

"Get in line," Leilani said. "We're close, you know. Worthington's still out there, but now we have motive, and we have Tanaka's testimony. We can tie it to the theft ring. We might get Interpol to move."

Isaac's smile was small, but true. "Not without the help of the FBI, and I think Chen stripped your name from her Christmas card list. You still want to chase him down?"

"Let's finish this," she said.

His hand, the unbandaged one, reached across the covers and found hers. They sat that way, the city outside waking up, a new day seeping through the window like weak coffee.

After a while, the door opened, and Chief Mori walked in. She wore a navy suit with a black shirt. Her hair was tied back with surgical precision. She gazed at the two of them and smirked.

"I see you're not dead yet, Torres," she said.

He sat up straighter, winced, and saluted with two fingers. "Still here, Chief."

"You're costing the department a hell of a lot of money for healthcare," she said with a smile. "What's this make, three times now?"

Isaac nodded. "Yes, ma'am."

She shifted her gaze to Leilani. "You holding up?"

"Yes, ma'am," Leilani said, standing.

Mori crossed her arms, all business. "Good. Because the mayor wants a statement by noon, and I'm not writing it myself. Also, the press will sniff around. You two are going to be on TV, whether you like it or not."

Isaac made a face. "Is it too late to get shot again?"

"Way too late," Mori said. "I'm proud of both of you. We've still got some rot in the system, but if we keep at it, we might root it out before I retire."

She turned to go but paused in the doorway. "I'll send someone to drive you home, Detective. Try to get a shower before the ten o'clock news."

"Yes, ma'am," Leilani said.

When they were alone again, Isaac's eyes followed her to the window. The sun was higher now, slicing through the slats in gold strips.

He said, "Are you sure you're okay?"

She smiled. "No. But I will be."

He nodded. "Me too."

The beeping slowed, grew calm, the rhythm of two hearts catching up after a long, wild night. Outside, the city was wide awake, ready for the next mess. But for now, in this little room, they could breathe.

# Chapter Sixteen

## The Black Market Showdown

The hospital left a bleach stink in Leilani's nose for hours after she left, and every minute of the drive to the slipway, she caught herself looking for Isaac in the mirror. She caught herself about to text him, too, until the ache in her jaw reminded her he'd told her not to bother. "Don't do that worried face. I'll be fine," he'd said, voice half anesthetized, eyes still too bright. So, she didn't.

The owner of the Kaimana Gallery had given them everything they needed on Sam Worthington in exchange for full immunity. Leilani's team verified the information and allegations with several sources, including detective Tanaka, who was forthcoming when offered a deal that got his son into a treatment program.

By the following afternoon, her DA representatives had secured search warrants for Sam's house, the new cultural center, and his yacht. The house had been cleaned out, and almost every artifact in the cultural center had been obtained legally.

What those raids revealed, and Mrs. Kaimana confirmed, was that Sam was holding an auction on his yacht, off the coast of Oahu, in international waters. Leilani didn't hesitate to gather her team and coordinate with the Coast Guard, who had identified the location of the yacht and were keeping a discreet eye on it.

The SIU staging area was a strip of cracked concrete under a rusted awning, but tonight, it was like a war bunker. Tano ran the briefing in a low voice, walking the team through every deck of the yacht, pointing with a marker at each fire exit, each stairwell, each place someone could get lost or killed.

Tommy fidgeted with the Velcro on his vest, which he wore over a Hawaiian shirt that would have looked clownish anywhere else. The four plainclothes officers stood behind Tano in a line, three men and one woman, all silent, all wired for action. Akira sat on a toolbox with a laptop open, screen bathed in red night mode. Her hair was up in a ratty topknot, half the electric streaks fading into brown.

Leilani checked her SIG, popped the mag, eyed every round, and closed it with a sound she let echo. She holstered it, ran a thumb under the flap to feel the weight. The routine steadied her more than she liked to admit.

Tano closed the folder, eyed the group. "No heroics. We get on, we secure the crew, we secure the salon. Artifacts first, suspects next. If it goes loud, we cut the main and use the dark." He looked at Leilani. "You'll lead team two?"

She nodded. "If he's there, I'll find him."

"Copy that," Tano said, and moved on. He sounded calm, but she could see the set of his jaw, the lines around his mouth. Tano wasn't scared, but he didn't like the feel of this one.

Akira piped up, too loud. "Once we're close, I'll hit the Wi-Fi repeater and kill every camera on board. It'll take about twenty seconds to cycle, but they'll have no feeds and no alarms unless someone panics."

Tommy raised his hand, like a kid in civics class. "What about the panic button in the main salon?"

"Second floor, west wall. I'll have eyes on it," Leilani said.

Tano nodded, satisfied. "Anyone else?"

There were no other questions.

The boat waited for them at the end of the dock—a black Zodiac, outboard engine hushed to a purr. The air stung cold, whipped with salt spray, and in the ocean beyond, the target sat lit like a floating palace. She'd seen photos, but never in person: Worthington's yacht, the Aurora, three stories of pure money, decks lined in gold-trimmed rail and glass, the hull spotless under the pool of halogen floodlights.

They moved fast. Tommy took the bow, Leilani, and Tano behind; the others staggered. Akira cradled the laptop like a child and typed as they raced across the open water.

"ETA sixty seconds," she said, and killed the screen.

Leilani used the time to check her phone—no messages, but the tracker she'd set in Worthington's private crate pulsed steadily. He was aboard, or his things were. She thumbed the signal, let the map run, then blacked out the screen.

The Zodiac came up quietly next to the yacht's swimming platform. The ocean here was black as night and flat except for the zodiac's wake. Tano signaled, and Tommy sprang up, looped a line to the platform, and hauled them in tight. The boarding ladder was retracted, but Akira had an answer—she flicked a switch, and a quiet buzz let the stairs down, one rung at a time.

They boarded in pairs, guns low, flashlights off, feet bare on the cold planks.

Leilani's pulse doubled as she cleared the platform. She climbed first, using the damp handrails, and rolled onto the aft deck. White light bathed the space in a glow like day, but the shadows at the edges ran deep. The salon doors ahead were glass, locked, and vibrated with the sound of voices inside.

She waved Tommy up, and he crouched beside her, hands ready.

"Two in the kitchen, one on the deck above," he whispered, eyes scanning the dark.

Tano joined them, the rest behind. "Hold until Akira's signal."

Akira's voice came through their earpieces, a bare hiss. "Three…two…one…"

The floodlights above flickered and died. Every window on the yacht went dark. The voices inside spiked with confusion, then dipped. The only illumination now was the glow of the city and a handful of running lights.

Tano stepped to the door, tested the latch. Locked. Leilani raised her SIG, used the butt to punch the lower glass—tempered, but the impact spider-webbed it. Tommy pulled out a pocket-sized sledge and finished the job, both in before the alarm could finish chirping.

Inside, they found a kitchen fit for a hotel, all marble and steel, counters lined with silver trays of finger food. Two crew members in matching polos looked up, eyes wide. Tano flashed his badge and hissed, "Police. Hands behind your heads." The woman complied, but the man tried to move. Leilani waved her pistol at him, and he stopped moving.

Tommy cuffed them with zip ties and dumped them to the floor and peeled off to cover the main stairwell.

"Go," Tano said. "Main event's upstairs."

Leilani climbed the stairs, heart pounding, gun up. The next deck was half-lit by emergency strips on the baseboards, enough to cast everything in shadow and ice. Ahead, through glass double doors, the sound of laughter, of prominent voices, and the clink of glasses. She saw Worthington's profile in silhouette, silver hair neat, standing at the center of a packed room. He was at the head of a long table, ringed with people—collectors, brokers, at least one woman Leilani recognized from the museum's donor lists. Next to the table, a crate: her crate, the one she'd tracked here. The lid was off, straw packing spilling over, something inside she couldn't see.

Leilani's team scattered around the yacht, but she waited, letting the auction play out so the rich people could have their fun.

The main salon was built for fantasy: glass walls, silk couches, and a floor that shimmered as if it were poured from mercury. On every surface, a white-gloved steward had arranged flowers, crystal, and trays of miniature pastries so perfect they could have been cast in resin. No one touched them. The crowd was here for something else.

Worthington stood on a low dais, two steps up from the crowd, but every inch the ringmaster. His hair was brushed flat, his goatee trimmed so sharp it could have drawn blood. He wore a navy double-breasted suit, the pocket square a burst of gold. In this light, the lines on his face looked chiseled by design.

The guests assembled were the people who never waited in line for anything: aging movie stars, tech investors in spookily identical sportswear, a woman in a lacquered bob and four-inch heels who had once, Leilani recalled, donated a wing to the local children's hospital. All of them were here now, sipping champagne and hungry for what they couldn't buy in any store.

Worthington tapped a silver spoon on the dais. The sound cut through the murmur, and the room fell silent.

"Ladies and gentlemen," he said, his voice all gravel and East Coast oil. "It is my honor to welcome you to a truly unique occasion. Tonight, you have the rare privilege to take part in the preservation of history, rather than its destruction."

A titter of nervous laughter ran the perimeter.

Worthington gestured behind him. Two men in tuxedos wheeled out the first artifact, a helmet of bright yellow and red feathers, the crest so tall it brushed the chandelier. "The Kamehameha mahiole," Worthington intoned. "Worn in court, lost for nearly two centuries. Recovered with gratitude from the hands of those who would have let it rot.”

He let the helmet rotate on a mirrored base, every light in the room bending to worship it. “Provenance is impeccable,” he said, and here he ticked off details like a priest: “Acquired from a private estate in Sydney, verified against early daguerreotypes, with all the signatories.” He smiled, the audience wrapped tight around his finger. “Opening bid. Five hundred thousand dollars.”

The helmet belonged to the Bishop’s private collection, last cataloged five years ago. Someone had traced its entire journey—through theft, auctions, private hoarding—and put a bow on it for tonight.

Hands shot up: the movie star, the woman with the bob, a skinny man in a teal linen suit. Worthington ticked up the numbers with each. “Six…seven…eight hundred thousand. We have one point one. One point three.” His voice was electric, in love with the number. “Sold to our distinguished guest in the front.”

The crowd applauded, not for the helmet, but for Worthington himself.

The next piece was smaller—a set of shark-tooth knuckles; the cord was still stained. “A gift for the serious collector,” Worthington purred, and spun another story: a missionary family’s heirloom, liberated from a New England attic, traced through an old, yellowed ledger. The lies were casual, confident.

Each artifact came with its own myth, always just plausible enough. A Koa wood statue, three feet high, eyes inlaid with shell, and a band of tattooed lines running up its arms. A pahu drum—this one blackened with age, its skin drawn tight by rawhide and bone pegs, the one taken from her mother's halau. Leilani recognized the carvings on the sides.

Worthington made a show of the drum. "A sacred object," he said. "It should never have left the islands, but now, thanks to the generosity of tonight's audience, it can be protected and cherished. It has been passed down through generations. Shall we start at a million?"

He let the crowd gasp and watched as three different hands went up at once. He let the tension grow, and the numbers swelled. One million. Two. Two point five.

Leilani's pulse thundered in her ears.

On it went: more helmets, another war club, a kapa cloak bright as a wound, each piece paraded, praised, and sold to the highest bidder. The provenance changed every time. Sometimes it was "rescued from a closed museum in Auckland," sometimes it was "recently deaccessioned from a major North American collection." Each story is true enough to convince the hungry, each a knife for anyone who knew the truth.

She caught a look from the woman with the bob, who smiled, all teeth, and whispered to her date. Leilani recognized the date, too: a retired Senator from California, whose family tree had more poison in it than fruit. He sipped his bourbon and leered at the artifacts like he might eat one.

Worthington moved to the last lot of the night, a crate bound in heavy cords, the straw spilling out the sides. He took his time untying it, letting the anticipation build. When he opened the lid, the room went silent. Inside: a feathered god image, its face fierce and beaked, the plumage a radiating halo.

Worthington's voice was softer now, reverent. "There are only five known in existence," he said. "Three are locked away in European museums. One is rumored to have been destroyed in the war." He paused and let the weight hang. "This is number five."

He cradled the statue in gloved hands and raised it so the crowd could see. The camera flashes sparked. Somewhere, a single breathless "wow" floated above the silence.

He placed the image on a velvet stand and stepped back. "Bidding to begin at three million," he said.

The hands went up, almost in sync. Three. Three point five. Four. Four point two. The numbers were so big they sounded fake; a fantasy made of zeroes.

Leilani scanned the room, reading each face. Worthington's was the only one that wasn't hungry; it was satisfied, a cat who'd already eaten the bird and was just waiting to be thanked for it.

The bidding slowed at five point two. Worthington gave a little cough, as if to clear the air, and said, "Six." The room turned. It was the Senator who grinned, daring anyone to match him.

No one moved.

Worthington nodded and called, "Six million going once—" From the back of the room, a new hand rose. The man was pale, with a face built for forgetting, hair so dark it glowed blue in the light.

"Seven," he whispered.

Worthington let the silence bloom. "Seven million. A gentleman's bid. Do I have more?"

The Senator hesitated. His date squeezed his arm.

"Seven point two," the Senator said, but his bravado was leaking.

The blue-haired man smiled, shrugged, and said, "Seven point five."

It was over. Worthington didn't let it linger. "Sold," he said, "to the patron in the rear. Congratulations." The applause was tired. The crowd had seen enough history for one night.

Leilani counted the heads. She made a note of every buyer, every gloating face. She watched as the runners collected the payment slips and Worthington thanked the crowd, voice thick with pride and relief.

She waited for the show to end, for the crowd to drift towards the bar, and the ripple of afterglow to settle into the air.

The plan was for Tano to give the signal—a slow count of five, then hit the lights. The plan did not survive contact with Tommy's nerves.

He was looking through the window of the rear salon door, eyes on a security guard reaching for his earpiece. The guard looked at Tommy, looked past him, then started moving for the back exit. Tommy, concerned that this might be a hit or a robbery in the making, thought he saw a gun under the jacket. He drew, leveled his weapon, pushed through the door into the salon, and yelled, "Police! Down!"

It all unraveled at once.

The guard whipped out his sidearm and fired a wild shot into the ceiling, sending glass and plaster across the bar. The crowd screamed, half of them diving under tables, the other half frozen, deer-stare and mouths open.

Leilani and Tano pushed through the outside salon door. She pulled her SIG and dropped to her knee, zeroing in on the shooter, but another blast from the far side made her flinch. Someone returned fire, splinters flying from the wooden banister above.

Tano's voice roared: "Lights now!"

Akira, somewhere below deck, cut the main. The world went black, save for the throb of red emergency strips along the floor and a slow, ugly pulse from the city behind the glass.

In the confusion, the sound of running feet up the spiral staircase. Worthington, with a duffel in one hand, the carved god image cradled in the other, was already moving.

Leilani signaled to Tommy, who nodded and hugged the wall, his gun up. She swept the room: guests sprawled on the floor, hands over their heads, some crawling, some weeping. The Senator cowered behind a sofa, one hand white-knuckled on his phone.

She followed Worthington.

The upper deck was chaos. The emergency lights bled blue and red across the teak, strobing every shadow into a demon. Leilani hugged the curve of the wall, careful to avoid the open windows, careful to check each corner. A single bullet ricocheted past her head—cracking the glass, raining pieces over the deck. She kept moving.

Above, the helipad. Worthington was running for it, legs pumping, face twisted in panic and rage. The bag bounced against his hip with every stride, but he never let go of the statue.

He hit the hatch, tried to push it open, but the lock was magnetic, and he had lost his key card in the melee. He slammed it with his fist twice, spun, and saw her.

Their eyes met.

He sneered. "You don't quit, do you?"

"Never," she said, and closed the distance.

He waited, coiled. When she was two meters out, he swung the duffel hard. The bag was heavy, filled with cash or worse. It caught her on the shoulder and knocked her sideways into the railing. He was fast—faster than she'd pegged for a man pushing seventy. He followed up with a straight punch, old boxer style, and caught her in the mouth. She tasted blood, spat it, and countered with a knee to his gut. He grunted but didn't buckle.

He jabbed the god image at her; the beak digging into her cheek. She slapped his wrist down, ducked, and hit him in the kidney twice in rapid succession. He dropped the statue, howled, but he still had the bag.

He swung it again, wild now, and she stepped in, twisted his wrist, and tore it away.

She had a half-second before he barreled into her, slamming her into the wall. His elbow went to her throat, pressure cutting off air. She punched up, caught him in the jaw, and the pressure faded. He staggered back, wiping blood from his mouth.

"You're not built for this," he growled.

"That's where you're wrong," she said.

They circled. He went for a tackle—sloppy, desperate—and she let him get close, then used his momentum to flip him over her hip and onto the deck. The thud was wet and final.

He tried to rise, but she was on him, arm locked around his neck, hand on the back of his head. "Don't move," she hissed, "or I'll break your teeth on the deck."

He struggled, legs kicking, but she shifted her weight, pinning him. She reached for her cuffs, fumbled them, and that was when he tried his last move.

He twisted, snapping his head up into her jaw. She saw stars, tasted metal in her mouth, and he was half free, reaching for the bag, for anything. She recovered barely, and kneed him in the spine, pressed him to the floor, and snapped the cuffs on his wrists with a loud, vicious click.

He howled, pain and fury mixed. "You don't get it, do you? There's always someone next in line. You stop me, it grows back."

She hauled him up by the elbow. "Likely," she said. "But you're out of business."

She could hear the chaos below—more gunshots, more screams—but her focus tunneled to

Worthington's face, and he looked scared. Not of her, but of something he'd never named, maybe never believed in.

She walked him to the rail, held him there. Below, police boats lit up the water, floodlights sweeping the hull. The city was a distant arc of gold. The night air cooled her skin, her lip throbbing, blood running down her chin.

Worthington spat over the side and turned. His voice was almost pleading. "Don't be a martyr, Detective. This is just money. This is business."

"It's more than that. It's every story you tried to kill."

He laughed, but it caught in his throat, and he stood there, cuffed and shaking, while the lights from the city reached them at last.

The deck door banged open. Tommy and Tano emerged, Tommy's shirt ripped and bloody at the shoulder, Tano dragging a dazed guard by the collar.

"Got him?" Tano asked.

"Yeah," she said, and handed over the cuffs.

Tano nodded, calm as if they were back in the case room, not on a floating battlefield. He took Worthington and marched him below.

Tommy lingered. "You good, boss?"

Leilani touched her face and the split in her lip, the crust of blood. "I'll live," she said. "How about you?"

He smiled. "You should see the other guy."

She laughed, raw and sharp. "Let's get the evidence and lock it down. Then we go home."

Below deck, the guests had been herded into a lounge. They sat draped in blankets, shivering, furious. The woman with the bob smoked through a pack of cigarettes in thirty minutes, never looking up from the glass table in front of her. The Senator barked into his phone until a uniformed officer took it away. As the police boats ferried Worthington's guests to shore, Leilani stood at the bow, hands on the rail. The sky was bruised and purple, the first edge of dawn rising over the city.

She stared at the island, at the stretch of sand and the green rise of the mountain, and it looked safe. Not perfect, but safe.

She thought of Isaac—probably watching the sunrise from a hospital window or dreaming of it. She thought of her mother, the pahu drum, the long, tangled line that had brought her here. She let herself smile. It wasn't over. It would never really be over. But tonight, they won. She stood there, letting the wind salt her wounds, and let the future come as it would.

Dawn hit the Aurora with the force of an interrogator's lamp. Every surface reflected light: the salt-polished rails, the glass doors, the deck still slick with a scatter of blood and something like victory. Two police boats nosed up on either side of the yacht, blue strobes painting everything in pulses. By the time the sun cleared the horizon, the party was over and the hangover had begun.

Worthington sat cuffed on a patio chaise, his hair

matted with sweat, suit stained with whatever had spilled on the floor in the melee. He glared at the HPD team working through the main salon, watched the officers bag every artifact, every slip of paper, every scrap that might be spun into evidence. He said nothing, but his eyes tracked the moves like he was still in the auction room, bidding for control.

Tano walked the deck with a legal pad, clipboard in hand, ticking off every box, every crew name. "Nothing leaves this boat unless it's tagged and signed."

Tommy, arm bandaged and already stained, boxed up the artifacts himself, careful with the labels, calling out each to Akira, who entered the inventory in a chain of quick keystrokes. "No deletes, no edits," she said. "I'm mirroring to the station and an off-site server. If it disappears, it's on you."

Leilani moved through the scene like a ghost, present but untouchable. She kept to the periphery, letting the team do the talking, letting the protocols roll. Instead, she drifted toward the back of the salon, where the last crate—her crate—waited.

She opened it slowly. Inside, the pahu rested on a cradle of straw, the wood still cold. The skin had a patch of familiar pigment, the drumhead taut and unblemished. She forgot about the pain in her mouth and the bruise along her jaw. She stood and let her hand fall on the rim, sensing the fine dust on her fingers.

She remembered that her mother showed her how to play. How to keep the rhythm with the heel of her palm, and how to press the beat into the air. She remembered how her mother had cried when it was stolen, the hollow left behind.

She lifted the pahu from the crate, arms trembling a little, and found a clean cloth in the evidence kit. She wrapped the drum like a baby, reverently. It felt right. It felt like it was coming home.

"Sweet reunion?" Worthington said from the lounge chair.

She looked up, eyes flat. "You wouldn't get it."

He shrugged, the cuffs clinking. "People always pretend these things have meaning. They're objects. Replace one, there's a dozen more waiting."

Leilani walked over, drum in hand, and stood above him. "It's not the object," she said. "It's what you tried to take. What you never had."

He looked up at her, the sun in his eyes. She noticed something like regret. But it passed.

"You have no idea what you've stepped into, Detective," he said. "You think you're a hero, but the people behind this—behind me—they'll eat you alive. You think I'm the problem? I'm nothing. I'm the delivery boy."

She held his stare. "Doesn't matter. You're the one in cuffs."

He smirked. "You'll see."

She turned away, not out of fear, but out of boredom. His story was over, and she had work to do.

She took the pahu to the bow of the yacht, found a spot in the sun, and sat. She unwound the cloth, let the light hit the drum, and the air dried the tears she didn't know she'd started. The island glowed on the horizon, sharp and green, and the city's towers glittered behind a haze of gold.

She felt the burden of the case, the fights, the pain—but she also sensed the echo of the drum in her chest, the memory of her mother's laugh, the certainty that this piece of history, at least, was safe.

Behind her, Akira came up and dropped into a sprawl, phone already out, snapping pictures of the sunrise.

"Hey, boss," Akira said, voice rough from the night. "You good?"

Leilani nodded, not trusting her voice. After a minute, she said, "Yeah. I'm good."

They sat in silence for a while, let the waves hit the hull, and let the new day build itself out of what was left. Two Coast Guard officers stepped on board and found Leilani.

"Detective," said the older one. "We're here to take the yacht to the secure berth at Pearl Harbor. Do you have everything you need?"

She gazed at the drum and smiled. "Yes, we do."

Tano eyed Leilani. "Would you like to do the honors?"

She did. She grabbed Worthington by the elbow, not roughly, but not gently either. She walked him to the side of the room. "You knew we were watching. You knew it for weeks. So why get cocky tonight?"

He shrugged, eyes on the Pacific outside. "Because I could."

She smiled. "You're not untouchable anymore."

Worthington's grin held, but his eyes had gone hard. "You have no idea what I'm untouchable from, Detective."

"Try me," she said. She looked down at him with contempt.

"We're done here," she said.

Worthington and the last of the guests were loaded onto the police boat. The ocean was blacker now; the yacht stripped of its lights and illusions. Akira had grabbed all the phones, the laptops, and the cloud sync, each file a nail in Worthington's coffin. Leilani handed the pahu to the evidence officer, made sure it was logged, and watched as Tano and Tommy loaded the last crate onto the police boat. Akira lingered, holding the laptop, eyes scanning the horizon.

Tano made the last check. He joined Leilani at the stern. "Are we good?"

She nodded her head.

They loaded Worthington last. He was silent, his eyes fixed on the island, now a low shadow in the distance.

Leilani watched him and checked her phone one last time. The tracker still pulsed—steady, unblinking.

"Ready?" asked Tano.

She nodded. "Ready." The team climbed aboard the Zodiac tied to the swimming platform. Leilani took one last look at the yacht and took her seat next to Tano. She pointed towards the island with her hand.

As the Zodiac pulled away, leaving the yacht behind, Leilani let the salt air hit her face, and let it sting her eyes until she could see the truth. Sometimes you didn't win. Sometimes, you only survived. But winning was so much better.

# Chapter Seventeen

## Homecoming

Leilani drove past the split-rail fence and into the lot behind her mother's halau as the afternoon sky broke open, a single shaft of gold flaring down like stage lights. She killed the ignition and shoved her phone into her back pocket, ignoring the five unread texts and the call from the Chief. The pahu sat in the passenger seat, swaddled in a quilted moving blanket and banded and wrapped with orange chain-of-custody tape.

The courtyard looked different than it had a couple of weeks ago. It was cleaner and brighter, with new gravel crunching underfoot where before there had only been mud. The scent of sandalwood and charred ti leaf hung low in the air, blending with the smell of the ocean that rode over the fence from two blocks away. The concrete walls had been freshly painted; the words Ka Hale o Nā Kumu Hula, The House of the Hula Masters, arced in navy script above the entry. The double doors were open, and woven mats fanned out from the threshold in wide concentric circles, bright as the summer sun.

A dozen elders stood scattered across the mats, their feet bare, eyes on the open sky. She recognized three of them. Uncle Moke, who'd retired from the bus depot but still wore his MTA polo; Tūtū Lani, whose braid was so long it brushed her calves when she walked; and Kahu David, hands behind his back, shirt pressed, the gold cross at his throat visible under the collar. The rest were strangers or faces she'd only seen in fading photographs: pillars of the community, summoned like jury foremen to witness what came next.

The hula students—keiki in flowered shirts, teens in black tank tops and pareos—clustered behind the elders, hands clasped in front, their voices wound tight by so many grown-ups. Someone had made a lei stand in the corner, and dozens of yellow 'ilima leis hung from the rungs, blossoms dense and perfect. Two of the aunties fussed with a lauhala table at the head of the mats, covering it with a red tapa cloth and setting out bowls of poi, salt, and squares of dark, spongy kalo.

At the center of it all, on a low bamboo platform, a round wooden cradle waited: empty, except for a triangle of barkcloth and a sliver of sun.

Leilani swallowed, slid out of the car, and lifted the pahu with both arms. It was heavier than she remembered. The Koa body was cold and smooth through the blanket. Its gut taut with tension and the old, persistent scent of smoked hide and earth. She took one step, then another, every eye in the courtyard shifting to track her movement. Her palms sweated against the blanket, her breath tight and brittle in her throat.

Her mother met her halfway across the gravel. Naalei wore a simple black mu'umu'u and a rope of shell lei that draped almost to her waist. She was barefoot, as always, and her gray hair was down around her shoulders, wild as a storm front. She gazed at the bundle, at Leilani, and at the elders. She nodded once—a subtle tilt that could have been a greeting or warning.

"You brought it home," Naalei said, her voice lower than usual.

Leilani shifted her grip on the pahu, careful not to let her hands shake. "They said it would be safest here until after the court date. I, um, signed it out with a release." She fumbled in her pocket for the folded pink slip and held it out to her mother.

Naalei didn't take it. "Does it still sound?"

"I think so. I didn't want to—" Leilani's voice wobbled, and she stopped, clutching the blanket tighter. "I didn't want to try it without you."

Silence rolled over them. Leilani watched as one by one, the elders nodded, slow and deliberate, like judges in a hula competition.

Naalei lifted a hand and smoothed the blanket over the pahu. "We'll do this together. If that's what you want."

Leilani could only nod.

Her mother took the lead, turning to the platform and signaling with her eyes for Leilani to follow. The walk was the longest Leilani had taken in years, each step marking time, the crowd of elders and students parting before her. She saw Tūtū Lani's mouth twist in a sly smile; she saw the hard glint of Uncle Moke's gaze; the pride buried under layers of skepticism. They were all there for her—or for the pahu, which would outlast every person in the yard.

At the base of the bamboo platform, Leilani paused and waited for her mother to speak.

"Loosen the straps. One at a time."

Leilani did as she was told. Her fingers found the old laces, dry and frayed, the knot as she remembered it from the last time her mother let her play. She worked the cords free, then slipped the blanket off, folding it over her arm. The wood was brighter than in the photos, alive with the glow of hand oil and salt air.

Naalei gestured for Leilani to lift the drum into its cradle. The elders watched. The keiki had gone still, barely blinking. Leilani settled the pahu onto the woven lauhala and stepped back.

Her mother nodded. "Now, the tapa."

Leilani reached out, palms sweaty, and lifted the barkcloth. It moved like a cloud, feather-light, and underneath, the skin of the drum shone with a fine sheen, the surface stretched tight as memory.

"Go ahead," Naalei whispered, close enough that only Leilani could hear. "Give it a voice."

Leilani raised her hand, heart shaking in her chest. She remembered how her mother taught her: never slap, always caress, let the hand bounce and breathe with the drum. She brought her palm down gently at first, a whisper of contact. The sound was low, almost hesitant. She tried again, firmer. This time, the note was deep, round, a pulse that ran through the air and settled into the ground beneath the mats.

She saw Uncle Moke's head lift. She saw the kids lean in, eyes wide. Leilani put her hand on the drum. She tried to breathe. The world seemed to shrink to just the two of them, mother and daughter, the old wound, and the new hope.

Naalei stepped up and placed her own hand beside Leilani's on the pahu.

"Together," she said, and their four hands played the next beat as one.

The sound rolled across the courtyard, bounced off the fresh paint, and hovered, suspended, for the length of a prayer. Naalei sang a short chant—her voice hoarse but clear—praising the return of the pahu, the ancestors who guarded it, the courage of the child who brought it home.

When she finished, the elders bowed their heads, and Tūtū Lani wiped her eyes with the back of her wrist.

Naalei turned and faced her daughter. She took a lei from the table—'ilima, bright as the inside of a mango—and slipped it over Leilani's head. The petals were cold, wet from the morning dew. In a move so quick Leilani nearly missed it, her mother pressed a kiss to her forehead and pulled her into an embrace, one arm around her shoulders, the other still resting on the drum.

Leilani breathed in the smell of sandalwood and salt, and the hard edge she carried from the case, from the city, from the years spent running away, went soft.

"You did good," her mother whispered. "You did what I couldn't."

Leilani wanted to speak, but all she could do was squeeze her mother's hand and nod.

Behind them, Kahu David stepped forward and sprinkled sea salt around the drum, a benediction in three careful passes. He bowed and signaled for the crowd to move in. The keiki surged first, eager and unafraid, touching the drum with reverence or tracing their fingers over the lauhala mat. The elders moved slower, each one nodded at Leilani or placed a hand on her shoulder.

Uncle Moke said, "You brought it back better than most."

Tūtū Lani whispered, "Your mother is proud, even if she won't say."

The students lined up to take photos, the youngest ones giggling at the sight of the big-city detective in her wrinkled, coffee-stained shirt, a lei askew around her neck.

After the initial wave, the courtyard settled into a rhythm of laughter and low conversation. Aunties filled plates with poke and lomi salmon, poi flowed like water, and the pahu was played by every hula teacher present. Each beat, each song, stitched the drum tighter into the fabric of the afternoon.

Leilani stood by the side, breathing it all in. She watched her mother laugh, hug the keiki, and swap jokes with the elders. She watched as Naalei—her mother, her kumu, her island—reclaimed the pahu not just as a symbol but as a promise. The old stories said the drum was the heart of the halau; now, the heartbeat was stronger than ever.

She let herself be pulled into the group photo, arms around Tūtū Lani and one of the keiki. The sun baked her face, and the salt air stung her eyes. The laughter, the chant, and the slow, steady thump of the drum drowned out the city for a little while.

She didn't check her phone until the party wound down, and the courtyard was littered with plumeria petals and the husks of old stories, ready to be swept into the future.

She read Isaac's text—only three words, but enough: **Case is closed**.

Leilani glanced at her mother, at the pahu, and at the circle of friends and family that had grown a little bigger today.

She didn't reply to Isaac, not yet.

She picked up the drum, found her mother's gaze, and let the rhythm carry her home.

***

Isaac liked the case room best when it was empty, the battered desks and glassed-in evidence lockers washed in the lazy haze of late sun. The building always felt older at this time, worn out and a little forgiving, like an uncle after a second beer. He sat at his corner desk with a pen in one hand and a folder in the other, cross-referencing the last of the chain-of-custody logs with the intake reports from the yacht bust. The desk was clean for once: no takeout, no bloodstained witness forms, not a stray bullet casing or loose paperclip. He'd stacked the legal pads at a right angle, as if the entire force of his attention could change existence into order.

The wall behind him was a quilt of mug shots, inventory photos, and Post-it notes—half of them scratched out now, their subjects either booked, bailed, or vanished to parts unknown. He paused at the photo of the Kamehameha helmet, feather crest bright as sunrise, and set it aside with a small nod. In the return to sender pile, the pahu drum rested, its image circled twice with a Sharpie. Isaac ran a thumb over the photo, remembering the way Leilani had wrapped it in the moving blanket, the care she'd taken to keep the wood from chipping on the ride back to her mother's halau. The sight still made him smile, a real one this time, wide and reckless as an open window.

He finished the last report, checked the signatures, and stamped CASE CLOSED in bold red on the cover sheet. The sound of the stamp made him laugh, low and private, like the punchline to a joke only he would ever hear.

He leaned back in his chair, laced his fingers behind his head, and let out a long, contented breath. The chair creaked, the room held still, and he noticed the fierce, impossible calm that only came after the best kind of disaster. No one from the Bureau had called. No one from Internal Affairs had asked for a statement. The only message in his inbox was a calendar reminder for the new Detective Orientation, which, judging from the empty coffee urn and the faint echo of snoring down the hall, no one else had remembered either.

The moment didn't last. Chief Mori walked in, shoes soft on the linoleum, and her dress uniform sharp as ever. She looked at Isaac, at the pile of folders, and at the CASE CLOSED stamp. She said nothing, picked up the Worthington file, thumbed through the inventory sheets, and set it down again.

The silence lingered, and her eyes locked on him.

"Good work," she said.

Isaac straightened in his chair, unsure if he was supposed to salute or nod. He settled for a nod.

Mori cracked the briefest smile. "You made the right choice, Torres."

He watched her for a sign—a flicker, a slip—but she was stone. He wanted to tell her it had never been a choice, not really. He'd known from the start that the Bureau would always be someone else's island, that he belonged right here, in this sun-bleached bunker with its chipped paint and broken AC.

He didn't say any of that. He said. "Thank you, Chief."

Mori tucked the folder under her arm and left as quietly as she'd come in.

Isaac waited until her footsteps faded, stood and stretched. He rolled up his sleeves, ran a hand over his head, and stared out the window as the sun slumped toward the mountains. He imagined the sound of drums, the kind that didn't wake you from sleep but called you home.

He checked his watch. Five forty. Leilani was late, but that was her style. He pulled out his phone, saw her **Be there soon** text, and laughed again. This time, it sounded normal.

She showed up at a dead run, badge still clipped to her belt, hair pulled back in a hasty braid that somehow made her look more like a cop than the uniform ever had. She was still wearing the 'ilima lei, though the flowers had gone soft and wilted in the heat.

Isaac met her at the door, holding out a paper cup of coffee.

"Bribery?" she asked, raising an eyebrow.

"Insurance," he said. "If you bail on the debrief, you owe me a new desk."

She grinned, took the cup, and sipped. "Let's make this fast. I have a dinner to get to."

He didn't ask with whom. He had a guess, but it was none of his business, not anymore.

They sat at his desk, the leftover case files between them. She rifled through the inventory, checked his math, and whistled low.

"I can't believe we pulled this off," she said.

"Team effort," he replied.

She glanced at him over the rim of her cup. "You really staying here?"

He shrugged. "I like the view."

She smiled slowly this time. "I like the company."

He let the silence settle, not awkward, but comfortable. They'd run the gauntlet together, and the scars fit.

"How's your mom?" Isaac asked.

"She cried at the ceremony," Leilani said matter-of-factly but with a smile. "Sang three chants, hugged everyone, including the aunties who talked shit about her in church."

Isaac laughed. "Sounds like a win."

"It is," she said, looking at her hands. "You ever get that feeling—like you closed the loop on something you never knew was open?"

He thought about it, about all the half-finished things in his own life, about the badge he'd given up and the one he wore now, and about the friends he'd left behind and the family he'd built here, if he'd never admitted it out loud.

"Yeah," he said, "I do."

She nodded, and they sat there, the city noise fading behind the double pane.

Finally, Leilani set down her coffee. "Come on. Let's get out of here before the Chief changes her mind and gives us a new case."

He snorted. "Dream big, Detective."

She pulled him to his feet, grabbed the evidence binder with the final signed page, and placed it in the outgoing mailbox, to be delivered to the U.S. Attorney. He followed, and together they passed through the echoing corridor, the still-sleepy lobby, and out into the evening air. The sky was streaked in every shade of orange, the kind that never made it onto postcards but would stick in your memory forever.

She stood next to her car, hands on her hips, looking at the horizon. "You know the real reason I stayed?" she asked.

He shrugged. "Why?"

"Because I like a good ending," she said.

He smiled wider than before and nodded. "Me too."

They stood in the glow of the setting sun, partners in silence. She got in her car, rolled down the window, and called back, "See you tomorrow, Torres."

"Wouldn't miss it," he called after her.

She drove off, dust curling behind her. Isaac watched until the car rounded the corner. He turned and headed to the station, ready for whatever came next. He didn't need the old badge to know who he was. He felt like he was home.

# Chapter Eighteen

## Justice and Healing

The federal courthouse looked like it belonged to another century, all polished Cherrywood and glass that let in more morning sun than anyone could reasonably need. The benches were packed—some with men in rumpled suits, some with journalists, and more than a few faces Leilani recognized from her own beat. The glare bounced off the marble floor and left sharp stripes across the shoulders of the jury box. She tried not to squint, adjusted her badge strap, and focused on the way her suit's sleeves barely brushed the wristwatch her mother had given her for high school graduation.

Isaac sat near the front, hands folded tight in his lap, spine straight as if he'd never left the Bureau. He looked at her when she entered the room, offered the tiniest nod, and fixed his gaze on the witness stand as if he could calm her from across the room. She noticed it too, the electric thread that ran between them after so many months in the field, after everything with Worthington, after everything that followed. The thought almost made her smile.

She didn't, though. Not here.

The case had drawn three solid weeks of headlines—THEFT RING BUST, CULTURAL HERITAGE SAVED, SORDID AFFAIR IN HIGH SOCIETY—peeling back another layer of Worthington's empire. The newspapers reprinting the same wire-service photo of Leilani carrying the wrapped pahu out of the Zodiac, or the blurry shot of Isaac in a sling after the evidence room shootout. It was a circus, but at this hour, the circus seemed cowed by the solemnity of the place. All the noise had squeezed down to the careful clearing of throats, the whisper of programs folded and unfolded in nervous hands, the dry scrape of the judge's gavel as proceedings began.

"All rise," called the bailiff.

Everyone did. The judge entered, stately and unsmiling, glasses perched at the edge of his nose. He seated himself, ran his hand over his notes, and nodded for them to begin.

The U.S. Attorney started with a monologue, of course. They always did. Something about the integrity of the American justice system, the invaluable legacy of indigenous culture, and the heroes in this very room who risked everything to bring down a global smuggling syndicate. Leilani tried not to let the words sink in. She kept her eyes fixed on the row behind the prosecution table, where a glass case displayed three of the most notorious artifacts, each tagged, bagged, and now as famous as their own wanted posters. Centered in the display was the helmet, the one Worthington had nearly gotten out in a diplomatic crate. Flanking it were the pahu and the feathered idol, the god image whose provenance Worthington had tried to forge and nearly succeeded.

When her name was called, Leilani rose, walked to the witness stand, and took the oath with both hands flat on the rail. The bailiff's voice was softer than she expected, almost fatherly.

The prosecutor, a sharp-featured woman in green, did not waste time.

"Detective Kealoha," she began. "Can you briefly state your current role and your involvement in this case?"

Leilani squared her shoulders, feeling the warmth of her suit against the chill of the air. "I'm a Detective with the Honolulu Police Department, assigned to the Special Investigations Unit. I led the local task force responsible for identifying and recovering artifacts stolen from state and private collections, including items found in the possession of Mr. Worthington and his associates."

She glanced involuntarily towards the defense table. Sam Worthington looked smaller here, hunched in his suit, the famous gray goatee trimmed but less dapper, less wolfish. He met her eyes once, a single flat look, then returned his focus to the legal pad before him. He tapped the pen, a metronome of nerves.

The prosecutor moved to the real meat fast.

"I'd like you to walk us through the chain of custody for what has been referred to as Exhibit A— the feathered helmet," she said.

Leilani did carefully. She listed the initial discovery on Worthington's yacht, the way Mele's team had photographed and tagged the artifact, the unbroken chain from the gallery to the evidence locker, the after-hours attempted breach, and the secure transfer to the FBI's regional office. She kept her hands still on the rail, voice low but clear, never giving the defense an opening to pounce.

The prosecutor brought out several documents, each marked with the telltale red evidence label, and slid them across to the witness box.

"Detective, are these the log sheets and digital records for the helmet?"

"Yes, ma'am."

"Are they accurate in your recollection?"

"They are."

"Your Honor, I submit Prosecution exhibits 3 through 11."

The defense attorney rose, eyes narrowed. He wore the classic bow tie, the affectation of a man who'd spent too many years enjoying the spotlight.

"Objection, Your Honor. The relevance of some of these logs—especially the post-recovery handling—is in question, as the artifact had already changed hands multiple times prior to police involvement."

The judge raised a snowy eyebrow. "Overruled. The jury will consider the entirety of the custody chain."

The prosecutor didn't glance at her opponent. She asked Leilani to read aloud the relevant entries: each line, each timestamp, each signature. The courtroom was so quiet you could hear the slap of every page.

"Detective, were you present during the attempted evidence room breach on March 24th?"

"I was."

"Who was involved in that incident?"

Leilani met Worthington's eyes, not out of defiance but because it was the truth. "It was orchestrated by one of Mr. Worthington's local contacts, but communications traced back to an encrypted line owned by the defendant."

More questions. The provenance of the pahu. The coordinated attempt to falsify export documents. The methods the Worthington crew used to launder the artifacts through third parties, then route them to foreign destinations. Leilani outlined each step and each memo. She described the undercover buys, the audio wires, the forensic match on the signature stamps Worthington's men had used to create fake provenance.

The defense circled back, hoping to find a seam.

"Detective, isn't it true that many of these artifacts were already considered lost by their original owners?"

"Some were lost, yes," Leilani said. "But not forgotten. Each one was part of an open investigation or had claimants waiting for their return. The defendant's actions prevented those claims from being honored."

"So, you're testifying that the crime here is one of… paperwork? That the state's claim to these artifacts is superior to that of the collector?"

Leilani kept her voice steady. "The crime is theft, sir. And the attempted laundering of stolen goods. The paperwork just proves the case."

A ripple of laughter that was quickly silenced. The judge glared over his glasses, but he allowed himself the faintest curl of a smile.

"Nothing further," the defense said, sitting.

The prosecutor ran Leilani through a few more points and rested. As she stepped down, Isaac gave her another nod. His turn came next: FBI cooperation in an international investigation, the chain of digital evidence, the wiretaps. He handled it with the old professionalism, steady and efficient, never overplaying the drama. The two of them worked like clockwork, always handing off, always closing ranks. The jury watched them, and more than once Leilani caught one or two of them looking back and forth as if waiting for a cue.

The week slipped by in a blur of exhibits and objections. When it was time for closing arguments, the prosecution kept it short.

"Ladies and gentlemen," she said. "The law cannot protect the soul of a place. But it can protect its history, and the people who would see it restored. This case is about more than money. It's about who we choose to be as a country, and who gets to tell our stories."

The defense appealed to reason, to property rights, and to the complexities of cultural exchange in a global world. He called the artifacts "ambassadors of aloha," which made Leilani bite her tongue to keep from snorting.

The judge charged the jury, gaveled them out, and called a recess.

Leilani stepped into the hall, rolling her shoulders, not caring about the sweat that prickled under her arms.

Isaac joined her, paper cup of burned court coffee in hand.

"We killed it," he said.

"I hope we did enough," she replied, but she let him see the pride on her face.

They stood in the hush, shoulder to shoulder, like two statues carved to match. They said nothing.

"You ready for this to end?" Isaac asked.

She turned to look at the window; the sun cutting long shadows across the seal of the court. "It never ends. But this helps."

He nodded, and when she didn't move away, he bumped her elbow with his own. "After this, drinks are on me. Win or lose."

She smiled, her lips formed in a line. "Win or win, you mean."

He grinned. "That's the attitude."

Jury deliberation lasted longer than anyone expected, and after three days, they were called back in. The jury had reached a verdict.

Inside, the courtroom was more crowded. Someone in the press pool had texted ahead; two camera crews set up outside the double doors. Leilani made her way to the front, settling in behind the bar. Isaac was three rows behind, but she could feel the heat of his gaze.

The jury filed in. The foreperson, a woman with silver hair and a suit older than some of the bailiffs, rose and handed a form to the bailiff, who walked it over to the judge. The judge read the document and handed it to the bailiff, who returned it to the foreperson.

"Madam Foreperson, has the jury reached a verdict?" asked the judge.

"We have, Your Honor."

He nodded. "Please read it."

She unfolded the slip, and her voice was clear as crystal. "In the matter of the state of Hawaii vs. Samuel Worthington, we the jury find the defendant guilty on all counts."

No dramatics, no outbursts. Worthington sat unmoving, eyes fixed on the seal behind the judge. The only sign of life was the subtle twitch of his jaw as he clenched, relaxed, then clenched again. When the judge asked if he had anything to say, Worthington shook his head.

Leilani gripped the rail in front of her, knuckles white. She exhaled, slow and silent. The judge thanked the jury, dismissed the parties, and set a date for sentencing. The gallery broke into murmurs. The case was over.

She stood, gathered her things, and threaded her way out. Isaac caught up to her on the courthouse steps.

"See?" he said. "Win or win."

She laughed genuinely. "I guess so."

They walked side by side, neither quite ready to leave, and not saying the obvious: that they'd done it, the artifacts would go home, and the whole insane cycle might, momentarily, be at rest.

From the corner of her eye, Leilani saw Worthington led away, his head held low, and she felt lighter than air.

She turned to Isaac and said, "You still owe me that drink."

He smiled, a crooked smile that always meant trouble. "Name your poison."

She did, and together they walked into the light, ready for the next thing—whatever it might be.

***

They set up the stage in the museum's new courtyard, under a halo of yellow-and-white plumeria strung between the beams like bunting. The weather, for once, cooperated: trade winds muted, clouds off at the horizon, and the sun sharp enough to bleach the memory of any bad day. Folding chairs stretched in neat rows, filled with city officials, the press and a dozen faces Leilani had only ever seen in the newspaper's society pages. She'd have run if she could, but Naalei had insisted she wear her best slacks and the blue button-down with actual cuffs. Isaac looked like he'd stolen his jacket from a wedding and like the cover of a men's magazine. She caught him pulling at the collar and grinning at Kai, who sat beside him in a too-big blazer, feet swinging, hands in the popcorn Akira had snuck in for him.

Tano sat next to Leilani, wearing a new suit, and looked like he'd be more comfortable in board shorts and a T-shirt. Tommy looked sharp in a black suit, shirt and tie. Akira got into the act, wearing her best ripped jeans, a wrinkled aloha shirt and flip-flops. They were quite a sight and a hell of a team.

Chief Mori took the mic, her suit deeper navy than the backdrop behind her. The crowd quieted in a single breath. Mori kept it short, which was her style.

"This community owes much to its storytellers," she began. "Today, we honor the work of those who returned our stories to their rightful place, and in doing so, brought us all a little closer together."

She gestured to the cases on display behind the podium: the helmet, the pahu, the gods, all set in clear acrylic, the sunlight catching on the old wood and feathers. Reporters craned for a better angle, but the crowd's eyes stayed on the artifacts. They looked smaller out in the open. More vulnerable, but also more at home.

Mori continued, voice steady. "It's my privilege to present this commendation to the Special Investigations Unit under the command of Detective Inspector Leilani Kealoha, for their role in the recovery of priceless heritage and her commitment to justice for all citizens of Honolulu." She paused, letting the applause fill the courtyard. "I am especially proud to acknowledge our partnership with community leaders, including Leilani's mother, Kumu Hula Naalei Kealoha, whose dedication to culture and truth inspired this entire effort. Thank you all."

Leilani walked onto the stage, the sound of clapping hitting her harder than she'd expected. The commendation was framed and heavy, their names spelled out in careful script. Mori shook her hand and murmured, "Well done, Lei," so only the two of them could hear, then moved aside for the next in line.

A museum director said a few words in Hawaiian, then in English, stepped back, dabbing at his cheeks. Leilani stayed put, staring down at the glass and gold leaf of their award, unsure what to do with her hands.

Kai solved the problem. When the ceremony ended, he broke from his seat, jacket flapping, and launched himself onto the stage. He wrapped her legs in a bear hug, the crowd's laughter soft and not unkind.

"Mom!" he said. "You look so weird up here!"

She tousled his hair and tried to look stern, but the effect was ruined by the grin she couldn't suppress. "That's 'Detective' to you, kiddo."

He stuck his tongue out, letting her pull him onto her hip for the photo.

Isaac followed, carrying a second maile lei looped with strands of white tuberose. He set it around her neck, careful not to snag the badge, and said, "For luck. You're going to need it when this hits Instagram."

She elbowed him. "You're jealous they didn't make you do the speech."

He leaned in quietly. "I'll take my reward in drinks and good company."

"Deal," she said.

The press took their shots of the team and the artifacts, after which the crowd was let loose for food and stories. Classic Hawaiian music played on a small stage by the palm trees. Aunties circled with trays of manapua and musubi. The elders from her mother's halau lined up to see the pahu, each one draping a fresh lei over the case until it looked like the drum was drowning in flowers.

Naalei found her when the crowd thinned, face flushed from pride and probably a little too much guava punch. She hugged Leilani tight, the way she had when Leilani was a kid: ribcage to ribcage, arms firm, like she could keep her there by force of will.

"You made me proud," her mother said. "Your tutu would have loved this."

Leilani blinked. "I hope I can keep it safe."

Naalei smiled through her tears. "You did already. That's what matters."

They hugged again, let go, and just like that, the old wound seemed a little lighter.

Kai tugged her sleeve. "Can I go get more popcorn?"

Leilani looked at her mother, who winked. "I think the detective deserves a treat," Naalei said.

Kai took off, a blur of blue, and Isaac moved to stand beside Leilani. They watched as Kai worked the snack table, conning more popcorn from Akira, who rolled her eyes but gave it to him, anyway.

"You okay?" Isaac asked.

She nodded slowly. "I think I am. Weird, right?"

"Not at all. You closed the loop."

She laughed. "Or we get a breather before the next one."

He bumped her shoulder, let his hand linger at her back, and looked over at the stage where the artifacts stood, glowing in the sun.

"I'd say you've earned it," he said.

Leilani caught her mother's gaze—saw the pride, the hope—and for once, the future didn't look scary at all. She smiled at Isaac, at her son, at the family she'd fought so hard to keep together. The applause and music drifted over the courtyard, soft and full of promise. For now, that was enough.

# Chapter Nineteen

## A New Chapter

Kai tried not to look at the room, because if he looked at the room he'd probably faint, and everything would be over before it started. Instead, he pretended the gymnasium at Washington Middle School was the deck of a spaceship, and all the grown-ups with their iPhones and clipboards were Martians, waiting for him to say something so they could shoot him with lasers.

It mostly worked until a bead of sweat rolled down his spine, and he remembered he was wearing a starched aloha shirt with a real collar and a button that poked his throat. There was also his mother, Detective Leilani Kealoha, seated three rows back and somehow scanning the crowd and beaming him full support at the same time. And beside her, arms folded and face stuck in a neutral expression, was Isaac Torres—her partner.

Kai looked down at his hands. They'd gone weird and clammy, like he'd dunked them in poi. He wiped them on his khaki shorts and focused on his project display, all color-printed photos and three-dimensional map pieces glued onto a tri-fold board. The title, bold and black at the top, read: MISSING VOICES: How Lost Artifacts Shape Modern Hawaii. His mother had helped him with the font, but everything else was his. The interviews, the research, the visits to Aunty Kalani's house. He'd gotten permission to record some of the stories on his phone, so he could get the words exactly right.

The table in front of him was stacked with his best findings. A hand-drawn timeline, a printout of the notorious Worthington Heist from a few months back, and a little laminated booklet of oral histories collected from the residents at the senior center. He'd set his display next to a poster about sustainable reef restoration, which had live coral samples in little baggies of seawater, and on the other side, a scale model of King Kamehameha's palace constructed from Rice Krispies Treats and royal icing.

He had to admit the palace was cool. It had a moat filled with blue Jell-O. But what he had was the pahu story. And the map. And the voices.

The judges walked the aisles, three of them, all in polo shirts, each with a clipboard covered in color-coded sticky notes. The lead judge—a guy with a faded dragon tattoo on his forearm and mirrored sunglasses perched in his hair—stopped in front of Kai's display and made a little humming sound. He tapped the edge of the tri-fold and smiled.

"You're Kai Kealoha, right? I read your proposal last month. That was some deep digging."

Kai's face went hot, but he nodded. "Thank you, sir."

The judge took a moment to flip through the booklet of oral histories. "Aunty Kalani is my neighbor. She said you brought her cookies and recorded her stories?"

Kai blinked. "Umm, yes. She said she'd only talk if I brought peanut butter haupia bars from Leonard's."

The other judges laughed, and the tattooed one winked. "You cracked the code. Smart."

He read through another page. "You mention here that several artifact thefts over the past twenty years led to major changes in state law. Can you explain that part to the panel?"

Kai took a breath. He'd practiced this in the mirror at home, with his mother standing outside the door making suggestions. "So, after the Worthington case, the Bishop Museum started using triple-custody for cultural artifacts. That means they must keep a video log every time something is moved or touched. The police also made a task force for tracking down black market artifact sales online. It all happened after some important things got stolen and almost shipped to China."

The lead judge nodded, looking impressed. "And what about the oral histories? Why do you think those are as important as the physical artifacts?"

Kai heard his mother's voice in his head: "Tell them what you told me." He cleared his throat. "Because if you lose an object, the story is still there. The elders remember. If you don't save stories, you're only saving a dead thing. It means nothing unless it's alive in someone's memory."

The judge put down his clipboard and clapped once, loud and sharp. "Strong answer. Okay, one last thing— if you could return one lost artifact, which would it be?"

Easy. "The pahu that belonged to the Kealoha Halau. My grandma's hula school. It got returned after the Worthington bust, but before that, they couldn't have ceremonies because it wasn't the same without their own pahu."

The judge smiled, wrote something on his clipboard, and motioned to the others. "Thank you, Kai. Good luck today."

Kai watched them walk away, his stomach making a weird flip that was part relief, part dread. He let himself glance at his mother. She was smiling now— barely, but he could see it in the crinkles around her eyes. Isaac leaned over and whispered something to her. She elbowed him, but in a friendly way. Kai thought about waving, but that would have been mortifying, so he focused on his project instead.

The gym was a low buzz of voices and shuffling feet and the squeak of marker boards being rearranged. Every table seemed to have a mini crowd: a knot of nervous parents, a couple of grandparents fussing over their grandkid's homemade volcano, and a teacher reminding two boys not to sword fight with their flagpoles. Above it all, the hum of the A/C struggled to keep up with the mass of bodies and anxious energy.

He recognized one kid from his class. Rachel Sato, who'd done the reef poster, waved at him. He waved back but looked away fast. He was supposed to act cool about this, but she was a year older and had a perfect science fair record.

A tall man in a blue volunteer vest came down the line, ringing a little bell. "Five minutes until the main presentations! Find your seats, folks!"

Kai straightened his display. The timeline had

peeled, so he pressed it flat. He lined up the laminated booklet, checked the batteries on the little audio player, and then stood behind his table with his hands folded, trying not to shake.

"Nice board," someone said beside him.

It was the kid with the Rice Krispies palace. He stuck out a sticky hand and grinned. "I'm Billy."

"Kai," said Kai, shaking the hand but wiping his palm on his shorts as soon as Billy turned away.

"I hope you win," Billy said, not unkindly. "My dad says your project is the best, but mine is tastier."

Kai snorted. "It looks good."

Billy shrugged. "My mom's a food chemist. It's not fair, really."

The bell rang again, louder this time. "Attention! Please be seated! Presentations begin in five!"

Kai watched as his mother and Isaac took seats near the center aisle. She looked calm now, but he knew she was still watching everything. She was always on alert, even at a middle school competition. He tried to remember the last time he saw her truly relax. Last Christmas, when she and grandma cooked laulau, and his mom tried to teach Isaac how to surf.

The lights in the gym dimmed, and the principal took the stage, adjusting the mic with a screech that made everyone flinch.

"Welcome to the 38th Annual Hawaii State Cultural Preservation Competition!" she said, voice amplified a hundred times over. "We have over seventy entries this year, from all the islands, and every one of them is a testament to the strength and beauty of our communities."

The next ten minutes were a blur of introductions. The winners from each category—oral history, visual arts, restoration, and research—were called to the front. Each kid received a paper certificate, a shell necklace, and a handshake from the mayor, who looked slightly out of place in a shiny aloha shirt and tan pants.

Kai's group was last. He watched as the names ticked by: Rachel took first for reef preservation; Billy got an honorable mention for architectural accuracy and most edible diorama. The principal cleared her throat and read:

"In the Special Research division, first place goes to… Kai Kealoha, for his work Missing Voices: How Lost Artifacts Shape Modern Hawaii!"

Kai stood there. He was pretty sure his heart stopped, then bounced back to life at twice the speed. He walked up onto the stage on legs made of jelly, nearly tripping on the last step. The mayor gave him a smile and a handshake, and the judges gave him a certificate in a plastic sleeve.

There was clapping—he heard his mother whistle, a sharp sound that rose above the general applause.

"Congratulations," the mayor said. "You did your family proud."

"Thank you, sir," Kai replied, his voice half a whisper.

Afterward, there was a flurry of photos. His mother flanked him, with her arm across his shoulders. He tried to look dignified but couldn't stop grinning. They included Isaac in one picture, and he cracked a real smile, not the polite kind he used on TV or in the office.

They stepped away from the stage and into a crowd of people: parents, kids, teachers, and a couple of local reporters. Kai fielded questions about his project—how long it took ("three months, but really my whole life"), what inspired him ("my grandma, and all the aunties and uncles who lost things"), and whether he wanted to be a detective like his mom ("I like mysteries").

After the crowd thinned out, the tattooed judge found him again.

"I hope you keep digging, Kai," he said. "Stories are how we survive."

Kai nodded. "I will."

By the time the gym emptied, Kai felt a hundred feet tall and so tired he thought he might collapse. He walked outside with his mother and Isaac. The afternoon light was golden, painting the grass and the lines of parked cars in long stripes. His mother reached down and squeezed his hand.

"You did good, bug," she said, her voice softer than he'd ever heard it.

He looked at her and saw something new on her face. Not the detective, not the mom who made him do chores, but someone proud and a bit amazed.

"I want to do more," he said. "About the family, and the stories. I'd like to help find the stuff that's still missing."

She nodded. "You will. But first—let's go celebrate."

Isaac pointed at the strip shopping center. "Liliha Bakery. I promised him Coco Puffs."

His mother made a face. "That's your idea of a healthy dinner?"

"Protein," Isaac said. "And joy."

Kai laughed, feeling lighter than he had in months. As they piled into the car, he thought about his project, the voices he'd recorded, and the artifacts that were still out there, waiting for someone to bring them home.

He closed his eyes as the car sped up the road; the world blurring past. He knew exactly what he wanted to do. Tomorrow, he'd start with Aunty Kalani. There were more stories to save, and he was going to be the one to do it.

The table was set with a blue-and-green flowered runner, four mismatched place settings, and more food than the three of them could eat in a week. It was Friday, and Naalei's house still smelled faintly of cleaning products from Leilani's pre-dinner panic sweep, but the star was the perfume of roasted pork, sea salt and the bright shock of lomi salmon. On the sideboard sat a big wooden bowl of poi, and behind that, a Tupperware mountain of haupia squares for dessert only, as Naalei had said, waving a wooden spoon at Kai with a warning face she only half meant.

The house was crowded, but not with people—more with the evidence of a family that refused to thin, after years of changing hands and addresses. On the living room wall hung a sepia portrait of Leilani's great-grandparents, the ones who, according to legend, built the first wooden lanai on the block and paid for it in gold coins from a forgotten mine. In the hallway, a framed collage of Kai's old report cards, next to a sun-bleached certificate from one of Leilani's first solved cases. Every flat surface seemed to have its own display: hula trophies, shell leis, postcards from mainland relatives, a single signed baseball Isaac had smuggled in as a joke, and no one had the heart to move.

Kai watched the kalua pork as it shredded under his grandmother's fork, the steam rising in curly tendrils. He thought about the phrase falling off the bone and wondered what it meant for something to let go so completely. He wanted to ask, but Naalei plopped a double scoop of pork on his plate and told him to wait for the rest, Mr. Hungry, so he grinned and nodded.

Leilani carried in the bowl of poi, purple and glossy, and set it next to the lomi salmon. "Careful, it's runnier than usual," she said, and then immediately laughed at herself. "Like anyone cares."

Naalei cut her off with a mock glare. "We care about everything in this house."

They settled at the table, and Naalei led the blessing, a mix of English and Hawaiian that Kai could follow only by rhythm, not by words. Her voice was strong, not quite musical, but with the conviction that made simple things sacred for the moment.

The meal started with the usual banter—updates on the neighbors, speculation about tomorrow's rain, a brief aside about whether the new mall would ever actually open. But Kai was too jittery to wait for his cue. Before the adults could dig in, he blurted: "I won the competition."

"You told us three times in the car," Leilani said, but she was smiling. Still proud.

"It was different this time," said Kai, trying to explain. "I didn't want to win. It felt like—like there was something I was supposed to do. I wanted people to remember."

"Remember what?" asked Naalei, genuinely curious.

Kai thought about the question, his fork tracing slow circles in his poi. "The real stuff. Not the tourist version. Like all the things that got lost or stolen. The aunties at the senior center knew about the pahu, and everyone still talked about it. It wasn't just a drum. It was like the heart of their group."

Naalei nodded, reaching for the lomi salmon. "The pahu was everything. My tutu said you could hear its voice from two streets away. It made everyone want to dance, including the ones with sore knees."

She glanced at Leilani. "You remember the old halau?"

Leilani's answer was a shrug and a distant smile. "I mostly remember having to help with costumes and getting glitter everywhere."

"And who always had to scrub it off your face before church?" Naalei asked, one eyebrow cocked.

"True," said Leilani, yielding the point.

Kai looked from his mother to his grandmother, a weird rush of pride and longing making his face feel tight. He tried to put it into words. "Sometimes I wish I were around back then. Before everything was digital."

His mother sipped her water, eyes a little soft. "You'd have survived. You're a survivor."

Naalei tilted her head, considering. "It's not about then or now. You're meant to carry it all forward. Not just the wonderful memories, but the hard ones too."

Kai nodded, but the question kept bumping around in his head. "Was it scary when the pahu went missing? When you lost it?" He glanced at his mother, then at his grandmother.

"It was," said Naalei. "Because you don't think about the drum until it's not there. Every beat is gone, and all you can hear is the emptiness."

Leilani's fork paused in midair. She looked like she might answer, but she put the fork down and glanced at the tablecloth. "I think I spent years pretending not to care about all this stuff," she whispered. "I wanted to be the tough kid, the detective, the person who fixes things instead of missing them."

She smiled at Kai, her face open in a way he'd never quite seen. "You changed that, you know. You and grandma."

Kai swallowed, a little embarrassed. "All I did was make a poster."

"You made a map," said Leilani. "You found voices."

There was a long silence, comfortable as a blanket. Then Naalei took over, as she always did.

"You know, Kealoha means the loved one, but also the beloved voice. That's what the family was known for long ago. Kumu hula, chanters, and storytellers." She pointed her fork at Kai. "Not only cops and detectives, but those are useful, too."

Kai grinned. "I could be both."

"You will be," said his grandmother, as if it were already decided.

Leilani looked at her mother. "You two. You're already planning his life for him."

"We're giving him options," said Naalei, spooning more kalua pork onto Kai's plate.

They ate for a while in companionable silence, each bite pulling them closer together, each dish a history lesson that tasted like comfort. When the food was mostly gone and only the desserts remained, Kai asked the thing he'd been thinking about all day.

"Can I visit the museum again?" he asked, almost shy. "Not the new exhibits, but the artifacts from before. The old ones. And spend some time at the halau," he said to Naalei.

His grandmother put down her fork and took his hand. "You can go anywhere you want. Remember, the old places aren't gone. They're waiting for you."

Leilani watched her son and her mother, the two of them leaning into each other, and realized something was shifting. The old worry—that the past would pull her under, that her own failures would become her son's—was fading. In its place was a strange relief, a belief that the best way to keep something safe was to share it, loud and proud.

She reached across the table and squeezed Kai's hand, her fingers rough but warm.

"You want to know about us?" she asked. "Ask anything. I promise to tell you the truth, including the weird parts."

"The parts about Tutu sneaking fireworks into her dance shows?" Kai asked, smirking.

Leilani laughed, a sharp, happy sound. "Especially those parts."

Kai looked at them and felt something click in his chest. "I want to learn everything. The dances, the chants, what it means to be a guardian."

Naalei nodded, her eyes shining in the soft light. "We'll start tomorrow. Sunrise on the lanai. I'll teach you the opening oli."

Kai could hardly wait. For the rest of the meal, he thought about what it would feel like to say the words, to beat the pahu with his own hands, to make his own kind of history.

He finished his last bite of dessert and pushed the plate away, full to the brim with hope. Across the table, his mother watched him, a smile beginning to grow.

She didn't say it, but he could tell she was ready, too.

***

The lanai faced east, catching the gold wash of sunrise and all the trade winds it could handle. Most mornings, it was just a place for coffee and slippers and maybe a stretch before the day got serious. But today, Naalei had turned it into something more—like a church, or a time machine, or the starting line for a new family relay.

She'd been up since dawn, brushing off the old lauhala mats and scrubbing the salt spray from the wood rail. She'd borrowed extra folding chairs from next door just in case, though she told herself she didn't really expect anyone but her own. On one side of the lanai, she set a low table with heirloom photos, feathered kahili, a bowl of polished kukui nuts, and her old hula skirt, neatly bundled and smelling faintly of ti leaf and coconut oil. In the very center she placed the pahu, the drum that had left and come home, its hide still marked from decades of ceremonies and more than one near-disaster.

Naalei gave it a loving thump with her palm and felt the note vibrate clear through the deck and into her bones.

She put on her black mu'umu'u and her best shell lei, and sat quietly, waiting for her students.

Kai appeared first, already dressed in a tank top and shorts, barefoot, hair sticking out at all angles. He was bouncing on the balls of his feet, nervous energy leaking from every pore.

"You ready, little lion?" she asked, using the old nickname.

"Been up since four," he said. "I practiced my ollie. On YouTube, I mean."

She laughed loudly. "It's not ollie like on a skateboard, but oli—a chant. No skateboard required."

He grinned. "Good. Because I'm terrible on skateboards."

Leilani was next, looking way more put together than either of them, but still blinking away the last of sleep. She wore yoga pants and a faded T-shirt, but Naalei noticed she'd also put on her own special lei, the one with the gold beads and plumeria blooms. She looked at the setup, then at her mother, and almost smiled.

"This is a lot," she said. "Are you expecting a crowd?"

"Just you two," said Naalei, "but the ancestors are always invited."

Leilani rolled her eyes, but with affection.

"Okay," said Naalei, standing. "First lesson, you need the right spirit. You can't chant on an empty stomach."

She pulled out a thermos and three mugs, pouring hot cocoa and topping it with whipped cream from a can. She handed one to Kai and another to Leilani, who shrugged. "Breakfast of champions?"

Naalei lifted her mug in salute. "Breakfast of kumu hula."

They sipped in silence, the light soft and clear, the city waking up in the distance.

When the cocoa was gone, Naalei brought out two fresh leis, simple strands of ʻilima picked from the side yard. She draped one over her daughter's head and the other over her grandson's, then told them to sit cross-legged in front of the pahu.

She joined them, taking her own spot behind the drum.

"Before we begin, you need to know who you are," she said, voice low and serious. "And not the names on your mail, but the old names, the line that brought you here."

She held up a faded photo, the kind that looked like it had survived a hundred hurricanes. It showed a row of men and women in full hula regalia, faces stoic and proud, every one of them standing at attention in front of a royal palace. At the center was a girl of maybe fifteen, eyes bright, and her hair pulled back in a perfect bun.

"This was your tutu, Leilani. Your great-grandmother. She danced for Queen Liliʻuokalani. She was the first in our line to hold the pahu at a state ceremony. She taught my mother everything, who taught me, and I taught you, even if you didn't always want to learn."

Leilani took the photo, holding it with a reverence she probably didn't realize showed on her face. "She looks like you," she said.

"She looks like you, too," said Naalei. "That's the

point."

She set the photo on the mat, then pointed to the pahu.

"And this," she said, "is your inheritance. Your kuleana. Our family guarded this for generations, even when people tried to say it belonged in a museum or to someone with more money or power. Your job is to keep it alive, not just with your hands, but with your voice."

She motioned to Kai. "Go on. Touch it. It's yours now, too."

Kai reached out tentatively, then tapped the drumhead. The sound was sharp, not loud but full, and he grinned, eyes wide.

"It's so cool," he said. "Is it always this loud?"

"It's louder when you believe in it," said Naalei.

She turned to Leilani. "Your turn. You used to do this, remember?"

Leilani laughed, a little embarrassed. "Barely. I was always scared I'd mess up and you'd glare at me in front of everyone."

Naalei smiled. "Then I did my job."

She reached out and struck the pahu twice, letting the beat settle. "See? Still works."

The three of them sat quietly, listening to the echo.

Then Naalei began the lesson.

"First, you must learn the oli kahea—the opening chant. It's what you say to ask permission to enter a sacred space, or to start a ceremony. Simple words, but you must say them from here," she said, pressing a hand to her chest.

She recited the chant slowly, voice carrying just enough to rise over the rustle of the palms and the distant sound of traffic.

Kai repeated it, fumbling the vowels, but getting louder and more confident each time. Leilani followed, her voice unsure at first but stronger by the third go.

Naalei nodded in approval.

"Now, the hands," she said. "Every oli has a gesture, whether it's a lift of the chin or an open palm. It's how you tell the ancestors you are serious."

She showed them, moving her hands in a slow arc, palms up, then down, like gathering light from the sun and planting it in the earth.

"Try it," she said.

Kai did, awkward but determined, his eyes locked on his grandmother's every move. Leilani copied, more precisely, but still a little self-conscious.

"Not bad," said Naalei. "Remember, it's not about being perfect. It's about being present."

They practiced the chant, the hand motions, and both together. At first, it was like an exercise, but after a while, the rhythm caught, and they moved as one. Naalei kept time on the pahu, soft at first, then louder as the voices joined and grew.

On the fifth try, she heard it—when the three of them synced up, breath to breath, word to word, hand to hand. She closed her eyes and let the sound wash over her. When they finished, there was silence, but it was a good one.

Kai looked at his mother, then at his grandmother, and asked: "Can we do it again?"

"Always," said Naalei.

For the rest of the morning, they practiced. Sometimes they laughed—when Leilani mispronounced a word or when Kai clapped off-beat. Sometimes they sat, letting the sunlight warm their skin and the trade wind tangle their hair. Naalei told stories, old ones about queens and voyagers and the first pahu ever made. She explained the meaning behind each word, each gesture. She reminded them that tradition was not a museum piece but a living thing, something that grew and changed with every generation.

By the time the sun was high, they were sweaty, hoarse, and happier than they'd been in weeks. At the very end, Naalei made them sit together on the mat.

"One last thing," she said. "When you go out into the world, people will ask you who you are. You tell them you are Kealoha. You are loved, and you are the beloved voice of your family."

She hugged them both, pulling them tight. She felt young again, not a kumu hula or a grandmother, but a girl on the edge of the future, wide open and ready.

When they broke apart, Leilani wiped her eyes and laughed. "See? You got me to cry on the first day."

"Part of the lesson," said Naalei.

Kai grinned. "Best school ever."

They sat together, the three of them, with the pahu at their feet and the sun shining through the fronds. In the distance, the city went on as always, but here, on the lanai, they made their own history, one beat, one word, one morning at a time.

# Acknowledgments

A special thank-you to my daughter Christina J. Morgan, my unofficial collaborator.

Any mistakes the reader may find are solely the responsibility of the author.

Special thanks to my daughter Stephanie Morgan, my beta reader. Stephanie has read every novel in its rough stages and rarely gets to see the completed product. Her insight and critique have been critical in making sure the stories make sense.

Also, I would like to thank my family for their encouragement. I have been telling them stories since they were little, and I always told them that someone should be writing this stuff down. I decided to write it down myself.

I want to thank my closest friend, Trish Moakler-Herud. She has been encouraging me for years to write my stories down. I hope this will make her proud.

A special thanks to my late wife, Jane. She pushed me for years to become a writer, and my biggest regret is that she didn't live long enough to see it happen. I love her with all my heart and miss her every day. I think she would be pleased.

Finally, thanks to the readers. Without you, none of this would be important.

# About the Author

**2019 Pacific Book Awards Best Mystery Finalist . . . *Crime Delayed.***

**2020 Pacific Book Awards Best Mystery Winner . . . *Crime Denied.***

**2020 Chanticleer International Book Awards: 1st Place Blue Ribbon, CLUE Book Awards for Suspense, Thriller Fiction . . . *Crime Denied.***

**2021 Chanticleer International Book Awards Finalist, CLUE Book Awards for Suspense, Thriller Fiction . . . *Crime Conspiracy.***

**2021 Chanticleer International Book Awards Finalist, Book Series, CLUE Book Awards for Suspense, Thriller Fiction . . . *Crime Series, The Buck Taylor Novels.***

**2022 Chanticleer International Book Awards Finalist, CLUE Book Awards for Suspense, Thriller Fiction . . . *Crime Exploded.***

**2022 Chanticleer International Book Awards Finalist, CLUE Book Awards for Suspense, Thriller Fiction . . . *Crime Spree.***

**2023 Chanticleer International Book Awards Finalist, CLUE Book Awards for Suspense, Thriller Fiction . . . *Crime Scene.***

**2023 Chanticleer International Book Awards Series Finalist, Mystery & Mayhem Book Awards . . . *Crime Series.***

**2025 Reader's Favorites Book Awards…Crime Fiction…Silver Medal…*Crime Unraveled.***

Chuck Morgan attended Seton Hall University and Regis College and spent thirty-five years as a construction project manager. He is an avid outdoorsman, an Eagle Scout and a licensed private pilot. He enjoys camping, hiking, mountain biking and fly-fishing.

He is the author of the Crime series, featuring Colorado Bureau of Investigation Agent Buck Taylor. The series includes *Crime Interrupted, Crime Delayed, Crime Unsolved, Crime Exposed, Crime Denied, Crime Conspiracy, Crime Unknown, Crime Exploded, Crime Spree, Crime Family, Crime Scene, Crime Victims, and Crime Unraveled.* He is also the author of *The Assassin's Heart, a romantic thriller, and Preserve, Protect, and Defend,* a political thriller.

He is also the author of *Her Name Was Jane*, a memoir about his late wife's nine-year battle with breast cancer. He has three children and four grandchildren. He resides in Lone Tree, Colorado, with his Siberian husky.

# Other Books by the Author

Dear Reader, thank you for reading this novel. Please enjoy the other books in this series and follow Colorado Bureau of Investigation Agent Buck Taylor and his team as they investigate new and sometimes unusual crimes in the Colorado mountains. Each novel is a separate story, and they can be read in any order, but you might find it more enjoyable to read them in order.

Happy Reading,

*Chuck Morgan*

"*Crime Interrupted: A Buck Taylor Novel by Chuck Morgan is a gripping, edge-of-the-seat novel.* Right from page one, the action kicks off and never stops, gaining pace as each chapter passes." Reviewed by Anne-Marie Reynolds for Readers' Favorite.

Finalist . . . 2019 Pacific Book Awards Best Mystery

*"**This crime novel reads like a great thriller.** The writing is atmospheric, laced with vivid descriptions that capture the setting in great detail while allowing readers to follow the intensity of the action and the emotional and psychological depth of the story." Reviewed by Divine Zape for Readers' Favorite.*

*"**Professionally written in the style of a best-selling crime novelist, such as Tom Clancy, Crime Unsolved: A Buck Taylor Novel by Chuck Morgan is a spellbinding suspense novel with an environmental flair.** Intriguing subplots of fraud, survivalist paranoia and murder weave their way through the fabric of the plot, creating a dynamic story. This is an action-filled, stimulating tale which contains fascinating details that are relevant in our present climate." Reviewed by Susan Sewell for Readers' Favorite.*

*"Chuck Morgan has a unique gift for plot, one that makes Crime Exposed: A Buck Taylor Novel a hard-to-put-down book.* From the start, readers know what happens to Barb, but they become curious as they follow the investigation, wondering if the characters will find out what happened to her. The descriptions are filled with clarity, and they offer readers great images. The prose is elegant, and it captures both the emotional and psychological elements of the novel clearly while offering vivid descriptions of scenes and characters. This is a fast-paced thriller with memorable characters and a criminal investigation that is so real readers will believe it could happen." Reviewed by Romuald Dzemo for Readers' Favorite.*

**Winner . . . 2020 Pacific Book Awards Best Mystery**

**2020 Chanticleer International Book Awards: 1st Place Blue Ribbon, CLUE Book Awards for Suspense, Thriller Fiction**

*"It's really progressive to see a female serial killer portrayed with such intelligent writing and depth of character*, and the cat and mouse chase dynamic is thrown off nicely by the switching of genders. What results is a really enjoyable thriller and crime mystery novel, and overall Crime Denied is certain to please fans of both hard-boiled detective tales and action/adventure crime novels." Reviewed by K.C. Finn for Readers' Favorite.*

**2021 Chanticleer International Book Awards Finalist, CLUE Book Awards for Suspense, Thriller Fiction . . . *Crime Conspiracy***

*"This makes for a truly dynamic story where anything is possible, and a hero you can root for even when it looks like all is lost." Reviewed by K.C. Finn for Readers' Favorite.*

*"This is a book you can't put down, which will entertain you on many levels, and at times make your skin crawl; the kind of book that remains in your thoughts long after you*

**2022 Chanticleer International Book Awards Finalist, CLUE Book Awards for Suspense, Thriller Fiction . . .** *Crime Exploded*

*"**Action-packed and fast-paced, I was sucked into the story the moment I opened the novel.** The author built the story to perfection. Chuck Morgan gave just the right amount of suspense, mystery, and action to keep readers' attention on Buck and his team. There was never a dull moment in the story. The narrative ran smoothly until the end; it followed the development of the story and the pace set by the characters. I enjoyed the twists and turns. What I loved more than anything else in the plot was how calculating Buck was. He was smart; he didn't let the FBI discourage him and kept his head in the game. The action gave me an adrenaline rush. Absolutely brilliant!" Reviewed by Rabia Tanveer for Readers' Favorite.*

"**Crime Family is the tenth book in the Buck Taylor series. Chuck Morgan had me hooked from the first page until the end.** There was never a dull moment with all the action; one chapter flowed into the next. The story was fast-paced and kept me on the edge of my seat. I kept turning the pages to find out what would happen next. I was intrigued, and with all the twists and turns, I could not predict what was looming. The characters were well-developed. Each had a background description, and it was fun getting to know some of them. The story was excellently written with a fitting ending." Reviewed by Alma Boucher for Readers' Favorite.

"**Crime Scene is a must-read for lovers of mystery sleuth and**

**murder tales with a touch of conspiracy."** *Reader's Favorite review.*

**"Crime Scene has a carefully designed intrigue that deepens with every unforeseeable turn of events and a dynamic narrative."** *Reader's Favorite review.*

**"This is a great book. Holds your attention and you don't want to put it down. I would recommend this book to anyone who loves a good crime novel."** *Amazon review.*

**"Spellbinding, gripping, powerful, and relevant are just a few words that come to mind after turning the last page of Crime Scene: A Buck Taylor Novel, Book 11, by Chuck Morgan."** *Amazon Review.*

**"A riveting plot and good pacing keep the reader in suspense as Buck Taylor and his team establish evidence beyond a reasonable doubt.** *The author sustains interest by skillfully showing the art and intuition involved in crime investigation and the science behind it, as well as the elements that can delay or confound it. There are a lot of quirky characters in the novel and the author gives them mannerisms, voices, and descriptions that make them distinctive and realistic. The details and descriptions of the work and everyday life of the players are both pleasantly appealing and revolting, depending on the scenario. What's most captivating and intriguing about the*

character development is the backstory of the unhinged characters and how the author uses them as part of the perplexing trail of a horrendous crime. Themes of sadism, cruelty, grief, forensics, police procedures, and even a little bit of romance can be found in this installment of the Buck Taylor series. Highly recommended for crime story fans who especially enjoy the information as well as the twists, turns, and the untangling of intricate and cold case crime sprees." Reviewed by Carmen Tenorio for Readers' Favorite.

★ ★ ★ ★ ★ If you are looking for a mystery murder novel with a touch of crime, Chuck Morgan's Crime Unraveled is just what you should be looking for.

★ ★ ★ ★ ★ Chuck Morgan took me on a roller coaster ride with Crime Unraveled. The action started on the first page and continued until the last.

★ ★ ★ ★ ★ Filled with suspense and action, Crime Unraveled: A Buck Taylor Novel, Book 13, by Chuck Morgan delivers a compelling and realistic story with historical and legal elements.

★ ★ ★ ★ ★ The 13th book in the Buck Taylor series, Crime Unraveled by Chuck Morgan is a fantastic addition to the series. I've read a few books in this series and they never fail to leave me in awe. This is the type of high-octane, fast-paced thriller I've come to expect from this author.

Delia Cahill is one of the world's elite assassins, but her next assignment has gotten into her head. Will Delia carry out her assignment or risk everything, including her life, to protect her intended victim?

*⭐ ⭐ ⭐ ⭐ ⭐ If you are looking for a thriller with brains, heart, and just the right amount of edge, this one is a must read. 5 stars, no doubt.*

*⭐ ⭐ ⭐ ⭐ ⭐ Chuck Morgan's The Assassin's Heart will keep the reader's heart thumping from the first page to the last.*

*⭐ ⭐ ⭐ ⭐ ⭐ Overall, I enjoyed the novel very much. If you're craving a fast-paced, action-packed thriller, you will not be disappointed!*

*"Preserve, Protect, and Defend by Chuck Morgan was intricate and enthralling, grabbing my attention from start to finish. This fast-paced, action-packed story had me turning the pages as quickly as possible, afraid to miss a single detail. With each twist and turn, the plot kept me on my toes, continually surprising me*

*with its unpredictability. The suspense had me sitting on the edge of my seat, making it hard to set the book aside. The engaging writing style made it easy to immerse myself fully in the story, and the characters felt incredibly genuine and relatable. Mike was a powerful force, and Stevenson had no idea what was headed his way. This book was masterfully written and maintained my interest throughout. It surpassed all my expectations, and I enjoyed every moment." Reviewed by Alma Boucher for Readers' Favorite.*